HER

DYING

WISH

BOOKS BY CARLA KOVACH

What She Did

Flame

To Let

Whispers Beneath the Pines

Meet Me at Marmaris Castle

HER DYING WISH

CARLA KOVACH

bookouture

Published by Bookouture in 2021

An imprint of Storyfire Ltd.
Carmelite House
50 Victoria Embankment
London EC4Y 0DZ

www.bookouture.com

ISBN: 978-1-80019-713-8
eBook ISBN: 978-1-80019-712-1

One in two people will be diagnosed with cancer in their lifetime. That's a scary statistic. I'd like to dedicate my latest book to anyone who has been affected by, suffered from, or lost a loved one to this horrible disease.

PROLOGUE

EIGHT YEARS AGO

As I lie on the floor trembling and gripping my phone, I wait for a call. I need you more than ever but you're not there. I thought we were going to keep each other safe, look out for each other, but you left me and that hurts more than the wounds I tend to on my bleeding body. It's more than the wounds a person can see, it's deep within. A gnarling pain radiating from the core, one full of emotion that's fit to burst. It needs to burst but like I normally do in any situation, I keep it right where it is.

Nothing feels real anymore. Pinching my skin until it threatens to break proves how numb I am. Nothing hurts and that disturbs me more. As I tend to my cracked lip and clean up my bleeding head, I know that tomorrow I'll wake up as normal. I'll attempt to go for my run and I'll come home and eat breakfast. I'll wave at the neighbour as he walks his dog and I'll pop to the shop and buy a couple of magazines. Normal is the way it's got to be. Forgetting is the only option.

The mirror doesn't lie. Staring at my reflection, I question that thought. A mirror is nothing but a lie, a short spell in the house of mirrors could prove that theory. Right now, everything looks like it has a fuzz to it. My outline is blurry. It's not the mirror that is lying right now, it's my eyes.

One night. One damn night and everything has changed. My life will never be the same again. Trying to deny that is foolish. I flinch as I dab my lip again. The smell of rot emanating from the pores of my skin makes my stomach turn but there's no point in nauseating myself, I have nothing left to eject. The growling emptiness sounds like a monster is trying to escape. Maybe there is.

Staring at my phone again, I know it's not going to ring. Abandoned is what I am. I taste the saltiness of my tears that have dried above my top lip. The sudden sound of a wailing fox makes me jump, heart banging so hard it feels as though it may fly out of my mouth, so I close the window. I open up my messages again and I read that same message for what seems like the one-hundredth time and I shake. That phone needs to go, especially as they have my number. Slowly I sink to the floor and grip my knees. My head is full, like it's about to burst. The monster growls again in my gut and the voices in my head sound like they did only two hours ago. Those same words repeated as clear memories over and over again. My whole body feels as though insects are crawling under my skin. The sensation makes me scratch and slap my body but it won't go away.

It will never go away.

ONE

SUNDAY, 14 NOVEMBER

Sneaking alongside the hedge, I know no one can see me. Everyone is right where they should be, in bed. I mean, it's the middle of the night and that makes it the perfect time to do what I have to do. Petrol sloshes in the can and it's starting to weigh a bit but I don't have that much further to go.

The house stands grand and it's everything I'd love to own. Double-fronted, large well-manicured front garden that looks like it belongs in a copy of an *Ideal Home* magazine. Expensive executive car on the drive that I know has all the mod cons. I wish I was only here to visit. My head is light, knowing what I'm about to do.

As I pass the bird table that sits in the middle of the lawn, I place the tiny candle in a jar on it then I light it. It sits neatly on a layer of frost; the same frost that is set to melt very soon, to give way to the predicted floods. I shiver. It's such a bitter night to be out and I wish I were at home snuggled up. The bird table has a little roof so the candle will stay lit if there's a downpour. As I exhale, a plume of white mist fills the air, then I feel a droplet of rain on my face. I have to get this done and get out of here before the heavens open up. Glancing around, I catch what I think is movement in one of the windows opposite. I stare for a few seconds, stupidly holding my breath like that might help. Maybe I didn't see anything. My imagination is all over the place.

I creep towards the front door and the security light clicks on. I look up and see the camera that is meant to protect the house but I know it has no chance to stop what I'm about to do. The camera hasn't been active for ages. I'm wearing a scarf over my mouth and my hood falls low. I look like a cat burglar and I'm well padded, making me look bulkier than I really am. I did this knowing that I have to protect my life. No way can I get caught for this and there's no way I can't do it, even though it's killing me inside. I have too much to lose if I get caught.

As I remain still in the open porch, I wait for the security light to go off and when it does, I hear nothing. There's not a stir when I lift the letter box. The house is as silent as me. As quietly as possible, I begin to unscrew the petrol can then I insert the pouring spout through the letter box. Then comes the good bit. I hear the liquid sloshing in the hallway, and still not a stir comes from within. I know he's drunk every night and he sleeps on the settee. He won't feel a thing as he dies in his sleep, at least I hope that is how all this will go. I might be wrong. I imagine the skin melting from his body, dripping like a candle and my stomach lurches. Taking a moment, I force that thought from my head. There's no point overthinking this, then the only question I need to answer comes into my head. What wouldn't I do for my own flesh and blood and the answer is, nothing.

Pulling a lighter from my pocket, I strike the rag to post it. Whoosh! The whole house begins to crackle as the fumes ignite. It spreads across the hall, up the coats and I know it's only a matter of time before the place goes up in flames. My heart flutters as I step back. It wouldn't be long until the fire brigade was alerted, or the fire alarm started to sound. I wait a few seconds, imagining how loud it might be, but there is no alarm. So many people don't check the batteries in their alarms. My heart hammers as I run in my trainers back up the drive and along the path, keeping close to the hedge-lined gardens. I try not to knock the bin that I crashed into on the way here. The last thing I need is attention on me. I think of what's at stake again and I know I have to hurry away. Through a gap in the trees, I catch a glimpse of my candle where it burns brightly on the bird table. I did everything I was meant to do and nothing has gone wrong. I only hope no one saves him or all will be lost. Flames begin to lick away and I see an orange glow coming from the upstairs landing and in the living room. It's spreading rapidly and there's a putrid smell in the air.

A few lights flicker on in neighbouring houses and I hear a door slam. Voices begin to call out and a woman shouts out that there's a fire. It's all happening now. I slip down a path that leads to another street, far enough away from the commotion, then I keep going trying not to slide on the icy patches. More rain begins to fall. The storm is coming so I'm about to get soaked. My car is parked far away so that no one would see me leaving this part of town. In the distance, I hear sirens. It'll probably be too late for him now. I made sure that plenty of petrol went into that letter box. Failure to complete the task was not an option. I shudder. If he is pulled out alive, I've had it. No, I shake my head. Too much time has passed now. Everything is going to work out and I can go back to normal.

Before I know it, I'll be tucked up in bed, waking up to the news that there has been a fire in our lovely little town. I'll look so, so sad as people talk about it while my stomach churns inside. My heart flutters. What if they save him from the house and he lives? I shake my head. No, he won't live. He can't live. He was drunker than ever when I saw him earlier, that's how I knew things would work out. My heart is yearning for what it's missing so badly and all I want to do is cry.

I only hope I've done enough and this whole nightmare is over.

TWO

Detective Inspector Gina Harte tossed and turned, unable to sleep in her sweat-drenched bed. Her legs had tangled in the sheet and she'd lost half of her quilt, but that didn't stop her from slowly drifting off into another dream. That's when in her disturbed nightmare she saw reporters, Lyndsey Saunders and Pete Bloxwich, kissing hard then turning to stare at her from the end of the same dark corridor that had plagued her dreams. She went to turn and run but the brick wall left her with no way out. It was either face the reporters or rot in the dark, brick corridor.

With a sharp intake of breath Gina bolted upright in bed, gripping a pillow. Her brown hair stuck to her sweaty cheeks in rat-tail strips surrounded by frizz. Rain, maybe even hail, slammed against the windowpanes, adding to her disorientation. Her cat, Ebony, meowed, and then jumped onto the floor. She placed a hand on her chest, feeling every pounding beat until her breathing returned to normal. She wished her nightmares were nothing more than that but there was something she had to deal with. Only then would this worry leave her alone. The big question was, how was she going to deal with it? She was as trapped in real life as she was in that stupid dream.

Lyndsey Saunders had been suspended from reporting and

slimy reporter, Pete Bloxwich, was now working for the *Herald*. He was certainly making himself known to her in every way possible. She grabbed her phone and glanced at the email he sent again, skipping to the part that she found most disturbing.

Too many people are willing to talk, Gina. Mummy-in-law, Hetty, and brother-in-law, Stephen; they have so much to say. When people aren't listened to, they talk louder. You need to get in first with your side of the story.

This is more than a news article by the way. It's not a tacky front pager for some local rag. You are going to star in my investigation. Tell me, did you scream for him to stop when he went too far that night? Was he hurting you? I know he was a drunk from what people said. Even his own family mentioned that he had a problem with drink.

Everyone loves a true crime story. You only have to check out the most popular programmes and they're full of it. I hope you're ready for the infamy. Hmm, Terry Smithson meets the innocent and pretty Gina Harte. She's at college and he's a tyre fitter. Love's young dream. You can tell me about that or I can make a bit up, add a bit of spice to the story. Maybe your first kiss was at a bus stop as he groped your arse, who knows? If you tell me, I won't get it wrong and I don't want to get it wrong. You deserve to be represented truthfully and I can help with that.

You know you want to talk. It must be hard carrying such a heavy load. Unburden yourself. Face it and let the truth out. What happened on the night of your husband, Terry's, tragic death? The public deserve to know that the very person who is meant to protect them could be dangerous. Are you dangerous? Call me.

She dropped the phone on the bed and leaned against the headboard, trying to get the vision of Lyndsey and Pete out of her head. No, she was not trapped in a doorless corridor and Pete had nothing on her. She knew that because Hetty and Stephen had nothing concrete either, but they weren't stupid. She'd underestimated the mother-son duo. At Terry's funeral, she hadn't looked like the grieving widow and they knew. Whatever they told Pete, it was all just guesswork on their part but one thing was for sure, they were never going to let it go and the more they shouted about it, the more doubt would be cast on her. If enough people questioned her version of events on the night Terry died, she could end up losing everything. Talking to the likes of Pete Bloxwich wasn't going to make things easy for her. The best thing she could do was to keep ignoring him. Threaten him with a libel case. Proclaim that everything they said was a lie.

She almost fell out of bed as her phone rang.

It was DS Jacob Driscoll. 'Alright, guv?'

'I was. What's happened?' He would only ring in the middle of the night if it was something really bad. For a second, she wondered if it could be about her. Had Pete Bloxwich unearthed some evidence to prove she killed Terry?

'Arson attack.' She exhaled and closed her eyes as she continued to listen. 'Man dead in house fire. I'm heading over there now and forensics have been called. It's a mess at the moment as the fire department are still in there with their hoses.'

'On my way. Can you text me the address?'

'Will do. See you soon.' Jacob ended the call and a few seconds later the address pinged through.

Gina threw all her sheets and blankets into a pile on the floor and hurried to the shower, shivering in the bathroom as she turned it on.

Are you dangerous?

Those words at the end of the reporter's email rang through her head. She had after all not saved Terry when she probably could have. She alone made the decision to wait until he'd died before calling an ambulance. She was dangerous, more than she ever thought she could be and the worst thing was, she'd do it again. Maybe Pete could see that when he looked at her. He wouldn't fully understand the cruelty she'd endured at Terry's hands and the fact that she'd feared for her own life every day. He has children, though. He had to know that a parent would do anything to protect them.

It was going to be a long day and she was under no doubt that she would see the reporter loitering at the scene at some point, trying to get answers before the press conference took place. He still had to earn his bread and butter money in between writing his alleged awful article about her life. Between him, Stephen and Hetty, they were doing their best to take her down.

THREE

As Gina drove down the twisty built-up street, she stopped behind
the ambulance. Early morning birds chirped even though darkness
still blanketed the sky. At least the rain had eased off a little but
rainfall was forecast so they all had to work quickly. A couple of
firefighters stood at the back of the fire truck while others came and
went. Shadows bounced back and forth on the road ahead – a
product of the portable lights that had been set up everywhere. She
glanced up, looking for signs of fire peaking above the conifer line
but there was nothing left, only the smell of smoke lingering in
the air.

Stepping onto the path, she glanced about, searching for
witnesses, and there were plenty of people. Neighbours stood
around in nightwear and coats, holding umbrellas. Some held out
their phones, filming the action. A couple of children peered from
behind their bedroom curtains. PC Kapoor stood behind the
cordon tape, keeping them all back as PC Smith finished tying the
last piece to a lamp post.

Gina wondered what state the body was in and she scrunched
up her nose knowing it would be left there to preserve evidence.
Burned bodies were never pleasant and the smell? Her stomach
began to turn a little as the acrid whiff seeped up into her nostrils.

Glancing up, she saw Bernard Small, the crime scene manager, standing beside the entrance to the drive. There was still too much commotion going on for him to be able to enter. As she waved at him, she spotted Jacob coming from the drive.

'Morning, Bernard.' Gina hurried down the path and glanced at the house. The long winding drive led to what would have been a beautifully presented house. She knew that The Meadows was one of the most expensive parts to live in Cleevesford. It was named The Meadows as it was once all meadow. Many of the meadows still existed but instead of being the main feature, they acted as a surround for the new estate.

'DI Harte. I hope you're not expecting too much from me yet, we haven't managed to get in to start our work and because of the nature of it all, everything outside has been trodden on. When we arrived, the lawn was covered in firefighters. The victim was already dead when we arrived. I did catch a look at the body, it's burned badly. I can't confirm the actual cause of death until we do the post-mortem. We don't know whether he was dead before the fire or the smoke or fire killed him.'

Gina nodded, knowing that was all Bernard would know at this point. 'Only opening him up will give us the answers we need.'

'Yep.' He glanced over to see if he was being called over but the firefighter in charge turned away.

Jacob flattened his short back and sides with his hand as he stared at the house. 'Guv, there is something that we found at the scene?'

'What's that?'

'There was a little tea light burning in a glass jar. Someone left it on the bird table.'

'Like a candle that people leave at vigils or light in church when remembering the dead?'

Jacob nodded. 'Yes, exactly like those.'

'Do we know anything about the victim?'

'We think it's thirty-three-year-old Glen Chapman. The victim is definitely an adult male and the only adult male registered at this address is him.'

'His next of kin will be called. We'll need that positive ID. Did he live alone?' Gina glanced up at the house, drenched and smoking out of the top windows. The acrid stench hit the back of her throat, then she caught sight of a child's trike leaned up against the fence.

'From what the neighbours have told us so far, he's married with two young children but it's common knowledge that they had a noisy argument a few days ago and Mrs Chapman left with the children.'

'Is there a chance that they came back?'

'No other bodies have been found in the house.'

Gina stopped clenching her teeth and exhaled, relieved that the rest of the family weren't in the house. 'We need to get hold of her. What other evidence do we have that the fire could have been started on purpose?'

Gina almost jumped as a tall, stocky firefighter came up behind her. 'Accelerant. I smelled it on arrival and on the surface it looks like the point of origin was at the letter box. The fire investigation officer should be speaking to the crime scene manager soon. I'm sure they'll have more later when the fire investigator can confirm the cause and ignition source. They have to rule out all other possible sources first.'

Gina nodded and thanked the man, knowing she could discuss this with Bernard when he'd had the chance to work through the scene and in turn speak to the fire officer. 'So it's looking like someone poured the accelerant through the letter box, lit it and ran?'

Jacob rubbed his sore-looking eyes. 'It looks that way. The smoke is really playing me up.' He blinked a couple of times and wiped his eyes. The red rims looked sorer by the second.

'Okay.' Gina turned back to Bernard. 'The crime scene. That bird table and the area around it is central to what we can preserve.'

Bernard ran his fingers through his pointy grey beard. 'That would all be well and good but, as I said, so many people have trampled all over the garden, dragging hoses and equipment through too. I know from the off this is going to be tough. The rain hasn't helped either. The garden is boggy. This scene is going to be a nightmare to process but you know us, if it's there to find, we will find it.'

The fire investigator interrupted, 'You can go in now. We've done all we can and we'll obviously help you with the investigation and making the building safe to enter. Stick with the grounds for now until we give you the go-ahead to enter the house.'

'Thanks.' Bernard smiled at the man. 'We best get on with it. I'll call you when we have some news.' Bernard turned to the van and waved at the officer inside. 'Dogs have arrived. Hopefully they'll be able to pick up on some trace evidence. Speak soon.'

Jacob smiled as Jennifer and a couple of other crime scene assistants appeared from around the corner, all dressed in their white crime scene suits, ready to go searching for evidence that could help the investigation. She smiled back. The happy couple had been together for quite a long time now and often met at crime scenes. 'See you later, Jen.' As Jennifer passed, Jacob turned to Gina. 'Who knows what time that will be?'

'All part of the job. It looks like we're not going to get much from forensics or the fire service yet, but let's look at what we do have. We know the fire was started using an accelerant so it was lit on purpose. Someone left a candle in a jar at the scene. Why and what does that mean?' Gina glanced at the property and spotted a shiny dome fixed to the corner of the house. 'CCTV. Hey, Bernard?'

The man glanced back.

'When you go in, if there's any way of getting hold of that CCTV, any hard drives, computers or devices that it might be recorded onto, please preserve it as best you can and get it sent over to the techies as soon as possible. We might just have our murderer caught on camera.'

He held a gloved thumb up. 'Will do.' With that, he pulled over his face mask and hair covering, ready to work the scene.

Jacob stepped away with Gina and zipped his coat up to the top. 'It's so cold. It makes you wonder why all these people aren't in their cosy homes, keeping warm.'

'And I wonder if one of them saw or heard anything?' Gina caught PC Kapoor's attention.

The young PC finished talking to the neighbours while PC Smith remained in place to keep the scene log. Her black ponytail flicked from side to side as she hurried over, calling in her Brummie accent. 'Hi, guv. We've arranged the door to doors. There are officers knocking as we speak and the good news is, we have a witness.'

Gina smiled at Jacob. 'That is good news. Which one?' She glanced at the pale woman in the puffa jacket, then the man in his lounge pants, then the rest of the residents.

'See that man?' Kapoor said.

Gina nodded.

'His son. The boy is only five.'

A child. Gina only hoped that the boy would be able to tell them enough that could help. She shrugged. 'Well, that's a good start.' She glanced for a little longer wondering if their murderer had remained at the scene to review their handiwork. 'While I'm speaking to them, would you try to find out if anyone has Mrs Chapman's number? We really need to contact her asap. She should be told before people start talking about it on social media.' So many people had their phones out. She wondered if the footage was already online.

Kapoor nodded as Gina and Jacob followed her to the outer cordon. That's when Gina spotted Pete Bloxwich with his camera around his neck and his phone held out, ready to record.

'DI Harte. I hear that we have a victim. Is this murder? Only I know how common murders are around here. In Cleevesford, I mean. I wasn't referring to you.' The man grinned widely as he chewed gum, the bottom of his chin buried in his zipped-up leather jacket.

'You'll have to attend the press conference later, which I'm sure DCI Briggs is working on as we speak. You know the rules. An appeal for witnesses is always helpful.' All she could think was, *don't let him get to you.*

He sniggered. 'It appears I do know the rules. Some people don't though, do they, detective? I mean, we're all on the same side. All I want to do is get dangerous people off our streets, just like you do.'

'You're all heart.' Gina bent and shuffled under the cordon, then she nudged the reporter out of the way as she passed him.

'Why was there a candle on the bird table?'

'We'll see you at the briefing with all the other reporters, Mr Bloxwich.' She glanced back and watched as he stepped back and held his hands out, leaving her with a huge smile, which was totally inappropriate for the scene. Then he turned and began speaking to the loitering residents.

'What was all that about, guv?' Jacob turned to her as he caught up.

'He's just a slime, that's all.'

He shrugged his shoulders.

Gina looked beyond the man in the lounge pants at the young boy sitting on the window ledge in their bay window. He looked so tiny, Gina felt a twinge of sadness that he had possibly witnessed a murderer in action. She'd have to tread lightly with him and his father, who would naturally be concerned. The boy rubbed his eyes and gripped his teddy bear.

FOUR

'Hello, I'm DI Harte and this is DS Driscoll. My colleague tells me that your son may have seen someone at the scene before the fire started.'

The man wrapped his coat tighter round his body. 'Yeah. I don't mind you talking to him but I don't want him upset with this. He already has nightmares and I can't get him to sleep in his own room. I don't need him scared. If he looks even a bit upset, I'll have to end it.'

Gina glanced up at the window again, taking in the innocent boy, knowing that there was no way she'd intentionally want to scare him. 'I'm a parent myself and I have a granddaughter about his age.' She smiled to put the man at ease.

'So you know what it's like. Follow me.' The man led the way up his drive. His thick dark curls tightened by the dampness in the air.

'Wait.' Gina stopped beside the car. 'May we speak first, before going in and seeing your son?'

'Of course.' He nervously frowned.

Jacob wiped his eyes one more time with a tissue, then sneezed. 'Excuse me. The smoke has really set me off.' He pulled his note-book from his pocket.

Gina stood under the security light that clicked on. 'May I take your name?'

'Aiden Marsh,' he replied as he pulled a pair of woollen gloves from his pocket and put them on. 'It's freezing out here, can we go into the kitchen at least?'

'Yes, sorry. I just need to speak to you first before we include your little boy in the conversation. The kitchen will be fine.'

The man pushed his front door open and Gina felt the warmth hit her. She could hear the boiler firing up as the radiator clicked. The little boy padded through from the living room in his monster-themed pyjamas.

'Daddy, I want some breakfast. My tummy's hungry.' The boy grinned, showing the gap where his front teeth would have been.

The man crouched to the boy's level and moved his black fringe from his eyes. 'I'll sort it in a minute, son. I just need to speak to this nice man and lady. Can you go and sit in the lounge with your blanky for a few minutes?'

The boy looked up at Gina and stared. She smiled. He then hurried into the living room, diving onto the settee and Aiden closed the door. The kitchen diner was huge and airy, bifold doors at one end and a skylight above. The darkness was beginning to lift and the beginnings of a new day were showing.

'Take a seat. Do you want coffee?'

Gina checked her watch, knowing that they had so much ground to cover and getting back to the station to update the team was a priority. 'No, thank you.' She glanced at Jacob, who also shook his head. Aiden continued to boil the kettle.

'How well did you know the Chapmans?'

'My son, Elias, had an occasional play date with their son, Harvey. On a personal level, I didn't know them well at all. I know they had a turbulent relationship.'

'What makes you say that?'

'The arguments and...'

'And what?'

'He'd call her names.'

'Mr Chapman.'

Aiden nodded. 'I've seen her flinching as she got in and out of her blue Volvo a couple of weeks ago. It doesn't take a genius to see what was happening. I'm sure he's hit her before. I hear the neighbours talking about it too. I was tidying up the front garden and I heard someone stop with a dog and talk about Glen and Faith. Faith, that's his wife's name. He's not a nice person... wasn't. I guess that the body bag coming out of the house meant that he's dead.'

Gina nodded. 'Why do you think it was him in the body bag?'

His hands shook as he placed a cup on the worktop. The sound of him swallowing broke the silence, then the kettle began to boil. 'What? Am I being formally questioned here?'

'Sorry, Mr Marsh. I'm just doing my job. I didn't mean to upset you.'

He shrugged and sat at the table with Gina and Jacob, leaving his drink unmade. 'No, I'm sorry. I understand that you have to ask these questions. I knew he was the only person in the house at the moment. Faith left him quite dramatically two days ago and the whole street saw and heard what was happening. She was crying and yelling, dragging the kids into the car. It was all rather upsetting because Elias saw Harvey. They were red-faced like they'd been crying.'

'Was Mr Chapman there too?'

Aiden shook his head. 'Not at first but he did stagger out after she'd buckled the kids into the car. Glen was really drunk which is why I think Faith managed to make an easy escape. I heard her shout the word divorce a couple of times, then he swore and went back in, slamming the door – I remember that much. Before I managed to ask Faith if everything was okay, she'd already got into her car and driven off. She wasn't okay though, I did see that she had a sore-looking lip. She hasn't been back since as far as I'm aware. That's why I thought that the only person who could be in that body bag was Glen.'

Jacob scribbled away, trying to get as much down as possible.

Taking her overcoat off, Gina leaned back a little to allow some air to circulate under her clothing. She'd heated up since coming into the warm house. 'Have you seen anyone hanging around or looking suspicious?'

Aiden shook his head. 'No, only my son did. I'd left him sleeping in my bed when I came down to nap on the settee, that's why the blankets are still strewn all over the place. Since his mother died over a year ago he joins me most nights, and tends to take over my side too and I can't sleep. His car bed isn't big enough for me either. Apparently he was awake and nosing out of the window because he heard a noise. He's the lightest sleeper I know.'

'Do you have Mrs Chapman's phone number?'

Aiden bit his bottom lip and scrunched his brow. 'Yes. It was for when we arranged the play dates; that was all. She'd call up and suggest times and dates, like when we met at a soft play centre. There were other parents there too... so we weren't alone. I mean, it wasn't a date or anything... for us. It was a date for the kids.'

Too much information. Gina wondered if there was more to Aiden and Faith's relationship than he was letting on. 'Mr Marsh, were you and Mrs Chapman in any kind of relationship?'

He sat bolt upright, the wooden chair creaking under his shifting weight. 'No, not at all. Never. I was concerned about her and offered her the chance to talk, about what was happening at home. I was worried about her so I just reminded her that I was a stone's throw away if she needed help.'

'How did she take you saying that?'

'Okay and she never asked me for help. I'd done all I could, I just hoped she'd find the strength to leave him.'

Gina knew that leaving was easier said than done. As she saw it, Mrs Chapman would definitely and justifiably like to see the end of her abusive husband and neighbour, Aiden Marsh, had personally got involved. He clearly felt something for her and he was keeping that back. Both had a motive. First, she needed to know what the little boy had seen. She smiled to try to put Mr Marsh at ease. 'May we speak with Elias now? Maybe we could all go into the living room together, where he's comfortable.'

Aiden nodded. His chocolate-brown eyes still meeting Gina's, a worried look fixed on his features. He forced a smile and tapped his fingers on the kitchen table before standing. 'Yes.' He led the way through, gently opening the door.

The boy lay under several blankets while clutching a stuffed bear. He dropped his picture book onto the floor. 'Can we have breakfast yet, Daddy?'

'In a minute, son. Budge up.' The boy shifted a little and let his dad sit next to him. Aiden placed an arm around him and the boy snuggled up to his dad. 'This nice lady and man just want to talk to you for a minute, is that okay?'

The boy grinned and hid his face with a hand, then peered through a gap. 'Who are they?'

Gina cleared her throat and kneeled in front of him. Jacob sat on the chair that was positioned in the bay. 'My name's Gina and this is Jacob. What's your name?' She smiled widely and tilted her head.

'Eli,' he shouted with a squeak before sucking his thumb. His rosy cheeks and sweet grin made her heart melt.

She looked at his book that was left open on a page where a friendly illustrated rabbit was raiding the kitchen cupboards. 'My granddaughter loves this book. She likes the bit when Rabbit eats all the carrots and has to lie on the floor all day because his trousers won't do up.'

The boy giggled. 'I like that bit too.'

'Your daddy told me that you woke up really early this morning, so early it was still very dark. Not like now, it's starting to get light.'

Elias nodded in an exaggerated way. 'I woke up.'

'Do you know why you woke up because it was still sleep time?'

He tittered a little. 'I heard a noise.'

'What sort of noise?'

'A bang.' He clapped his hands and laughed.

'Okay, that was a very loud bang. Do you know what could have made that noise? Did you have a look out of the window to see?'

He nodded again and placed his hands on his rosy cheeks. 'There's a bin on the path. The naughty person must have bumped into the bin and knocked it over. I saw them picking it up.'

'Naughty person?'

'They should have been in bed.' He giggled.

'I see.' Gina licked her lips and smiled again. 'You're right. People should be sleeping in the night. Did you see the person?'

'Yes, but it was dark. They had a hood and trousers and they were big like a grown-up.'

'Could you see if it was a man or a woman?'

The boy shook his head.

'Can you look out of the window and point to the bin that this person banged into?' Several bins lined the path.

He slid off the settee and ran to the window pointing. 'That one.'

'Thank you, Eli. You've been really helpful.' Gina glanced at the bin and saw that a few bits of litter were on the floor around the bin, which would back up the little boy's story that the bin had been knocked over.

He placed his knuckle in his mouth before turning to Aiden. 'I'm really hungry, Daddy. My tummy hurts because it wants food.'

'Of course, son.' The man ruffled the boy's hair and kissed his head before standing. 'I think that's all he knows. He came downstairs and woke me just after.'

'What time was that?'

'Let's go back in the kitchen. Eli, I'll do your breakfast and you can have it here. Stay here and keep warm under the blankets, okay, mate? It's cold so I want you to keep warm.'

'Okay, Daddy.' The boy gripped a little square of frayed blanket and snuggled it.

Gina stood and smiled. 'And thank you again, Eli. You've been very helpful and it was lovely to speak with you.' The adults headed back into the kitchen.

Aiden leaned against the worktop, finally pouring the hot water into his coffee. 'Eli woke me around two forty-five, so it must have been just before then. He then just came and snuggled with me on the settee, that's until I heard the commotion going on outside.'

Gina waited for Jacob to make a note. 'Thank you. If I could just take Mrs Chapman's number, that will be all for now. This is all just routine and we'll be speaking to your other neighbours too.'

He began scrolling through his phone and then scribbled a number down on a Post-it note. 'Here you go.'

'Thank you, shall we let ourselves out?' Gina popped her coat back on, ready to head back out into the cold.

Aiden nodded.

As they left the house, Gina turned to Jacob. 'He definitely liked her more than he's letting on. With every mention of her name, he seemed a little distant. I suppose we best break the news to Mrs Chapman next but first things first. I want that bin secured. Can you call Mrs Chapman, let her know we're on our way?'

Jacob nodded as he took the Post-it note from her and headed to the edge of the drive.

Gina glanced back at the house and watched as Aiden passed Elias a bowl of cereal, then Aiden's gaze met hers for the briefest of moments before he looked away. The feel of warm breath on her neck made her freeze then she slowly turned. 'What do you want?' she asked the reporter.

'The neighbours have been gossiping away while you've been in there. Poor Mrs Chapman. Domestic abuse. She had such a strong motive to kill him. I mean it was either her or him, one of them was going to end up dead. Just a guess. Oh, and don't worry, I won't be publishing that... not yet. I like to get my facts straight.'

Pete Bloxwich grinned and sniffed sharply, before rubbing the bottom of his nose. 'Class this as me helping you. Sharing information from the street. I help you, you help me. We can get to the truth together. The truth will set you free... as they say.' He burst into laughter as he turned away.

He was wrong, the truth would be the end of her.

FIVE

The little boy doesn't know why he's been placed in this room, alone, but he promised not to make a sound, so he won't. If he makes a sound, the monster downstairs will come for him and he doesn't want that. His voice is funny and he can't say real words, just loud scary grunts and he smells real bad.

It's a funny room and not like any room in the house the boy lives in. It slopes down at the sides and he's in the roof. There's a tiny room at the end with a toilet and washbasin in.

He lies down on the floor bed and thinks of where they got to in the story. He wonders what happens next. It's a good story, much better than the ones his teacher tells and better than the ones he reads in his books. He wouldn't tell Mummy, but it was better than her stories too. Mummy would be upset if he told her that so it would be their secret.

He glances around the room. It's quite long and there are boxes stacked up at the other end. It's also dusty but he's stopped sneezing now. The room is okay for an adventure, which is what this is, but he misses his own bed with all his favourite toys and especially his iPad games. He also misses his TV programmes too: *Beat Bugs* and *PAW Patrol*. If he was at home he could watch them now. Mummy always let him watch his programmes whenever he wanted. Here, he had other things, mostly jigsaws. He'd already done the one with the apples and bananas but it was too easy and didn't take long. There are colouring books and lots of crayons. Maybe he'll do some colouring or draw a picture for Mummy.

The lamp in the corner of the room has been left on all night and he's happy about that. If it went off, he wouldn't know what to do, after all he couldn't leave; the door was locked. It was for his safety though and he understood. A shiver ran down his back as he thought of what was outside that door. He wants his friend to come back and finish the story so that he can go home but he doesn't want to see the scary man again. Sometimes the man wails and that's scary. Mouth dry, he grabs the glass of juice that has been left for him and he takes a sip, but not too much. It tasted a bit funny and it makes him sleepy.

Barefooted, he pads across the room, careful not to hit his head on the sloping ceiling. The joggers he wears are far too long and he keeps tripping over the dangling material.

He flinches as something crashes against the window above. Running, he launches his body onto the bed, burying himself deep in the blankets. His heart judders like a train.

Be brave, he tells himself. *Take a little peek.*

With shaky hands he pulls the thick blanket away from his eyes and looks up expecting to see the monster man, but it's okay. It's only a pigeon strutting on the roof window, pecking for food that isn't there. Mummy says we shouldn't feed pigeons but sometimes he throws a bit of food in the garden for them, especially his crusts that he doesn't like. The pigeon stops and for a moment it looks like it's looking at him. That's when he hears the roar and the clanging.

The monster is coming. It's time to hide.

SIX

Gina pulled into the car park of the Mount Hotel that sat on the dual carriageway leaving Cleevesford. It wasn't a traditional hotel, more like a two-storey motel, the rooms laid out in a long, detached building situated away from reception. She saw the restaurant lights flick on and a man begin to set tables. Breakfast service was starting.

'She said she was in room ten. Should we park over there?' Jacob pointed to the parking spaces next to the accommodation block.

'Yes... actually, no. Let's talk to the night manager first. I want to know if Mrs Chapman left here in the night.' Gina pulled the car up to the entrance and they stepped out into the bitter November morning. A ray of light burst through the rain clouds, drawing attention to the prickles of frost on the roof tiles. As she walked, they shone like a carpet of diamonds. She yawned, tiredness working its way through her aching bones. There was nothing like a sleepless night to make a person feel totally out of sorts. Add on to that the problem of Pete Bloxwich and that was a recipe for disaster. He was another problem she'd have to deal with but she had no idea how she was going to go about that. The automatic doors slid open and a gust of hot air blew down, greeting them both with warmth as they entered.

'Morning. Are you checking in or is it just breakfast you're after?' The man in the burgundy waistcoat and tie looked up from his computer.

'I'd like a word, if possible. I'm DI Harte and this is DS Driscoll.' She held up her identification.

The man squinted as he read. 'I don't recall any problems in the night. Has something happened?'

'I hope not.' Gina smiled as she spotted his name badge. Michael – Manager. 'We've come to speak to one of your guests but it's okay, she knows we're coming. I just thought I'd pop by and ask you a couple of questions first.'

'Well I don't know what it is I'm meant to know. Nothing's happened here. I haven't reported anything and I've been here all night. In fact, I'm due off in half an hour.' He picked his glasses up and put them on.

'We just need you to confirm when Mrs Chapman checked in.'

'Okay, let me see. It was Friday but I don't know what time as I didn't check her in.'

'That's okay, thanks for confirming that information. Have you been at your desk the whole night?'

The man nodded. 'Apart from taking a toilet break, I haven't moved from this chair.' Gina spotted a copy of *Lord of the Rings* on the desk, the bookmark in the middle. 'I've been here all night, mostly reading.'

A woman burst through, dragging a vacuum along.

'Did Mrs Chapman leave between midnight and three this morning, on foot or by car?'

He scrunched his brow. 'No, but I wouldn't see anyone leave anyway. They park in front of their rooms and there's another way out of the car park.' He glanced at his computer screen. 'Ahh, Mrs Chapman, she's the one with the two children in room ten.'

'That's right. Do you have any CCTV covering the other access road?'

'No, I'm afraid not. We have dummy cameras to try and deter trouble. Not that we get any. This is a really safe hotel.'

There was no way to confirm if Faith Chapman had left in the night, maybe her room would tell a different story. All it would take would be the smell of smoke in her hair, on her clothing. Would she leave her young children alone to burn her abusive husband down? Whose side was Gina on? Cases like this were the worst for her. If Mr Chapman had been hurting her and Mrs Chapman had done the deed, Gina wouldn't enjoy making this arrest. If her own truth came out and Mrs Chapman was guilty, Bloxwich would enjoy putting that in his article.

'Shall we speak to Mrs Chapman, then?' Jacob made her flinch as he brought her out of her thoughts. The manager had already gone back to his work.

'Yes.'

Murky pools of water settled on the road and they were beginning to frost up. With every exhalation a plume of white mist filled the air. It was getting chillier and... Gina almost slipped on the slabs underneath.

'That was close. You nearly landed on your arse.' Jacob laughed.

'Not funny.'

He sniggered.

'Okay, it's just a bit funny.' She stopped talking as they approached the block, an air of seriousness replacing the jokiness. 'I hate delivering news like this, I mean really hate it. I see number ten, bottom row.' They hurried past the frost-coated cars that were parked up. Gina spotted the car she knew to be Mrs Chapman's Volvo. It too was covered in frost, suggesting that it hadn't been driven recently. The engine in that car hadn't recently warmed up. She wondered how the woman would take the news of her husband's murder. A line of large conifers stood on the opposite side of the road providing a screen from the dual carriageway. Fast moving vehicles sped by and the smell of fumes hung in the air.

Gina knocked on the door and Mrs Chapman opened up. Her grey yoga pants clung to her ample middle. Straggly mousy hair fell down to her large bust. The first thing that hit Gina was the sour smell. It was like she hadn't washed for a couple of days.

'Come in.' The split on Mrs Chapman's lip looked like it was healing. 'Kids, can you go and brush your teeth? Harvey, help your sister. We don't want to go and see Nanny and Grandad with stinky teeth, do we?'

The television blasted out with the local weather report, more frost and potentially black ice was predicted as temperatures were set to plummet. The boy took his little sister's hand and led her to the bathroom. Then the water began to run and the kids giggled and screamed as they played.

Mrs Chapman walked over to the bathroom and closed the door on the little ones. 'What's going on?'

Gina swallowed. 'We have some bad news. Would you like to sit down?'

'No, not really. Are my parents okay?'

Holding her hand out, Gina bit her bottom lip. She hated these calls more than anything and, at the moment, there was nothing she could see in the room that made her suspect Mrs Chapman of murdering her husband. It definitely didn't smell of smoke and amongst all the clothes that were strewn everywhere, there were no hooded items. That didn't fully put her out of the picture but her involvement was looking less likely. 'You're parents are fine as far as we're aware.'

'Well, what's happened?'

'It's your husband, Mr Chapman. There was a fire at your house and I'm afraid he's dead. We're really sorry for your loss.' Gina paused to allow the news to sink in. 'Is there anyone I can call to be with you?'

The woman shook her head, then she sat on the end of the double bed. 'How? A fire. My house... How am I going to tell Kiara and Harvey that their dad is dead?'

'I know this has come as a shock, Mrs Chapman. I'm also really sorry to say that we have reason to believe that the fire was started on purpose. We need to ask you a few questions.'

Tears began to stream down her face, removing a streak of old make-up down her cheek; that's when Gina saw the scratch on her chin. 'I can't talk about this right now... my children. I need my mother.' She grabbed her phone and called a number. No one answered. 'Come on.' She tried again. 'Mum.' Faith Chapman burst into tears as the kids ran out of the bathroom.

'Mummy, why are you crying?' Kiara sat next to her mother and Harvey jumped on the bed behind her, wrapping his arms around her neck from behind.

'Something bad has happened and Mummy just needs a word with Nanny.'

Gina picked up a stuffed giraffe from the floor. 'Maybe you could tell me what this lovely giraffe's name is?'

The kids came over while their mother took the phone into the bathroom.

'He's called Pickle,' Harvey said.

'Pickle, that's a funny name,' Jacob said wide-eyed with a smile.

The boy laughed and grabbed another toy from the floor, a plastic dinosaur. Gina looked at the children and wondered how far Faith would be prepared to go to protect them. After all, Gina knew exactly how it felt to be trapped in a violent relationship with a child.

Kiara ran towards the bathroom on her chubby legs and began to bang on the door. Gina knew they were going to have to give Faith a little time to absorb the news and see to her children.

A few minutes later, Gina stood with Jacob by the car. 'That was tough.'

'At least she's agreed to talk to us in a bit.'

'I guess thinking she might be able to talk now was a bit too much.' Gina's phone rang and she answered. After a bit of agreeing and nodding, she ended the call. 'That was Briggs, urgent briefing now. Bernard has just called him. They found something at the scene and it might just lead us to the murderer.'

SEVEN

DC Harry O'Connor brushed past, biting a croissant between his teeth while holding a coffee in his hands. His head reflected the light in the corridor as he entered the incident room.

'Morning,' Gina called.

'I hope there's plenty of coffee on the go.' Jacob wiped his eyes again. The redness had completely gone now.

'Me too. I'm absolutely parched and in dire need of caffeine.'

As they entered the incident room, DCI Chris Briggs stood by the board. Some of the crime scene photos had already been pinned to it. DC Paula Wyre scraped a chair on the floor and sat at the table, her black plait swishing as she sat. It was barely gone nine in the morning. The room had a bleak feel to it. Cold strip lights occasionally flickered and the fan heater whirred away. Not that the heating didn't work – that had been fixed properly a while ago – it simply wasn't up to the task of heating the room. Condensation trickled down the inside of the windows that looked out onto the car park. Wyre zipped up her jacket and shivered as O'Connor finished chewing on his croissant. He clapped his hands, releasing a pastry mist all over the table.

Gina grabbed one of the cups of black coffee that had been left in the middle of the large table and took a sip, enjoying the bitter warmth as it slipped down her throat.

Briggs stood and tidied his hair with his hands, his firm arms exposed as he'd rolled up his shirtsleeves. Gina knew he rarely got cold but this room was freezing. She wondered how he could bear to have so much exposed flesh. 'Right, take a seat all. Thank you for getting in so quickly. Gina, can you fill us in?'

She nodded and stood, bringing her coffee to the front of the room. 'Morning, yes, thank you for getting here so quickly. Jacob arrived at the scene with forensics first and I arrived a little after. Bernard and the fire investigation officer confirmed that an accelerant had been used to start the fire. The point of origin was the letter box. When I got there, the firefighters were still extinguishing the fire and making the scene safe, but one thing we did see in the front garden was a candle. It had been left on the bird table. This can't be a coincidence so I'm taking it that our killer left it there for us to find. It means something to them. The tea light was in a little jar.' Gina paused and she sipped her coffee again to lubricate her dry throat. 'Jacob and I managed to speak to the man who lives opposite to the Chapmans, his name is Aiden Marsh. He told us that Mrs Chapman left Mr Chapman on Friday after an argument, taking with her their two young children. He said that Mr Chapman may have been abusing his wife. He mentioned her lip being sore and we saw a cut on her lip when we went to the hotel. It's something the other neighbours had speculated about too.'

O'Connor leaned in. 'Do we have anything on Mrs Chapman? Could she have been at the scene?' He grabbed a biscuit from the plate in the centre of the table before offering the plate to everyone.

'It's possible but not as far as we know. Mr Marsh gave us her number and we went to the Mount Hotel where she has been staying with the children since she left her husband on Friday. There was nothing in her room to suggest that she'd set her own house alight, no smell of smoke or accelerant. Her reactions to the news seemed genuine too and her car was still frosted over. Not to mention that she has two young children. As for opportunity, they may have been asleep if she did leave them to set her own house alight.' Gina grimaced as she too grabbed a biscuit. Her stomach was almost sick with hunger and thoughts of Pete Bloxwich.

'Is there anything else?' Briggs stepped back.

'Yes, going back to Aiden Marsh. His little boy, who is only five, woke up in the night and saw someone outside just before the fire was lit. He described a person in a hood wearing trousers. He couldn't give us an indication of height or build or gender but we did secure a bin that he said the person he saw knocked over and banged into. I'm not convinced that Aiden Marsh's relationship with Faith Chapman was platonic. I don't have any evidence but I'm sure there was something he was keeping back from us. Mrs Chapman is coming here in a short while once she's settled the children in with her parents. I'm hoping we can find out more then.' Gina nodded to Briggs and sat.

Briggs ruffled the end of his tie and dropped it. 'Right, so on to what we do have. Bernard called with a brief update. The scene is a nightmare to process and the house has been drenched. In a wider search of the garden area, the crime scene investigators found a lighter. It was just under the shrubbery at the top of the drive and we've managed to obtain a good clean print. The bad news is that we don't have a match on the system but it's a start. There is, however, an engraving on the lighter. It says, *to my love, XXX.* Someone will miss this lighter, with its personal message. We need to find out who it belongs to. Right, fuel up on coffee and get out there. We need to obtain as much CCTV as possible and interview all the neighbours. Someone must have seen something.'

As the room erupted into chatter about the case, Gina hurried over to Briggs as he was about to leave. 'I'm in such big trouble. I don't know who else to turn to.' The colour drained from her face as he led her into his office.

EIGHT

'Sit. Do you want a drink?'

'No, I'm okay.'

He pulled his coat from the hook on the door and placed it over her shoulders. 'It's a bit chilly in here.' He turned the heater on. 'Are you going to tell me what's going on?'

'It's Pete Bloxwich, the reporter at the *Herald*.'

'Oh him. What's he done now? Was he interfering at the scene?'

'No more than usual. It's much worse than that.' Gina's forehead throbbed as the pressure began to build. She sniffed and took a deep breath.

'Okay. What?' He wheeled his chair close to Gina and sat in front of her, placing a warm hand on her shoulder.

She glanced up into his eyes and bit her lip. 'He emailed me. He's in talks with Hetty and Stephen. They've convinced him that I let Terry die and he wants my side of the story for some true crime article he's writing.' She pulled out her phone and opened up the email.

As he read it, she saw him swallow. 'They have nothing, not a jot.'

'But that isn't stopping him and them from shouting about

what they all think they have. This could ruin me. Where there's smoke, there's fire. The public aren't like us. We need evidence, they just need rumours. I can't go through this. I'll lose my job. I'll lose everything. Just when things were back on track with Hannah, she'll be convinced I'm lying to her too and I'll lose her all over again. We both know my daughter well enough to know that's possible.' She grabbed her hair in her hands and leaned over into her lap, fighting the urge to scream or worse, sob.

'I can give the case to Jacob if you feel you need a break? I know he'd like the opportunity to be senior investigating officer.'

She jolted up. 'No, I mean Jacob would do a brilliant job, but I need this case. I need to be at work. If I go home, I'll go insane. I need to carry on as normal.' She paused and stared at the wall behind him. 'The truth will come out one day, I can feel it.'

'The truth is, Terry was an abusive arsehole who came home drunk on that fateful night. He threatened you with violence and in a scuffle he fell down the stairs. His injuries were that bad, he died.'

She shook her head. 'I helped him down those stairs. It's different.'

'No. You have to get that out of your head. Look at me.' He gently touched her chin. 'We will get through this like we've got through everything else. It too will soon be history. One thing's for certain though, if you get too distracted while working on the case, I will have to send you home on rest. We have a dead man and our priority is to find out who murdered him and get them off the streets.'

She stood, almost knocking the chair over. 'I'm not going home to rest. I'm fine. All fine. As you say, it's nothing and I'm going to get on with my job.' Briggs was normally so helpful but now, his suggestion of her coming off the job was something she couldn't even risk happening. The only thing she could do was paste a brave face on it all. It was time to face the fact that maybe he'd had enough of her, her problems and all the drama she brought with them.

She went for the door handle. His strong grip enveloped hers as he kept her from opening the door. She felt his warm breath tickling her neck. 'I'm sorry. That all came out wrong. If he emails you again, tell me. Don't keep me in the dark. I promised you that we were in this together and I meant it. Sometimes, I just don't know what to do. All I do know is, everything will be fine.' He leaned his chin on her shoulder.

'Okay, I promise. I promise you too that it won't interfere with the case.' They both flinched at the loud knock at Briggs's office door. Parting, Gina stepped back and Briggs went over to the other side of his desk.

'Come in.'

Jacob entered. 'Mrs Chapman is here. I've put her in interview room one and given her a coffee.' He paused, his brow furrowing. 'Did I interrupt something?'

Gina smiled and cleared her throat. 'No, of course not. We were just discussing the press release. I'll grab some water and meet you there.'

Jacob smiled and left the room.

'I best go and see what Mrs Chapman has to say. I really want to know more about her and Aiden Marsh. I wonder if Aiden's own son could recognise his father in a hood in the dark. If he did have a thing for Faith Chapman, maybe he thought he was helping her by getting rid of her husband, or maybe they planned it together.'

'People will do a lot for love.' Briggs turned on his computer then ignored her as she left, leaving her to ponder his last statement.

NINE

Sonya headed over to the treadmill and started off with a steep incline to warm up. She was late. After a minute or so, she would start her twenty-minute jog with intermittent sprints, just like she did every time. The large mirrored wall reflected an image of herself that she didn't recognise. Her usually shiny brown hair was matted and scooped into a ponytail and her skin looked sallow. At the end of the session, she would go to the gym café with the others. She called them her motivation ladies. Heather, Kerstin and Faith; but Faith hadn't turned up today.

This gym had started off being her treat but now she needed it more than ever. It was her second home, her social life, her family but they didn't know she was in debt because of the membership. When she'd joined, she'd been with her son's father, Justin. They'd lived together, had two incomes coming into the household, now she had no maintenance because he was barely getting any work and sponging off some woman he'd left her for called Charlene. Things were tough and the gym would have to go soon. She glanced around. It was all super shiny, clean mirrors and the latest state-of-the-art equipment. Sauna; steam room; pool surrounded by sun loungers. The chill-out room played piped music and the treatments were extras on top of membership. She loved it here and knowing that it might all end soon brought a lump to her throat, but then all good things ended at some point.

Every Sunday, Wednesday and Friday, the motivation ladies met at the gym without fail. Excuses were never an option. Glancing across all the equipment, she waved at Heather, then across at Kerstin, but still Faith was nowhere to be seen. Heather and Kerstin hurried over with serious expressions on their faces. Kerstin began scrolling on her phone before passing it to Heather. It was no good, Sonya had to ask them what they were looking at. She ended her treadmill workout and headed over. 'Hey, what am I missing?'

Kerstin grabbed Sonya's arm and dragged her over to a bench. 'Look at this.' Her red ponytail swished as she thrust her phone into Sonya's hand. Heather followed and took a swig of water from her bottle.

'You want me to look at Facebook?' Sonya frowned.

'It's *What's Up Cleevesford*. You know, all the gossip and news seems to hit that Facebook page first.' Kerstin pointed at the screen, the pearly-pink nail tip clipping the screen.

She glanced at the post. 'RIP Glen. Who's Glen?'

'Glen Chapman. It's Faith's husband.'

'Oh hell.' She gulped and felt her heart rate pick up. 'Has anyone spoken to her?'

Heather put her hand up. 'I have, I mean I've tried to call her. I didn't get through. I've been calling for the past twenty minutes but her phone is off.' Heather sat the other side of Sonya on the bench, squashing her into what was left of the space. Her brown hair escaping the topknot on her head and mingling with the film of sweat along her hairline.

'What happened?'

'A fire, at the house.' Kerstin leaned into Sonya and scrolled a little further. 'Click on that link to the *Herald*.'

'Shit. There's an appeal for witnesses. Do they think someone did this on purpose?' Sonya gave the phone back to Kerstin, her heart banging away. Heather turned away from them and began tapping out messages on her phone.

'It looks like it. It doesn't mention Faith. She must have got out. What about the children?'

'Faith and the children weren't there.' Sonya flushed a little. Faith had told her not to tell the others what had happened and she felt guilty betraying her friend's trust.

'What? How do you know?'

'She called me yesterday.'

Heather stood just as her phone rang. 'I've just got to take this.' The door swung as she left.

'Sonya, rewind. Faith called you yesterday. What happened?'

'She's left him, Glen.'

'I know things weren't good between them but I had no idea she'd left him. Given what happened to their house, it's a good job I suppose.'

'Kerstin, whatever you do, don't tell Faith that I told you. She made me swear I wouldn't say anything. I think she wanted to tell you guys herself.'

'Did she say anything else, like why?'

Sonya scrunched her brow. 'Can you guess without me telling you?'

'She finally stood up to the bastard.'

'I can't confirm or deny but you're warm.'

'That's a confirmation.'

'It's not.'

''Tis.'

Heather scurried back in, gym bag over her shoulder, face draining of colour. Her trainers squeaked on the floor with each step. 'Got to go.'

Kerstin stood. 'Already. We need to get a drink. Our friend's husband has just been killed in a fire and you're rushing off?'

'Sorry, so sorry. My dad needs some things and I have to collect his medicine from the chemist. Catch you later. I'll call.' She held her fingers up to her ear in a phone motion before rushing out.

Shaking her head, Kerstin stretched her legs out in front of her. 'I think she forgot that she used the same excuse on Wednesday and Friday. Maybe I'm just being mean, I know her dad is sick but since she's been with Stephen, things haven't been the same. What's happening to us? You're not going to desert me, are you, Sonya?'

'No, hun. Let's ditch the treadmills and get that drink. We need to work out how we can help Faith. We know Glen was bad to her but at the end of the day, he was father to their two children and the fire happened at her house. I have her parents' number from when they bought my old car. Maybe we should give them a call, see if she's there.'

'Good idea. See you in the café. Ten minutes. I need a replenishing vitamin C smoothie to get me through this morning.' Kerstin grabbed her towel and headed out, leaving Sonya alone with her racing thoughts.

She shouldn't have said anything about Faith to the others. The less said the better, especially when she was told in the strictest of confidences not to say a word about anything. She swallowed, holding back all the anxiety and fear that was brewing in the pit of her stomach, the sense of loss eating her up from the inside. She'd never felt so alone in her whole life. She'd well and truly blown things now. All she wanted was to be at home cuddled up to her little boy, Erik.

Do everything you would normally do. Be a good girl and everything will be just fine.

TEN

'Mrs Chapman, thank you for coming to see us. I know this is hard for you.' Gina pulled out the few notes that they had and scanned them quickly as Jacob began to head up the statement. The recorder was rolling and a fan heater was blasting out warm air into the tiny room.

The woman sat hunched over, biting her nails. Her straggly hair had been tied up in a ponytail. 'I haven't told the kids yet. I don't know what I'm going to say.'

'Again, we're really sorry about what happened.'

She flinched as the skin on her finger bled a little from where she'd gnawed away at it. 'I still can't believe it. You say the fire was started on purpose. Do you know how?'

Gina nodded. 'An accelerant was used. The fire alarms didn't go off when the fire took hold. Can you please tell us a bit about your relationship with your husband?'

'I always nagged Glen to check them, but he never did.' She paused and bit another nail. 'We were going through a rough patch.'

'Did he ever abuse you?'

She shrugged. 'He wasn't always like he's been recently. It's as if something changed within him.'

Gina felt like sighing. Whatever may have been going wrong in Mr Chapman's life was never an excuse to hurt his wife, but she sat back and listened.

'He was stressed, really stressed. Kept saying it was work. I mean, he was never the most patient of people. If I did something wrong, he'd shout his mouth off at me but he'd never hit me before, he'd just throw a few things, push me out the way, punch a door – that kind of thing.'

As if that was okay. Gina felt the frustration in her chest building up. Shouting at his wife and pushing her because he was stressed wasn't okay.

Mrs Chapman stared at the table and wiped a tear from her eye. 'That was until a couple of weeks ago. I kept asking him what was wrong. I knew something had happened but he wouldn't say what. He caught me looking through his emails on his laptop and he went berserk. He pushed me out of the way and caught my cheek with his elbow. A couple of neighbours heard our shouting. It was an accident.'

'Did anything else like this happen after?'

'His drinking got even worse. I came home from seeing my mum one day last week and he was blind drunk, lying on the sofa slurring his words. The kids got upset and started crying and I had a go at him, saying that this couldn't go on. I mean, our marriage wasn't that good anyway. He'd been sleeping on the settee for ages. Anyway, he staggered across the room and pushed me away from the door so hard that I fell into the TV stand and made my forehead bleed.' She lifted her fringe to show the faint pink line. 'It's nearly gone now. He didn't mean it; I was standing in his way. That's all.'

'And your lip. What happened?'

She shook her head. 'That was Friday. I'd finally had enough and told him that I was leaving him and taking the kids until he sorted himself out. I don't know what caused this change in him and what he was hiding from me, but it was something bad. I've never seen him like he was that day before and it scared me. He gripped my chin that hard his nail dug into my lip until it bled. He said I couldn't go and take his children. In fact, he tried to push me out of the door without them. I had to wait three hours until he'd drunk himself into a stupor then I basically made my escape. He tried to stop me but he was too wobbly. That's when I left him and checked into the hotel with the kids. I didn't want to turn up on my parents' doorstep in a state. I needed a couple of days to get my head around everything that had happened.'

'Did you hear from Mr Chapman after that?'

The woman paused and began to twist the end of her ponytail between her fingers. 'Yes, he kept calling me and leaving me messages. At first he said he was sorry and that he missed us all and he loved me, but after a while of me not answering, it was all, you bitch – leaving with my children. You're going to pay.'

'Do you still have these messages?'

Faith nodded. 'Yes.'

'May I see them?'

'They're private.' She paused for a few seconds before handing her phone over.

Gina took the phone and gave it to Jacob.

'I need it back. My mother will probably try to call and all my phone numbers are in it.'

'Do you mind if we download the messages from it before you go?'

She shrugged and swallowed. 'Whatever, maybe you can find out what was going on with Glen.'

'Where were you in the early hours of this morning?'

'Really?'

'It's a routine question, Mrs Chapman. I have to ask.' Gina leaned back a little and the chair squeaked.

'I was obviously with my children in the hotel room. Kiara was crying half the night, she does that, wakes up all the time but with all that's going on, she had a rough night last night. She was missing her dad. The people in the room above me were banging on their floor and I think I told them to shove off in the early hours.

I didn't mean to sound rude but there was nothing I could do. I was already doing my best with the children and I couldn't cope so I banged on the ceiling back. This carried on for a while. The walls are paper-thin in that place.'

Gina watched as Jacob made a note to check what Faith was saying with the people who were in the room above.

'What did your husband do for a living?'

'He owns a plumbing supply company which has several branches around the Midlands.'

'Did he have any enemies that you know of?'

'It's hard to tell. He's not what I call a people person.'

'In what way?'

'He never used the words please or thank you. He claimed he was paying them and they should do their job. I remember one member of staff has a sick child and his boy needed chemo. He wanted to be with his wife when she took his son to the hospital but Glen wouldn't let him have the morning off. The man walked out and never came back.'

'When was this?'

'About a month ago. I just remember Glen coming home in a foul mood saying that he had a business to run. I tried to reason with him, saying what it would be like if it was Harvey in that position, but he wasn't having any of it. He just said it doesn't take two to take a kid to hospital and he didn't want to have his business disrupted. I think that may have been the start of it all. I really saw a side to Glen I didn't like from then on.'

'What was he like before that?'

'He's always been cold but never nasty in this way. Like I said, something changed in him. That may have been the start of it but over the last couple of weeks things got much worse, which is why I was looking at his emails.'

'Did you see anything that would explain his change in behaviour?'

'I wish I did but no. There was nothing out of the ordinary.

Whether he had another phone somewhere or a hidden email account that I have no knowledge of, I don't know.'

'What is it you do?'

'When the children are at school and nursery, I do the accounts for the business.'

'And was everything okay with the business?'

'It's doing really well. As far as I know, there were no problems, only the ones caused by Glen when it came to how he handled the staff.'

'Can I take the name of this employee, the one whose son was having chemo?' Gina swallowed. The more she was hearing about Glen Chapman the more she found to dislike him, but it was her job to find out who torched his house and killed him.

'Garth Shaw. I have access to the employee database on my work computer and his address and details should be there. He's no longer working for us after leaving. As I say, that was almost a month ago.'

'May we have access to yours and your husband's offices?'

Faith unzipped her jacket pocket and pulled out a set of keys. She removed a key and a fob. 'There's no one in today. Our offices are the first ones at the top of the stairs. It's GC Supplies on Cleevesford Industrial Park.'

'We will need to take yours and your husband's computers for analysis. Could you write the passwords down?' Gina passed her a pad and pen.

The woman sat up and began to write. Her teary eyes were now stark. 'What about the staff and the next payroll I'll have to run? I'm doing everything here to cooperate but people need paying. You can take my husband's computer if you have to but I really need mine back by the end of the week. As my husband is the victim here, I sincerely hope you'll make sure that happens.'

'We'll make sure you get yours back as soon as possible and we thank you again for everything you're doing to help us with the investigation.'

Exhaling, Faith sat back in her chair.

'Just another question, did your husband have any issues with the neighbours?' Gina wondered what Mr Chapman's views were on Aiden Marsh.

'He thought they were all nosey and asked that I keep away from them and don't divulge our business to anyone.'

'How about Mr Marsh across the road?'

Faith snorted and let out a half smirk. 'Glen hated him. He got so peeved when us mums used to meet him at soft play and the park. I kept telling Glen that he was being stupid.'

'So was Mr Chapman jealous of Mr Marsh?'

'I guess he was. I mean, Glen could have come too but he never seemed interested in being with us all at soft play. Aiden used to joke that Glen was giving him the daggers again but I told Aiden to take no notice.'

'What is yours and Mr Marsh's relationship like?'

'What kind of a question is that?'

Gina tilted her head slightly. 'It's routine. We just need to know of anyone that may have a motive to hurt your husband.'

'Well you're looking in the wrong place when it comes to Aiden. He's the kindest and gentlest soul I know. He wouldn't hurt a fly. He even told me to call him if I ever needed to talk about anything. He could see that I was stressed with Glen.'

Gina wondered if Aiden Marsh would have it in him to burn Mr Chapman alive. Maybe that kind and gentle soul had been pushed to his limits, especially if he had feelings for Faith and could see how unhappy she was.

'Look, I really need to go. I have to be with my children and my parents will be tearing their hair out. They were really unsettled when I left them. Please just get what you want from my phone, and then I need to get out of here.' The woman began biting her nails again.

'Sorry, we won't keep you long.' Gina began listening to the messages that had been saved. She shivered; each and every one could have been messages that Terry had left. So many sorry messages followed by a load of drunken insults. A creeping sensation tickled the back of her neck. She placed the phone on the table. Did Mrs Chapman have as much to hide as Gina had? There must be more to the story or maybe Mr Chapman had died at the hands of an employee to whom he didn't show an ounce of compassion? Or was it the love-struck neighbour?

Gina pulled out a photo of the lighter that was found at the scene and pushed it along the table. 'Do you recognise this lighter?'

Mrs Chapman's brow scrunched. 'I gave that to my husband on our first anniversary? It's his.' The woman began to scratch her neck and fidget. 'I have to go now.'

Something wasn't right. The woman stood and zipped her coat up as Jacob wound the interview up and stopped the tape. Gina knew now it was hugely important to contact the people who stayed in the room above Mrs Chapman last night, but first they had to question Garth Shaw. An employee of GC Supplies, the company that Glen Chapman owned. Had Mr Chapman's heartlessness pushed him over the edge?

ELEVEN

The satnav directed Gina to take the next right onto Fern Road. After leaving GC Supplies with the address that they needed, they'd left the team packing up the tech from the offices. Jacob stuffed the last of his sausage roll into his mouth and chewed loudly before stuffing the wrapper into his pocket.

The houses were tightly packed on this estate and however hard Gina looked, she couldn't see a door number but then she stopped outside the house where the bin had a huge number fifty-five painted on the side. 'Here we are.' She pulled up in the only space she could find, blocking Garth Shaw's car in.

A woman peered out of the window and moments later the front door flew open. 'You can't park there. Move now, please. I have a sick son and I'm fed up with everyone around here blocking me in.' She placed her hands on her hips. Straggly black hair fell over her shoulders and breasts and her bright red and pink jumper made her stand out in the bleak fog.

'Mrs Shaw?'

She paused and stared at Gina as she and Jacob stepped a little closer, locking the car.

'Who's asking?'

Gina pulled her identification from her pocket. 'Sorry, I'm

Detective Inspector Harte and this is DS Driscoll. Is your husband in?'

'What's he done?'

'We just need to speak to him about an incident. May we come in?' The last thing Gina wanted to do was to start discussing the murder on their doorstep with his wife. She needed to speak to Mr Shaw first.

Mrs Shaw took a step to the side and continued weighing them up. Eventually she continued walking up the uneven and broken slabs. 'Come in. He's in bed.'

Gina glanced at her watch. It was gone lunchtime.

'I know, I know. He's recently lost his job and he's not taking unemployment too well.'

Gina paused at the door. 'When we pulled up, one of the first things you asked us was "what has he done?" What did you mean by that?'

'I didn't mean anything. It's just, he hasn't been himself and he's started drinking a lot. When I've got home from work, I've found him in the kitchen, even on the floor in a stupor. I'm worried about him, that's all. Our son is sick too and it's taking a toll on both of us.'

'I'm sorry about your son.'

A thin boy of around five years old came down the stairs, wrapped in a velour blue dressing gown. A huge smile formed on his face. Despite losing his hair and feeling rotten after his chemo, this boy was still smiling and Gina smiled back.

'Hey, Lewis. Can you tell your dad that he has visitors and to get up.'

'Okay, Mum.' The boy ran up the stairs and Gina heard him crash through the door and onto the bed where she heard Mr Shaw stirring.

'Come through to the kitchen. Can I make you a drink?'

Gina nodded. 'I'd love a coffee. Black, please.'

'Same, thank you.' Jacob smiled.

As the woman prepared the drinks, they heard the bannister

creaking as Mr Shaw followed his son downstairs. He pushed the kitchen door open and yawned. His brown hair stuck out in all directions and the musty smell told Gina that he hadn't washed for a while. His wild-looking beard was possibly ageing him as Gina knew him to only be twenty-seven, but he looked to be in his late thirties. 'What's going on?' He patted his son's head.

'They're detectives and want to speak to you. Lewis?'

The boy looked up. 'What?'

She poured the coffees then kneeled in front of the boy. 'Can you go in the living room and watch your programmes while Daddy talks to our guests?'

The boy nodded and bit his knuckles before leaving the room. Moments later, the television was turned up and the squeaky voices of cartoon characters blared out.

Mr Shaw sat on the bench seating that was against the back wall and Mrs Shaw brought the drinks over. 'Take a seat.'

'Thank you.' Gina and Jacob sat on the loose chairs the other side of the table. Without the light being turned on, the kitchen was dark and dreary.

'What's this about?' Mr Shaw took a long drink of his coffee and scratched his head. His wife went to lean over to turn on the kitchen light and he held a hand up. 'Please don't. My head is killing.'

Gina could smell the staleness of some alcoholic drink oozing from his breath and pores. She wondered if the man in front of her could have drank too much and decided to make Mr Chapman pay in the heat of a drunken moment. Then she thought of the candle. What did it mean? Someone had left that burning for a reason. Was that too calculated an act for someone who was drunk and angry, acting without premeditation? 'First of all, we're sorry to disturb you but there was an incident that happened in the early hours of this morning. We believe you used to work for Glen Chapman at GC Supplies.'

'Yes, I left though. I haven't been there for a few weeks now. What's happened?'

Gina sipped the coffee. 'In the early hours of this morning, Mr Chapman died after someone set fire to his house.'

'Bloody hell.' He paused and seemed a lot more sober than he did a few minutes ago. 'Wait...' He glanced at Gina, then Jacob. 'You don't both think I had anything to do with it. I was at home all night, wasn't I?'

'Yes, he got in from the pub late last night and went straight to bed.'

Jacob pulled out his notebook.

'What time was that?'

The woman shrugged. 'I was asleep when he came in but he was so drunk he slept on the sofa for the first half of the night before coming up to bed about six. I know it was six as Lewis woke his dad up at that time.'

'Which pub did you go to, Mr Shaw?'

'The Angel Arms. I was there until close and I staggered home. There's no way I could have set his house on fire, first I was mega drunk and secondly, I don't even know his address.'

'We went to that barbecue last summer.'

Mr Shaw stared at his wife, a look of annoyance on his face. 'Oh yeah. He paid for caterers to placate his miserable staff last summer. I forgot, sorry. I can't remember where his house is though. We went once, last summer. It wasn't even his idea, it was his wife's. Faith was always lovely to everyone. But I was nowhere near his house in the early hours.'

'Can anyone confirm when you got home? Did you see anyone when you walked home, a neighbour maybe?'

'I don't know. I wasn't really taking any notice. Ask Elouise, the landlady at the Angel. I could barely stand when I left. I wasn't in a fit state for anything.'

Jacob scribbled a few notes to check with the Angel Arms.

'Tell us about why you left GC Supplies.'

Garth Shaw slumped back, his head leaning against the cream painted wall. 'Our son is really sick... leukaemia and he was due a chemotherapy session at the hospital. Mrs Chapman had said it was okay to take the afternoon off to be with him, but a few large deliveries had just come in and were clogging up the warehouse. Mr Chapman swanned in around lunchtime, saw the pile-up of stock and went mad. He said there was no way I was leaving early and that I had to help to put everything away. When I explained about my son, that me and my wife needed to be with him because he was scared, he just said that it didn't take two people to take a kid to the hospital and it wasn't like he was having an operation or anything.'

Gina clenched her hand under the table as she imagined how she'd react if they were talking about her granddaughter, Gracie, right now. There's no way she wouldn't be there to hold her hand. 'We're just trying to learn more about Mr Chapman at the moment. So, what happened after that?'

'I lost it. I kicked the boxes and it was like my head was going to explode. It wasn't the first time this had happened. I wasn't there for the last session and Lewis had been so upset. I mean he's five, for heaven's sake. Chemo would be scary at any age and he's my little boy. I said a few things that I can't remember, swore a few times and told him to stick his job. I said I'd had enough and I walked out. Never went back. My P45 arrived in the post after the next payroll had been done with a sorry letter from Faith.' The man grabbed a hoodie from the floor and pulled it over his T-shirt, shivering as he did.

Mrs Shaw placed her arm over his shoulders. 'Chapman was a horrible man, even treated his wife like shit. I wouldn't be surprised if he has enemies everywhere. He has no heart.' She laid her head on her husband's shoulders. 'Look at him. There's no way my husband would have had anything to do with what happened despite how he felt about that horrible man.'

Gina finished her coffee and asked a few more routine questions. Garth Shaw may have had a motive but she was unsure about the opportunity. For now, they would need to check the Angel Arms to determine how bad Mr Shaw was last night. Maybe their CCTV could tell them more. She truly hoped that the man in front of her had nothing to do with the fire. She listened to the boy giggling away over the cartoons and glanced at Mrs Shaw's watery eyes. The last thing she wanted was to see this family torn apart at a time when they all needed each other so much. 'Thank you for your time. I'm going to have to ask you to attend the station some-time today just to give a formal statement. Would you be able to do that?'

'Yeah. I'll get ready and head over this afternoon.' He stared at Gina with a worried look in his eye. 'I didn't do this; you have to believe me.'

She couldn't answer him. What Gina hoped for and what she got were two different things. It was her job to uncover the truth, however much that might hurt. She flinched slightly as she thought about Hetty, Stephen and Pete Bloxwich. That was exactly what they were trying to do and the only possible outcome if they were to succeed was total ruin of her life.

As they got back into the car, Gina stared out of the wind-screen. Tiny raindrops scattered over the glass and she turned on the demister as Jacob pulled his seat belt on. 'What did you think?'

'Glen Chapman wasn't a likeable person at all. That poor family, going through all that they're going through then had to put up with what that man said. I know he's our victim but bloody hell, at the moment, and between you and me, I'm on the side of the person that torched him. One look at that little boy...' Gina barely saw Jacob exposing his feelings like this but she totally agreed with him.

'Cases like this are hard. I don't know how I would have reacted if it were Gracie in that position and I wanted to be with her. I've always put my job first but some things are bigger. That would be bigger. Do I think he did it? Who knows?' She wanted to ask Jacob, if Shaw did do it, and there was any way they could ignore something that pointed to that fact, would he do so if he knew they could get away with it. Secretly, she wanted to know if her act of letting Terry die was something he could forgive her for should it all come out?

'Right, well the pub is open. Shall we head over there now?'

'No time like the present. The team are still at GC Supplies so we should hear from them later if they find anything that will help with the case. Wyre and PC Kapoor were going to organise speaking to the other employees too.' The windscreen had cleared but there was still a mist in the air. Soon it would become transparent and the road ahead would be clear for all to see.

TWELVE

'What happened next?' The little boy snuggles against his friend who pulls the quilt up to his chin and smiles while he rests on the comfy mattress.

'Your mother, that's what happened.'

'Mummy?'

'Ignore me. Let's get on with the story.' His friend picked up the spotty plastic dinosaur from the floor and held it up. 'Well, little Ziggy the dinosaur wanted nothing more than to enjoy the party with best friend, Topsy. They had lots of things, jelly, cake, ice cream and crisps. They didn't have the salad though – yuck. It was a party and who wants salad at a party? It was a day of fun and games. When the music started, all the little dinosaurs danced and had lots of fun. They enjoyed themselves so much, they never wanted the day to end. It had been perfect. The sun had shone and Ziggy was going to do lots of great things and this was the start of it all.'

'What was Ziggy going to do?'

'Little man, that's for another day. I have to go, but I will be back later.'

'Will the monster hurt me?'

'I told you before. You know, not all people that look like

monsters are monsters, and not all people that look like angels are kind and lovely. Sometimes you have to look at the person underneath.'

'What are you?'

'What do you think I am?'

'I think you're kind but I think the monster is scary.'

The boy's friend gives him a warm hug. This was one big adventure and when the story came to an end, all would be revealed. He loves an adventure and this makes him feel special. His friend says this is his very own adventure and it's just the start of all that's to come, but he has to be a good boy.

The new television flashes on and instantly his favourite cartoons play and he smiles. 'Drink your juice up. It's good for you. Full of vitamins to keep you strong and healthy like a big roaring dinosaur. Strong like me.'

He does as he's told and the juice is tasty too. He also enjoyed the sugar puffs he had for breakfast and all the sweets he has... he's never been given so much. Another jar sits on the table next to the Lego that he's been playing with, a mixture of chocolates and jellies. As soon as his friend goes, he will get them and lie in his bed while watching everything he wants, just like when it's Christmas.

Eyes drooping, he starts to nod off. Tired... so tired.

'Sleep well, sweetheart.' His friend kisses him on the head. One more yawn and he's gone.

THIRTEEN

Gina and Jacob stepped into the pub and the warmth hit Gina straight away. Jacob rubbed his hands and flicked the damp dew off his hair, splashing the door. The fire roared away and several people had huddled around it, one holding the lead to a Labrador that was licking beer off the floor. The queue was building up so they hurried to the bar before it could get even longer.

Gina stared into the flames as they waited, wondering what it was like to burn to death and she shivered. There was a faded scar on the side of her breast where Terry had stubbed a cigarette out on her, she couldn't imagine her whole body burning at that intensity. From what she'd heard, Chapman's body wasn't in too bad a state and Bernard had thought he'd probably died of smoke inhalation. That was still to be confirmed and she wasn't looking forward to the post-mortem in the morning. Maybe it wouldn't be a day for breakfast.

'What can I get you?' The young woman pushed her glasses up her nose and smiled.

'We're here to speak with the licensee. I'm DI Harte, this is DS Driscoll.' Jacob smiled and the girl bit her bottom lip, then smiled back at him. He was definitely what people would refer to as a looker but loyal as always, Jacob loved crime scene assistant, Jennifer. He cleared his throat and looked away.

'I'll just get her for you.'

'Looks like you made an impression there.'

'Can't help being a handsome beast.' He laughed.

'They haven't seen you run like a duck or stuff a sausage roll in your already stuffed mouth.'

'Jennifer has and she still loves me.'

'Must be the real thing.'

He smiled and the licensee came from out the back. She had her dyed black hair piled high on the top of her head with a spotty scarf tied around with a bow on the top. Red lips, nails and a flick of top liner finished the look. 'What can I do for you?' A group of darts players roared and one splashed his beer all over the floor. The Labrador pulled its lead a little until its owner gave it enough slack to reach the liquid on the floor.

'May we speak somewhere quieter?' Gina held her identification up.

'Of course. Come through to the office.' Gina and Jacob followed her through to the little room above the bar, up the narrow staircase. The woman grabbed a pile of invoices and delivery notes from the chair and threw them in an already overflowing pile on the floor. 'I hate paperwork and I'm still trying to get my head around everything. Take a seat.'

'Thank you.' Gina sat and Jacob shuffled behind her to the short wooden stool and he too sat and took his notebook out. 'It's Ms Nichols, isn't it?' The woman in front of her already looked much friendlier and less sleazier than the previous landlord of the Angel Arms.

'Please call me Elouise or Elle for short. Most people call me Elle. What can I do for you?'

'There was an incident early this morning and we just need to check the whereabouts of one of your customers last night.'

'Is one of them in trouble? I know most of the regulars really well.'

'Can you tell us how Garth Shaw seemed last night? In fact, take us through the evening until closing time.'

She picked up a pen and began twiddling it between her long fingers. 'I think he arrived about seven. He sat in his usual spot underneath the jukebox. He always sits alone and looks deep in thought. I went over and sat with him for a while because I know what he's been going through lately. We all know what he's been going through... the regulars I mean. His son is sick, his marriage is all but over.'

'His marriage is over?' This was a shock to Gina. When she saw Mrs Shaw with her head on her husband's shoulders, it didn't look at all like their marriage was over. She got the impression they were going through a bad patch because Mr Shaw had walked out on his job and their son was so sick, but they had seemed solid enough. Gina glanced at Jacob and saw that he'd popped a question mark at the end of his notes. He looked back at her with furrowed brows. Something wasn't adding up.

'Yes, they're only together because of poor Lewis. I don't know how they both hold it together but it's great that they can be amicable for their little boy.'

'So, what did you talk about when you sat with him?'

'Well, it was actually my night off and the staff were holding the fort. I grabbed myself a drink and joined him as I have done lately. He talks and I listen. He told me about how his boss had been mean to him and how his wife is fed up of him not having a job. He said he couldn't cope with even looking for something right now, that his head wasn't in the right place. At about ten thirty, he seemed quite merry and the conversation had lightened up a bit. He'd put a few tunes on the jukebox and seemed to be enjoying himself.'

'What happened after that?'

'Last orders were called. He bought two more drinks and got me one too, then everyone started leaving. That was about eleven thirty. I guess he went home.'

'How did he seem on leaving?'

'Very drunk. Staggering around the car park, in fact. I asked if he needed an Uber but he said no. Said he needed to sober up a bit so he'd walk.'

'Do you have the CCTV outside the front door for last night from six thirty to close of business?'

'Yes, why would you want that?'

'We need to see Mr Shaw coming and going.'

The woman paused. 'Dammit. I'm so sorry. I haven't been entirely honest.'

'Elle, what happened?'

'I'm so ashamed.' The woman stared up at the light and blinked back a tear. 'His marriage is over and I don't like being alone all the time. Garth is a really nice guy and quite mature for his age. I think we just clicked. I'd had too much to drink and so had he... you won't see him leaving at closing time because he was with me until at least four in the morning. I should have left him alone but we were both in a bad place. I'm new out of a relationship and it wasn't a great one. Bloody hell, I'm old enough to be his mother too. I don't make a habit of sleeping with my customers, this was a one-off.'

'We're not here to judge you and thank you for telling me the truth. When we look at the CCTV, will we now see him leaving at four this morning, is that correct?'

She nodded. 'You won't tell his wife, will you? Even if they're not properly together, it'll hurt and I don't want to kick her while she's down. How could I have been so selfish?'

'Sorry to ask, could we have the CCTV to the back entrance of the pub too?'

'Yes, with pleasure. I'll put it on a stick for you in a minute.'

'Thank you.'

A short while and a glass of cola later, Gina and Jacob were back in the car. Gina turned on the engine and began to demist the windscreen. A fine mist had fallen and visibility in the car park was poor. 'What did you make of that?'

Jacob exhaled and threw his pad on the back seat. 'The CCTV backs up what she said. He left just before four.'

'She was quick to tell us he left at eleven thirty and they had been talking about Mr Chapman that night. I wonder if there's a chance that she could have come around to his way of thinking and given him a cover story. It was a bit convenient that the camera to the back of the pub hadn't been working when she went to show us the footage.'

'I know she looked surprised and we haven't got enough evidence to bring either her or Shaw in at the moment but you never know.'

Gina checked her mirror and backed out of the parking space. 'It's something to bear in mind.' Her phone beeped. Before driving onto the main road running through Cleevesford, she glanced at it and saw that Pete had sent her a message. She pulled over. 'Bear with me, I just have to check this message.'

Come on, Gina! Either tell me what I need to know or I fill in the gaps. Remember, the truth always comes out.

Her heart began to bang and she swallowed.

'You okay?'

She dismissed the message. 'Yes, it's nothing. Just Hannah wondering if I'm free to chat. I'll call her later.' She wasn't about to tell Jacob what was going on with the journalist. 'Can you give O'Connor or Wyre a quick call and find out if Garth Shaw has been in to make a formal statement. It will be interesting to know if he tells the truth about being with Elle last night. If he doesn't, I want them to keep him there until we get back.'

FOURTEEN

Just as Gina reached her office, her phone began to ring and the number wasn't one she recognised. With shaky hands, she answered. 'Hello, DI Harte.'

'DI Harte.'

She recognised the voice of Pete Bloxwich and fell into her chair. 'You do know I can't give you any information on the case. There will be a press conference later today and stop messaging me.' She knew he wasn't calling about the case.

'I've just had a lovely conversation with Stephen. He had so much to say about his dead brother, well your ex-husband, Terry. Father to Hannah—'

'Leave my daughter alone.' She swallowed.

'I haven't done anything to your daughter, except maybe sent her a teeny-weeny message.'

'You're harassing me with your emails and phone calls. I have nothing to say to you. Leave me alone.'

'The problem is, Gina, if you don't say anything to me, I only have what dear old Hetty and the very cooperative Stephen have to tell me. If I don't get your side, that wouldn't be fair now, would it? I mean, Hetty says you were really mean to her. You went to her house and upset her, telling her how awful her son was. And

Stephen, he's convinced you almost looked happy at his brother's funeral... so, you can see, something doesn't ring true. Your behaviour wasn't that of a typically grieving widow and given that the circumstances of his death could have happened differently to how you told them, there's meat on the bones of that story. I mean, even if what they suspect isn't true, the public will think there's no smoke without fire. There's a way out of this though.'

Face flushing, she pushed the window open a little, letting the damp air in. A few flecks of rain hit the windowsill.

'Gina Harte has nothing to say. I'm guessing your little mind is ticking away, wondering how you can get out of confronting your past. The truth is, you can't. It's never going away and the longer you leave it to tell your story, the worse it will look for you. That's why you have to face it and only I can help you.'

'You're the person who is creating all this drama. Why should I trust that you can help me? You're a journalist, mostly specialising in clickbait. I will never trust you.'

'And that is your downfall.' He paused and sipped a drink. 'You only have one option as I see it. Tell me your side. I've spoken to some of the people who used to live by you all those years ago. They remember the screaming that used to come from your house. They were your screams. What did he do to you, Gina? People love a victim, well some do. I sense that most people will be on your side.' The next silent pause seemed to last forever. 'Did you watch him die? Had he hurt you that night?'

She ended the call and threw her phone on her desk. A tear ran down her cheek. Pacing back and forth, she continued biting her nail, flinching as it pulled away from her skin. There was a knock at the door. Wiping her eyes, she called out. 'Come in.'

Wyre entered and popped a coffee on Gina's desk. 'I thought you could do with this.'

Gina turned and looked away, not wanting her colleague to see her reddening eyes.

'Is everything alright, guv?'

'Yes.' She turned and yawned. 'Just tired, that's all.'

'Shaw is here. Do you want to speak to him?'

'Would you?'

'Of course.'

'Ask Jacob to lead as he came with me to speak to Elouise Nichols and apparently he was with her during the incident. He didn't tell us that this morning so he needs to be confronted with what we know. I want to catch the press briefing in a while. I know Briggs will be holding it soon.'

'I'll go chase Jacob up and we'll get onto it now.'

'As soon as you're done, let me know what was said.'

'Will do.' Wyre smiled and left.

Gina took a sip of the coffee and felt her stomach start to turn. There was less than an hour to go before Briggs addressed the press. She had to pull herself together. There was no way she could let Pete see that he'd got to her, especially now he was watching her every move and reaction. She pressed Hannah's number and her daughter answered after one ring.

'Mum? Glad you called. I've received a message from a reporter.'

She took a deep breath. 'He's harassing me. Your nan and uncle have been talking to him and from what he tells me, they are blaming me for your father's death.'

'But that's ridiculous. He fell down the stairs drunk. That wasn't your fault.'

'I know.' All the truths she'd told her daughter weren't enough. If Hannah knew how Terry had died, she feared she'd never see her or Gracie again. The sound of a child playing in the background made her heart sink. If she could never see Gracie again, life wouldn't be worth living. 'Hetty and Stephen seem to have it in their heads that it was my fault though. They've always blamed me. I wasn't a good enough wife. I was a bad mother.' Her head began to throb. 'I tried so hard with your father. All I wanted was for him to love me but...' She couldn't stop the tears that fell. Terry died. It was always going to be her or Terry and it was only a matter of time before Hannah got hurt. He would never have stopped terrorising her in their home and Hetty and Stephen did nothing but enable him. Hetty believed firmly that a woman should do everything for her man and it was her fault if she got a slap. Stephen was the same. Every woman he'd ever been involved with ended up being controlled by him. She was never quite sure if he was as bad as Terry behind closed doors. Maybe she'd never know if he was.

'You weren't a bad mother.'

'I wasn't there for you though, was I?'

'Mum, we spoke about this not long ago. I understand now. You were on your own, you had to work, for us, and I know I spent a lot of time being looked after by others when you did your night shifts or got called out but I understand now. I've grown up a lot. I think about it all the more now that Gracie is growing up a little. I mean, she's spent three days this week with three different friends of mine so that I can work and you know what, I've had five kids over this morning to pay them back. She might think I was a rubbish mother one day, farming her out to everyone but we do what we have to in order to manage. Greg works, I work; this is how we have to live for now. I'm sorry I was so selfish and spoilt all these years but I don't blame you, I was just being... I don't know... immature about everything.'

Gina bit her bottom lip and sniffed.

'Are you crying?'

'No, of course not.'

'About that reporter.'

'Did you reply to him, that's what I needed to know?'

'I did.'

Gina's mouth felt instantly dry and she couldn't swallow. 'What did you say?'

'You don't want to know.'

'I need to know.'

'It involved a lot of swear words and ended with don't you dare message me again – ever!'

Exhaling, Gina held the back of the chair. 'Thank you.'

'What are you going to do about him, Mum? I don't want him talking about you, me or Dad in the paper.'

'Stephen and Hetty are instigating all this. They approached him. He wants to know the ins and outs of my marriage to your dad. There are people around who have spoken; neighbours who heard what happened through the walls. There's not much of a story to tell but he'll make something of it, I know he will, that's why we can't say anything to him.'

Hannah paused and the sound of Gracie playing ended as she closed the door and went into another room. 'Stephen has called me too. He keeps saying that you could have helped Dad on the night he died but you didn't because you hated him. Do you promise me that didn't happen?'

'I promise and I didn't hate your dad. I was scared of him, there's a difference. There was a full police investigation at the time and nothing implicated me at all. Your dad was drunk and simply had a bad fall down the stairs. I know he hit his head hard. I called an ambulance and they arrived too late to help him.' Stomach knotting, Gina pushed her head out of the window, allowing the icy breeze to ground her. Why her and why now?

'I'm sure it will all blow over. I've got to go, I think Gracie is going through the cupboards looking for a biscuit and Greg is on his computer. Don't want her spoiling her dinner.'

'Tell her I love her and I'll drive down to see you both soon.'

'Will do. Take care. That reporter won't call me again, I've blocked his number.'

Hannah ended the call. Late for the press conference, she pulled the window closed, tied her wet hair back and took a couple of deep breaths. Time to face Pete Bloxwich. His attention wouldn't be on anything Briggs had to say about the case, it would be on her and she had to look like she was in control even though every cell in her body was screaming.

FIFTEEN

Gina hurried into the conference room and stood to the side of the podium where Briggs was wrapping up. 'So we'd like to appeal for witnesses. Maybe you have CCTV or you were walking your dog late at night. If you saw anyone around or heard anything, please call the number on your screen. Any questions?'

'Do you have anyone in custody?' one reporter called out.

'Not as yet which is why we need the public to come forward if they have any information.'

'Should the public be scared?' another called.

'We need everyone to be extra vigilant until this person is caught.'

'What are you doing about it?' Pete Bloxwich chimed in.

'An investigation has been opened and our detectives and officers are working hard on the case. We will hold another press conference when we have more information.' Briggs loosened his tie. Gina knew he always got hot when the stage lights were on him. Cameras clicked and a boom operator held the sound recorder up.

Pete pushed his way to the front. 'I was there this morning. I saw the aftermath of the fire and a man died in that house. Someone wanted to kill him. Can you assure the public that this killer is going to be caught and will not get away with murder? That would be the worst thing ever, wouldn't it?' The man grinned and glanced across at Gina as he spoke. Briggs looked at her and Pete glanced up at him.

'I can assure the public that we are following every lead and doing all we can. As I said, there will be another conference when I have more to tell you. Thank you.' Briggs unclipped the mini microphone from his tie and left it on the lectern, taking his notes in his large hands he headed over to Gina. 'That's the reporter you were talking about?'

She nodded. 'Yes, and he's staring at us.'

Briggs placed a hand on her elbow and led her towards the door. Gina looked over her shoulder and saw Pete making notes as his photographer took a snap of her and Briggs. Pete hadn't come about the current case, he was only interested in getting more information on her.

As they left the room, Briggs took her through the fire escape and out into the wet yard where nobody could see them.

'He won't leave me alone.'

'You haven't said anything to him, though.'

'No, not a word.'

'Good, keep it that way. Has he contacted you again?'

She nodded. 'He called me this afternoon trying to get me to talk about what Terry did to me. He's tried to message Hannah too but she sent a reply telling him where to go. I don't know how to stop him.'

'You can't. Just give him nothing to work with. That's all you can do.'

'How do I stop Hetty and Stephen trying to ruin me?'

Briggs shrugged and dropped his arms in frustration. 'We have to shut them up.'

'Shut who up?' Pete Bloxwich came through the door with a cigarette dangling from his lips, which he lit. 'Have you got something to tell me?'

Briggs and Gina remained silent. She felt a shiver running through her body and she wanted to do her coat up and run away.

'Look at the way you are with her.' Pete nodded at Briggs. 'I see the way you led her out, the way you look at her. Is it just sex or are you in love? This is getting juicier by the minute? Will you be next?' Pete dropped his barely smoked cigarette to the floor and stubbed it out with his boot. A few drops of rain began to fall on his nose. 'Nah, she only does away with guys who beat her, isn't that right, Gina?'

'How dare—' Gina was stopped from saying anymore as Briggs held his finger to her mouth.

'If you keep harassing DI Harte, she will make a formal complaint which we will have to investigate. Any more calls, we will take this further.'

He laughed and scratched his chin. 'I didn't expect anything less. Have a good evening.'

As Pete went back through the door, Briggs shook his head then checked to see if he'd gone. 'I seriously hate that man. He's dangerous.'

Gina stared at her feet. 'This is going to be my last case ever, isn't it? I can't see that this is going to end well.'

'Right, we best get back in and have a catch up on the case and if there's nothing more for this evening, I think we both need a bit of down time until morning. Do you want dinner tonight? You could come to mine.'

Gina shook her head. 'I think I need to be alone.' She didn't want company, she wanted to go home, have a shower and immerse herself in the case or anything to take her mind off the reporter who was taking up every corner of her mind.

'If you need someone to talk to—'

'I know.' She forced a smile and gently touched his arm before leaving him alone in the dark as she headed back towards the incident room.

SIXTEEN

Sonya sat rigidly at the kitchen table staring at her phone and occasionally refreshing her messages. Her muscles ached from the workout earlier that day. She hadn't felt like doing anything but she had no choice. Hands shaking, she ran her fingers through her hair. She still hadn't showered and her knotty hair was getting trapped in between her fingers but none of that mattered. She opened another bottle of wine and swigged from the bottle before slamming it on the kitchen table.

A loud bang on the kitchen window startled her. Even in the darkness, she couldn't mistake that outline for anyone but her ex. Heart pumping, she opened it on the catch. As she shuffled to get into a comfortable position, she knocked a glass into the washing-up bowl. 'What? I told you Erik was poorly today. He's fast asleep and you could have woken him up.' Her son's father stared at her, his face contorted with rage. He always did have a short fuse, often breaking things and shouting when a temper hit him.

'Sunday is my day with him and you didn't bring him over. Thanks for that, Sonya. Are you going to be one of those bitches that won't let a man see his child? If you try to stop me seeing him, I swear you'll be sorry.' He started to rub his close-shaved head. It always did look like he was wearing a close-cropped black hat on his head.

'No one is stopping you from seeing Erik. I told you, he's been sick. There's this bug going around.'

'Bug, yeah right. A bug is why you're talking to me through a window and drinking wine straight from the bottle. You just don't want me to see him.' He pointed with his thick finger.

'That's not true. I don't want you to catch it and take it back to... whatever-her-name-is.'

'Can't bear the thought that I've found someone else, can you? Can't accept that Erik likes her too? Charlene is so good with him you'd think Erik was her own flesh and blood. All too much for you, is it?'

She grabbed the wine bottle and placed it in the fridge. 'He will always be my boy. There's nothing quite like a mother's love.'

'Except when said mother doesn't let a father see his son. He'll hate you for it one day.'

'I told you, he's ill, that's all. Why don't you have him for longer next week, make up for it? Take your son out somewhere nice.'

'Because you know full well that Charlene and I are away next week.'

'Oh yes. Clubbing in Blackpool. You know, take the clubbing out of it, Erik would love a weekend at the seaside.'

'Just do one. It's you who stuffed up. I was meant to have him this weekend and I have plans next weekend. Get over it. Just because you don't go anywhere or do anything. You live in this sad bubble of work, a gym you can't afford and this oppressive house spending time with those air-brained bints you call friends.'

'You're really something, you know that. Poor Charlene will see you for what you are one day.'

He leaned on his elbows and looked through. 'And what's that? A man who cares about his son and respects women.'

'And calls them bints.' Sonya shook her head. 'A philandering misogynist. Are you already shagging someone else because if you aren't, I can guarantee that you will within... hmm, let me see. You've been living with Charlene for one month. I don't believe that there's no one else on the horizon yet. Still got your secret phone?'

He stood and glanced to the right. 'Look, just get Erik. I want to see him quickly. I haven't got time for this.'

'No. Why can't you accept that he's poorly? You can call him tomorrow, when he's awake. And for the record, I don't care who you're with or what you're doing.' She did and she'd cared a lot. He'd left her for another woman without warning, leaving her world in turmoil and now he wanted everything on his terms. She didn't know why she was arguing with him. Right now, he was the least of her problems. She could just shut the window in his face and walk out of the room. He'd get the message and leave.

'I don't want to call tomorrow, I want to come in now.'

'But,' she said, leaning over the sink and staring at him, 'I'm not letting you in so you best leave now before I call the police and tell them you were harassing me.'

'I'm not harassing you. You're just creating drama like you always did. Look, I know you were at the gym earlier. My mate said he saw you. If you were out, Erik can't have been that bad.'

'My sister watched him for an hour.'

'Your sister, the one you never really speak to? Right. You,' he pointed, 'denied me access and I'm not going to stand for it. This is just the beginning.' He banged on the window.

'Please, Justin. Stop making this a thing just because I won't wake him.'

'You're going to pay for this, that's a promise.' He leaned in and grabbed a glass from the draining board, then threw it to the ground before leaving her to pick up the pieces, but first, she needed a drink. It was the only way to get through the rest of the evening. She listened to her ex revving up as he pulled away in his car then she closed the window. Heading to the fridge, she pulled the bottle of wine back out.

Her whole body collapsed onto the kitchen floor as she burst into tears. She stared at her phone, willing it to ring, but it didn't. She needed to talk to someone and the only person she could trust was her oldest friend, Heather. After trying her number again and again, eventually her friend picked up. 'Hiya, Sonya. You okay?' Heather spoke in a whisper.

'No, can you come over?'

'Of course I can. What's happened?'

'I can't talk about it on the phone. I don't know if I can talk about it at all but I'm going crazy here.'

'Hey, Stephen. I'm popping out. My dad's really desperate for a loaf of bread.'

'Have you got to be somewhere else? I'm sorry for being a nuisance.' Sonya wiped her eyes.

'No, it's fine. Can't talk right now. See you soon.' Heather ended the call.

Sonya gulped the wine down and laid her head against the cupboards. Heather had always been there for her and as soon as she was fighting fit again, she'd help Heather to see that Stephen was no good for her. She could see that the loaf of bread was an excuse for her to get away from Stephen. Right now though, she had something much bigger on her plate and even though her friend had to lie to get out of the house, she had to deal with her own problems first.

SEVENTEEN

Gina finished the last of the family bag of crisps and threw the wrapper onto her bedroom floor. She glanced at the case notes again and exhaled. Elouise Nichols had been telling the truth about spending the night with Garth Shaw. The CCTV had showed him leaving out the front at around four in the morning, just like he said. Not only that, Garth had almost staggered down the path. It was looking unlikely that he had set fire to his ex-boss's house. He still wasn't totally out of the picture, there was an outside chance that he could have left out of the back, done the deed and come back to the pub where he drank more, leaving him staggering by four. She couldn't prove that he had but it would remain a possibility for now.

Gina's home phone rang. She jumped out of bed and ran down the stairs, grabbing it off the cradle in the living room. The embers in the log burner crackled as they burned out and the last of the orange glow in the room was about to die, leaving her standing there holding a phone in the dark.

'Hope I didn't wake you... wait... I hope I did.' She couldn't mistake that voice.

'Why are you calling me, Hetty? I said all I needed to say to you last time we spoke and as for making trouble with that journalist, I should sue you for defamation of character.'

'So sue me. You can only win if I'm lying and we both know you're lying.'

Gina recalled their last conversation, where she had whispered in Hetty's ear. '*Your son broke my bones. Your son raped me, repeatedly. Your son locked me in a shed. Your son used to shout so loud at his baby daughter I was scared he would kill her. Your son was a monster. You made that monster. That is exactly what happened. You could see that, Hetty, couldn't you?*' Even though Hetty knew that to be the truth, she was still coming at Gina with all she had.

'This again. Hetty, go back to bed and get a life.'

'My life is on hold and I will get a life when the truth comes out of your mouth.'

Gina wanted to say that Hetty was going to have to wait forever because it wasn't happening. On the night Terry died, a rapist and abuser was taken off the streets forever. Had Gina escaped him, he'd have gone on to terrorise more women and maybe even murder someone. He was definitely capable.

Hetty slapped her lips. 'I knew when I saw you at the funeral, and then at his memorial service, that you helped him to his death. That's a kind expression, isn't it, Gina? I didn't call it murder. Maybe you nudged him, maybe you watched him die when you could have saved him. You've always been vague about the details when I've tried to ask you about that night and you know how that makes you look? Guilty. That's how. Anyway, I'm digressing. When I saw you, I noticed the involuntary twitching of your muscles, the side glances and the nervous scratching. Then the drinking and avoidance of any conversation about Terry. The look on your face when people tried to express their condolences. You know the signs of guilt, Gina, you're a detective. When I look at you, I realise, I've always known that you're not innocent. I wouldn't be surprised if you exaggerated what my boy did to you, just pre-empting that all this might come out one day and bang, there's your defence. The poor battered wife... oh, and what do they call it now, coercive control. Terry wouldn't let poor Gina go out and see her friends. Terry kept all the money. Terry was a nasty drunk. Never a mention of how you antagonised him and wound him up. Poor, poor Gina.'

'Victim blaming again, Hetty?' A tear escaped from the corner of Gina's eye. She had hoped that from their last conversation, Hetty would have been able to think deeper about how her own husband treated her and how that rubbed off onto Terry and Stephen, shaping their views of women. 'You know what your son did to me.'

'I know what you told me.'

'You know first-hand, Hetty. Your husband did the same to you. Your sons were and are just like their father.'

Hetty paused. 'A mother will always put her child first which is why I won't rest until you pay. And now, I can't even see my great-granddaughter and it's all your fault. You've poisoned Hannah against me and she won't let me or Stephen see Gracie.'

'Hannah has finally seen your toxic family for what they are. If that's not a sign that you need to change then I don't know what is. Only one of us needs to face what's going on here and it's you. I agree with you on one thing. A mother *will* always put her children first.' Gina swallowed her tears away.

She could hear Hetty sobbing down the phone. 'No, Hannah's been turned by you and you alone. She's taken little Gracie from us and I will never forgive you.' The call ended. Gina placed the phone back in its cradle and padded through to the kitchen. She grabbed a sheet of kitchen roll and wiped her eyes and blew her nose. She stared at her sad reflection in the kitchen window, watching as another tear streamed down her cheek.

So that's what had started Hetty off on her crusade. Hannah had finally told the woman that she could no longer see Gracie. Pete had approached her for a story about Gina's past after a bit of digging and Hetty had been thrilled to drag Gina through as much mess as possible. Or maybe it was the other way around. Maybe Hetty approached Pete. Whatever, they were on her back now whether she liked it or not. If Hetty were to win the war and Gina were to confess, there would be no winners. Hannah would have the stigma of a mother in prison. Gracie would lose her grandmother. Hetty still wouldn't be welcome in Hannah's life. Everyone would be a loser but then again Hetty didn't care about that. She had lost, so it was now time to bring everyone else down with her. This wasn't entirely about justice. Revenge was what Hetty had in mind. Revenge for losing Terry and Gracie.

EIGHTEEN

MONDAY, 15 NOVEMBER

Kerstin wakes with a start and all she can hear is Cameron's gentle snores as he continues to sleep beside her. Slowly she gets out of bed, wondering what could have broken such a deep sleep. The noise comes again and now she hears it properly, it sounds like a squeak. She creeps along the bedroom floor, careful to avoid the creaky board. Waking the kids would be a disaster and there's no need to scare or worry anyone as it could well be down to the local wildlife. She pushes Leo and Dominic's bedroom door open and sees that her two tiny boys are fast asleep. That rules out that one of them is wandering around the house.

Standing as still as possible, she does nothing. She listens for a couple of minutes but the sound doesn't come again. Maybe it was nothing but a product of her imagination. She was dreaming about something weird but she can't remember what about now that she's awake. Or, maybe the sound is nothing more than a fox nudging the gate to get to their bins. It wouldn't be the first time she's caught one of the pesky creatures making a complete mess of the garden.

What if it's a burglar or... no. Now her mind really is heading off on a tangent. Her family have no enemies, not like Faith's husband.

She thinks of what happened to Glen. There's an arsonist on the loose and that thought sends a shiver along the back of her neck. It feels like there are insects crawling in her hair until the chill passes. Faith's husband wasn't the nicest of people. From what Faith said, his employees didn't like him and she was about to leave him. He didn't exactly make an effort to be liked or get on with people. She remembered one of the barbecues the Chapmans' had hosted the year before. Glen got drunk and started goading everyone there into a political debate, telling everyone that disagreed with him that they were sheeple and brainwashed idiots. He was convinced he was right too because he was the rich successful man and they were all just nobodies – Joe and Joanne average he called everyone. The barbecue had ended on a low with everyone making their excuses to leave and Faith apologising about him being drunk as they left.

Swallowing, she hopes what's happening is nothing to do with what Cameron told her... no... it couldn't be. She had to not mention that ever again, to anyone. There was no point in upsetting him and causing an argument as that's what inevitably would happen.

She hears another squeak so she grabs Leo's plastic golf club – not that this toy would really take down an intruder but right now, it's all she has. Knuckles white as she grips it, she heads down the stairs, not even daring to breathe. The only light coming in is from the moon. Heart banging, she stops as she sees a shadow through the glass-paned door. Then, she hears the clicking of a lighter. Through the glass, she sees flickering. The intruder has lit a candle. She goes to scream out for Cameron but nothing comes out. Instead, she runs to the front door as the intruder lifts up the letter box and she wedges the golf club through the gap and pushes it into their body, over and over again.

The intruder scarpers off and the gate slams.

'What the hell's happening?' Cameron turns on the landing light and rubs his eyes. 'What's with that?' He points to the plastic golf club.

Kerstin holds a finger to her mouth and opens the front door. That's when she sees the candle in a jar left on the little bench outside their house. 'Call the police, now. Someone was going to set fire to our house.'

NINETEEN

Gina pulled on the handbrake and got out of the car, greeting Jacob as she did. PCs Kapoor and Smith came out of the house. Gina spotted the police tape around the small bench by the entrance to the house and some more around the fence.

'I'm going to set up a cordon, guv. Forensics are on the way,' PC Smith said. PC Kapoor opened up a scene log form and began noting down who was there. 'It might be best if you go around the back.'

'Of course.' Gina totally agreed. The last thing they wanted to do was ruin any trace evidence that the perpetrator had left behind. She followed Jacob down the side path until they reached the large square garden.

The security light came on and frost twinkled like a diamanté carpet all over the grass. A teary-looking woman stood in the doorway exhaling white mist and shivering. As they approached, she moved to the side so that they could enter through the patio doors that led straight into the dining side of the kitchen.

'Mrs Godwin, I'm DI Harte, this is DS Driscoll.'

'Take a seat.' The woman stood in the kitchen area. 'Would you like a drink?'

'A coffee would be lovely, thank you.' Gina needed a caffeine jolt more than anything right now.

Mrs Godwin went to put the coffee into a cup but her trembling hand lost half of the granules on the worktop.

'Here. Let me.' Gina offered to take the spoon and the woman gave it to her. Gina continued making the four drinks that were laid out.

Mrs Godwin brushed her long red hair from her face, some of it still stuck to the corner of her mouth. Jacob slid the patio doors closed to keep the heat in.

'I can't believe someone out there wants to kill us.' Mrs Godwin bit her lip and scrunched her brow.

Gina placed the drinks on the table, leaving the fourth cup on the worktop.

'Kids are still fast asleep.' Mr Godwin entered and took the drink. The tall man had the squarest of jaws and Gina could see through his cheek that he kept clenching his teeth.

'Mrs Godwin, I know you're still in shock, but may we ask you a few questions?'

'Yes, and please call me Kerstin. This is Cameron.'

The man stood at the counter awkwardly.

'Kerstin.' Gina sympathetically smiled and sipped the coffee. 'Can you talk us through what happened?'

Jacob made a few notes at the top of the page and cleared his throat.

'Yes. I woke up. I mean I was fast asleep and I think I was woken by a noise. That's when I heard the squeak... or maybe I did. Now I know that noise was the gate in the front garden. At first, I thought it was probably foxes. We get a lot of them around here. I went down in the dark with the kids' plastic golf club to scare them away. That's when I saw the figure through the glass in the door. They lit the candle on the bench. They went to open the letter box so I pushed the golf club out over and over again until they ran away. That's all I saw.'

'It's good that you reacted so quickly. We will need to take the golf club for analysis. Can you tell me anything about this person? You say you saw a figure through the door.'

'It was dark and the glass isn't clear, it's frosted. All I can say is I felt they were average height but I can't even be sure of that. They were wearing dark clothes, much darker than their skin shade. They were white, I'm sure of that. I could only make out tones in the dark.'

'So a white person of possible average height?'

'Yes.' The woman rubbed her green eyes.

'Do you know what time this was?'

Kerstin scrunched her brow. 'After I called you, I noticed on my phone that it was three fifteen. I would say the noises started around three.'

'You've done really well, thank you. Do you know anyone at all that may wish to harm you?'

'That's the thing, we don't have any enemies. We get on with everyone, don't we, Cam?' Kerstin bit her bottom lip and her husband looked down. She'd emphasised the end of the sentence as if leading Cameron into an answer. Gina made a mental note that something seemed a little off.

'Yes, I have no idea why we've been targeted. We heard about what happened last night too. Could the same person have targeted us?'

Gina nodded. 'It is a possibility. Did you know Glen Chapman?'

'We're all friends,' Kerstin said. 'Well, I'm more friends with Faith. When we heard what happened, I tried to call her but Faith hasn't answered my calls. Could it be someone who knows us and the Chapmans?'

'That'll be something we'll be investigating. Tell me more about you and Faith.'

'She's my friend. We're not close friends, you know like best friends. We meet at the gym and we also take some classes together. Pilates and yoga.'

'Do you meet up with any other people at the gym or is it just the two of you?'

'There's normally four of us. We've been meeting there for just over a year and we've become close. We call ourselves the motivation ladies. It's silly really but it keeps us hitting our fitness goals. Well, you already know about Faith. There's Heather Walton and Sonya Baker. You don't think it's anything to do with our gym buddies. That would be ridiculous.'

Gina took a deep breath and smiled. 'We're just looking for any links at the moment. Could I please have the contact details of Heather and Sonya?'

'Of course.'

'I'll write their details down while you talk.' Cameron began to search for their details in his phone.

Gina wondered why Kerstin's husband would have all Kerstin's friends' addresses and numbers in his phone. 'You're friends with them too?'

'Oh God no. Sometimes we all meet up to go out together. I know Glen, Stephen and Justin. The partners and, well, one of them is an ex now. We used to sometimes have a few beers together while the footie was on. We're all Blues supporters. Or we are now that Glen is no longer with us.'

'Do you think my friends might be targeted too?' Kerstin began twisting the ends of her hair.

'We hope not but we will need to speak to them and their partners.'

'Which gym do you all go to?' Jacob asked.

'It's the one in Cleevesford Golf Club.'

Gina knew it as the large glass-fronted building that boasted a plethora of therapeutic treatments, sauna and steam room. It had expansive gardens that showed off the best of the Warwickshire countryside. It was the place to go if you wanted an afternoon tea or a champagne breakfast.

'Can you think of any incidents that have occurred there? Has anyone bothered any of you?'

'We haven't been bothered as such but one of the instructors is a bit creepy. When he's showing us how to use new equipment, his hands tend to wander. We call him the pervy instructor. Well—'

'Has something happened?'

'It's nothing.'

'Someone has killed Mr Chapman and tried to attack your family. It might just be everything and if it's nothing, he has nothing at all to worry about.'

'Has he touched you?' Cameron stepped forward. 'You didn't tell me about some creepy instructor at the gym.'

She flicked her red hair from the corner of her mouth. 'I didn't need to. It was nothing and no, he has never touched me.'

'It doesn't sound like nothing.'

'Cameron, could we please finish getting Kerstin's account of what happened?'

He ran his fingers through his full head of hair. 'Of course, sorry.'

'Could you tell us more about the gym instructor?' A member of staff at the gym would be able to access addresses.

'His name is Graham Pollard and he's only been working there about a month. He overheard Faith calling him a perv. I know he touched Faith's bottom accidentally on purpose, if you know what I mean, and she reported him. Since then he's left us well alone so I didn't think much more of it all. However, I did hear him mutter that Faith was a stuck-up bitch after she asked another instructor to help her with something.'

'Thank you again for being so helpful. Police and forensics will be here for the rest of the day but do you have anywhere else you can stay for now?'

Cameron stepped forward, tightening up the drawstring on his checked lounge pants. 'Really, I'm not having some gym saddo push me and my family out of our home.'

'Mr Godwin, we have no confirmation that he was involved in the incident tonight and secondly, we know someone came here tonight with the express intent to set fire to your house. We don't know if you are the target, if your wife is the target, or you both are. You also have two children to consider. We would advise that you stayed somewhere else while we investigate. If you have nowhere to stay, we can help to organise a hotel or safe house for you, just for a few days.'

Kerstin walked over and held his hand. 'Hun, we can't put the kids at risk. We can stay at my mum's for a few days while the police look into things, can't we?'

He leaned in and kissed her on the head. 'I think I'd rather be fried in my own home than stay with your mother and stepdad.' He paused and Kerstin let go of his hand. 'I'm sorry. That was uncalled for. Of course we can stay with your mother, love.'

'We'll need to take your mother's address so that we can keep you informed of any developments.' Gina smiled warmly, happy in the knowledge that the Godwins' were going to be leaving their house for a while.

After wrapping up the interview, Jacob and Gina headed back to their respective cars that were parked on the road. The early hour's breeze blew a chill across her neck. She buttoned her coat up further. Gina opened up the internet on her phone as she leaned on the door. 'That's handy, the golf course gym opens in two hours. We can head back to the station, update the system, grab some food and then head over to see if Graham Pollard is working this morning. At the moment, he's a potential link between the two victims' wives and definitely could have taken umbrage at being called a perv. After, we'll look into the other two gym ladies in the group. We need to speak to them and their partners to at least encourage them to be vigilant.'

Gina got into her car and rubbed her hands, hoping that the heater would kick in soon. The way Kerstin had looked when Gina had asked if they had any enemies kept flagging away in her mind. What wasn't she saying?

TWENTY

A lone robin bobbed on the golf course. Gina stood next to Jacob, rubbing her hands together, waiting for seven in the morning to come. That's when the doors to the gym would open. A light drizzle began to fall.

'It's so peaceful here. I could get used to being a member of a place like this when I've retired. Play a bit of golf, drink a few beers.' Jacob stared into the bare-branched trees in the distance.

'I didn't know you played golf.'

He laughed. 'I don't and I don't care about golf or gyms. It would just be nice to have a go and sit around in the bar. That'd be the life.'

'You'd be bored stiff after a day with no crimes to sink your teeth into.'

'You know me too well. Jennifer keeps saying I can never keep still. I'm like a fidgety toddler at home while she likes to lounge and do sod all when she's off.'

'It was interesting what we found out about Graham Pollard.'

'Certainly was. What a horrid excuse for a human being he is.'

A woman in track bottoms and a polo shirt opened the doors. She looked to be about twenty-five with long blue hair tied up. 'Someone's keen.'

Gina smiled. 'We're not here to use the gym. We've come to see a member of staff. Is Graham Pollard in?'

'And who are you?' She now looked suspicious.

'DI Harte and this is DS Driscoll.'

'Has something happened?'

'We are just making enquiries and looking for witnesses. We need to speak to Mr Pollard, that's all. I can't say anything about the ongoing investigation.'

'It's about the woman, isn't it? I don't know her name but she's a member here. I heard her husband died in a fire. Have you come to speak to Graham because he's a creep? He's running late. Called to say he must have eaten something dodgy as he was up in the night but he'll be in soon.'

Gina made a mental note to ask him about what exactly he was up to during the night.

'Come through to the staff area.' As Gina and Jacob followed the young woman, a couple of men in gym gear shuffled past them to get in.

They entered a room containing several tables, a vending machine and a microwave. The strip light flickered as the woman turned it on.

'Do you want to wait here and I'll send him through when he arrives?'

'Yes, thank you.' Gina pulled one of the plastic chairs out and sat. Jacob walked over to the vending machine for some coffee. 'You called Mr Pollard a creep, could I ask why that is?'

She leaned over the table, a few strands of blue hair falling forward. 'He's just a bit touchy feely and makes these jokes that aren't funny, like about blondes and women in general. He tries to play these up to the men but I think they get annoyed by him. From what I've heard, I think his days here are numbered as there have been a couple of complaints. He's asked a few people out, as in on a date, and he seems to get really angry when they turn him down.'

'Did he ever ask Faith Chapman on a date?'

'I caught him looking at her a few times and he'd say nice things about her like she was sweet and friendly, but I think she started asking some of the other gym instructors to help her when she needed something and he took the hump. He'd say she was like all the other women, just playing with the feelings of men. He'd go on about women holding all the power and just using men. I think he's some sort of sad incel who sits in front of a computer all night slagging women off, if I'm honest.'

'Has he ever made you uncomfortable?'

'A little and I've reported him, which is why I'd say his days are numbered.'

'How did he make you feel uncomfortable?'

'It's little things. He called me a dyke because of my blue hair and he said no man would touch me because I'm a gobby cow. Too right I'm gobby where he's involved. I replied with a few swear words. The good thing is, one of the gym users heard him having a go at me and reported him too.' She paused. 'It was Faith. She reported him for me.'

'You've been really helpful. Would you mind giving us a statement when you finish work?'

'No, I'd be happy to. Like I said, the man's a creep.'

'What's your name?'

Jacob placed the machine coffees down and took his pen and pad out.

'Alannah Patrick.'

'Thanks, Alannah.'

'Happy to help.'

As soon as Jacob had scrawled her name down, a man entered.

'Graham,' Alannah called out with a huge grin. 'You have visitors. The detectives would like a word.' Gina could tell that Alannah had enjoyed telling him that.

The man stood, rooted to the spot and stared right at Gina.

TWENTY-ONE

Gina introduced them and the first thing she noticed was, even though she outranked Jacob, the man kept fixed on him as if Gina didn't exist. His short grey beard and bald head looked quite large on his skinny body. Leaning back a little, Gina tried to catch a glance of his footwear under the table, wondering if there would be some telltale sign that he'd been wandering around with a petrol can in the night, rather than being close to the toilet like he'd proclaimed to Alannah. His trainers looked fresh and clean. However, the man in front of her smelled like his polo shirt hadn't been washed for weeks, but it didn't smell of accelerant. The man in front of her might be a creepy harasser of women but was he a murdering arsonist? 'Mr Pollard, we'd like to speak to you about the murder of Glen Chapman.'

'Who?' The man's nose twitched and he placed his elbow on the table.

'Faith Chapman's husband. She uses this gym. There was also another attack on another gym member's house a few hours ago. We're investigating whether the gym members were the targets.'

'So, you're jumping to a massive conclusion that I know what's going on?' He gave Gina a forced smug smile as he acknowledged her presence.

'There has been a report of a falling out between you and Mrs Chapman and we wouldn't be doing our job if we didn't investigate that. Apparently, she reported you when she heard you calling a staff member a name.'

'You're here because of that. The same staff member you're referring too had just had a swearing frenzy at me. Bloody woman has a right potty mouth on her and needed telling.'

'So, you were angry when Mrs Chapman reported you?'

'Too right I was angry.'

Gina leaned back and noticed that, again, the man answered all her questions as he looked at Jacob, once again ignoring her.

Pollard rubbed his beard and leaned back. 'You can't pin anything on me for simply being fed up about one sweary woman and saying my piece.'

'We have more, Mr Pollard.'

The man grinned at Jacob.

'Mr Pollard. I'm actually speaking to you.'

The man turned his head and sighed.

'We have another allegation. A witness mentioned that you touched Faith inappropriately.'

'That's the thing, I didn't. What we do here is close contact and I brushed against her by accident while I was helping her with the heavier weights. A man can't even do his job these days without some woman calling him a rapist. Then, it's like they're all ganging up on me, making up stories. That's what they do, women. Men are always suffering with false allegations and the woman is always believed.'

Gina sighed. 'Making up stories. Let's talk about the cautions that you've received for shouting abusively at a woman in a nightclub then spitting on her and the time that you got caught on camera rubbing yourself against a woman on a busy train.'

'Bloody liars, all of them.'

'That's not what the train footage showed. I saw it myself earlier. Does your current employer know about your past?'

Gina noticed that Pollard was clenching his fists as he stared at her without blinking. He didn't really consider the evidence against him when he spouted about false allegations and the man was lucky to have got off with a caution.

'Where were you this morning between two and three thirty?'

'At home with my head down a toilet bowl.'

'Was anyone with you?'

He shook his head and smirked at Jacob. 'I live alone.'

'How well do you know Mrs Godwin?'

'Perfect Mrs Godwin with her red hair. Not well at all. I know she's one of the group that are trying to get me fired.'

Gina wanted to say to the man that he was doing a fine job of making himself unemployable. He didn't need any help. It was men like him that made women scared to walk alone at night and the worst thing was, she could see that Pollard would never learn from his past or understand that.

'Wait, between my head being down a bowl, I was online throughout the night, chatting away on my home computer, not my mobile or any other device. You can check. My computer is my alibi.'

'What site were you chatting on?'

The man ignored Gina.

'Mr Pollard,' she said in a raised voice. 'Site?'

'The *Boyz R Takin it Back*. That's what it's called. Nice group of lads that recognise that women are out to stitch them up. It's a good job I was talking to them, isn't it, otherwise you'd have me for something I didn't do? Ironic, a woman would be stitching me up. I was chatting to someone called the VenMan.'

'We will need your computer.'

'You can have it. I've got nothing to hide. In fact,' he shouted at Alannah as she came back in and opened her locker, 'I didn't do anything. I know it upsets you that I'm innocent. I have to go out and help these lovely detectives with their investigation. You'll have to hold the fort while I'm out and don't lie to the bosses and say I shirked off.'

'As if!' She stuck her fingers up at him and left the room.

'Right, as a man who has nothing to hide, I'm ready to go to my flat and hand over my computer to you right now. In fact, I want you to have it. My alibi is coming up.'

As much as Gina didn't like Mr Pollard, she was pleased that he was making certain aspects of the investigation easy for them but the proof was still to come. When was he communicating online? Was he definitely using the computer he says he was using and not logging into an app elsewhere? What was said and would he have enough time to nip out and attempt to set Kerstin Godwin's house on fire? At the moment, he had motive and only their technical experts could answer her questions.

'There's something else but you didn't ask. Too busy suspecting me.'

'Go on then. I'd love to hear what you have to tell me.'

'That Faith Chapman, she isn't as rosy as she makes out.'

'What does that mean?'

'Ask her who she's been shagging? I saw her meeting someone around the edge of the golf course while I was on a break. A drip of a man with dark curly hair. She had her tongue down his throat. Maybe you should be arresting them and leaving innocent people like me alone. Looks like they wanted to get hubby out of the way.'

TWENTY-TWO

Sonya stood outside the factory where she worked as a purchasing assistant and leaned against her car. Head banging, she had been grateful for Heather's company but disappointed that her boyfriend had constantly tried to call while she'd been trying to confide in her. Needless to say, she'd only harped on about her encounter with Justin rather than the things that really mattered. Her phone rang and she instantly answered. 'Kerstin, slow down. Start at the beginning.'

'We're at my mother's. Someone tried to burn us down last night, the same person who killed Glen.'

'Are you sure? I mean, how would you know?'

'How many other arsonists are on the loose at the moment and we know Glen. I'd say that was too much of a coincidence. They could have killed us all. You have to be careful. I think it's to do with the gym. They were asking about Faith and Glen and me, and how we were connected and I mentioned the creep at the gym.'

'Graham.' Sonya exhaled and continued to listen.

'Yes, him. You have to admit he's weird but to try and kill us, that's something else. I reckon he wanted to kill Faith for calling him a perv but he wouldn't know that she wasn't with Glen that night. He'd also have all our details on our gym memberships. I'm waiting for an update. I would have told you all this at the school gates but I've kept the boys off nursery and school.'

Sonya bit her bottom lip and tried to hide the pain that she was keeping inside. It was all getting too much.

'Do you understand, Sonya?'

'What?'

'You have to be careful. You live alone with Erik. Have you got somewhere to go or somewhere you could stay?'

Sonya's manager stepped out of his car and waved. She noticed it was two minutes to nine and if she spent any longer talking, she'd clock in late. 'Yes, I'll sort something, don't worry. Me and Erik will be fine.' She already knew that to be a lie. She and Erik were anything but fine and things were set to get much worse. 'Got to go, my boss is watching.'

'Okay. We'll speak soon.' Kerstin hung up.

Sonya placed the phone in her bag and wiped the beads of sweat from her forehead. Her phone beeped and she pulled it back out, hands shaking as she clicked on the Snapchat message.

You're all I had and you weren't there. You're going to fry and your son will die.

Sonya fell to the ground, breathless and gasping as it disappeared. Her manager looked out of the window and came out of the main door. Her phone beeped again.

Or maybe, I'll give you a lifeline... Hang tight, so-called friend and remember, act normal.

Her manager caught up. 'Are you okay? I thought you'd fainted.'

Control it. She took a deep breath in and held. Blood pumped through her veins and thudded in her head with every beat. A sickness washed through her and she was sure if she tried to stand, she'd pass out. She placed a hand over her mouth and closed her eyes for a few seconds.

'Shall I call first aid?'

She shook her head. 'No, I just slipped on the ice and it knocked me sick. I'm okay now.' She was far from okay but she had to be okay if she'd ever see Erik alive again.

He held his hand out and helped her back onto her feet. 'Okay, but I want you to go to the canteen and grab yourself a drink. Sit there until you feel better, okay?'

'Thank you.'

Her phone beeped again. As her manager turned she quickly glanced at the message from Justin.

If I can't speak to my son later, I'll be logging this with my solicitor. Obstructing access isn't on.

She wanted to scream down the phone at her ex. She wished she could do nothing more than let Erik go to his dad's or give him a call. *You're going to fry and your son will die.* She followed her manager into the building, acting on autopilot through the worst moments she'd ever lived through. Last night, she'd wanted to tell Heather everything but she couldn't do it. She couldn't risk Erik's life. All she could do was wait for another message.

TWENTY-THREE

'Pollard has made a statement and his tech has gone off to the experts. I'm sure they'll let us know when they've had a chance to look at everything.' Gina turned into the neat little new estate road with its well-pruned communal gardens. 'Do we have on file where Sonya Baker works? Shame she wasn't in.'

Jacob nodded. 'Yes, she works at a company on the industrial park that make car parts.'

'When we've spoken to Heather Walton, we'll head over there. Both them and their families could be in danger so we need to warn them. Ah, there's number seventy-two.'

Gina pulled up on the road and they both got out.

Jacob grabbed his overcoat from the back seat and pulled it over his suit. 'Nice houses.'

'What do we know about Heather?'

He glanced at his notes and flipped over a couple of pages. 'Twenty-nine. She has an IT business and works from home. Fixes computers, gets rid of viruses – things like that. That's all we have.'

'Great.' Gina began walking down the drive, past the red Mini and knocked on the door. A young woman answered. 'Ms Walton.' Gina introduced them and held her identification up.

'Come through.' Heather opened the door fully and the smell

of toast escaped. Heather pulled the sleeves of her black jumper up and Gina almost wanted to do the same as she went through to the warm kitchen. Two empty plates peppered with crumbs sat on the side next to a pile of orange peel and a cereal bar wrapper. 'Take a seat at the breakfast bar while I clean up.' She started to pop the plates in the dishwasher. 'I've had a call from Kerstin so I know why you're here. I can't believe everything that's happened.' The woman stopped fussing over the mess and checked the coffee pot that was dripping away. 'I'm so sorry about the state of the place. How can I help you?'

'We'd like to ask you a few questions.'

'Of course. I didn't really know Glen though so I don't know how I can help.'

'You know Faith and Kerstin so we can start there.' Gina smiled to put the woman at ease.

'Yes, my motivation ladies. That's what we call ourselves. We meet at the gym, a lot. Kerstin told me that she mentioned Graham Pollard, the instructor. I don't know what else I can add.'

Gina felt the stool swivelling of its own accord so she gripped the worktop. Without asking, Heather poured out three black coffees and handed them out, leaving a bottle of milk in front of them. Gina took a cup. 'Thank you. That's most welcome. Can we start with asking you about Faith and Glen Chapman?'

'Of course. I'd like to help in any way I can.'

'How well did you know them?'

'My partner is friends with Glen.' She paused. 'I mean was. Sorry, I still can't believe what's happened. It's a lot to take in.'

'It's okay. We understand that this is hard for you.'

'My partner knows Glen; they've been friends for years. I've known Faith and Kerstin for four months now after meeting them all on a night out with our partners. I mentioned wanting to join a gym and we all became friends after that. Sonya and I met a few years ago but we didn't know each other that well before. Cleevesford is a small town in that respect. Sorry, I'm waffling. After meeting the motivation ladies and joining the gym, I ended up going to the café in the building afterwards, for drinks with them all. We've become pretty inseparable. I joined because, well, I work alone at home in IT and I was vegetating here. Thought I could do with some company and exercise. I wouldn't really say I'm close friends with Faith but she was always nice to me, really friendly.'

'How about Mr Chapman?' Gina noted that Heather looked a little drained. Dark circles made her eyes look tired.

Heather scrunched her nose. 'He alienated people with ease. His drinking would always get out of hand and he was quite mean to Faith. When I've seen them together, I've quite often heard him making snide little comments under his breath, like he'd call her fat if she went to eat something or he'd start arguing with her over the news. I won't be the only one to tell you that. He regularly made a display of himself in front of everyone, that's why I'm sure that whoever attacked their home was trying to get to him. Faith wouldn't hurt anyone.'

'Do you know if either Mrs Chapman or Mr Chapman were having a relationship with anyone else?'

Heather licked her teeth and looked down and a few curls escaped from her clip. 'I don't like to gossip.'

'Someone has murdered Faith's husband and as you've spoken to Kerstin, you'll know that there was an attempted attack on her family too, and we're worried that this same person might hurt someone else.'

'You really need to speak to Faith. I'm not supposed to tell anyone. It's not my business and I don't want to knock her when she's already going through so much.'

'Please... may I call you Heather?'

Heather nodded and Jacob leaned back on the bar stool, hands on the counter, waiting for her to answer.

'What do you know, Heather?'

'Faith asked me to look after her kids once and she came all dressed up. It was about a month ago. I pressed her on what she was up to and she caved in and told me. Please don't judge her, her husband was horrible to her and she deserved to be happy. She met up with one of her neighbours at a hotel out of the area, Stratford-upon-Avon I think. I don't need to spell out what they probably did, do I?'

Gina shook her head.

'She said she couldn't go to his house as they were neighbours and she didn't want anything to get back to her husband. She said she didn't know how Glen would take it and she wanted to leave him so badly but he made it hard. He used to tell her that she was his for life and if she ever tried to leave, she'd never see their kids again.'

'Do you know this neighbour's name?'

'Aiden something. I don't know his second name but he's the opposite of Glen. He's a lone parent and from what Faith says, really gentle and kind to her. I feel like an awful friend now. Faith will never forgive me for telling you all that.'

'I know that was hard but you did the right thing in telling us. Can you tell me how well you know Kerstin?'

'Again, I only know her from the gym and I've seen her a few times socially when we've gone out as a group. I know she has two boys and is really happy with her husband, Cameron. I really don't know much more and I don't know who'd want to hurt her family.'

'Have you ever seen anyone acting inappropriately towards Faith or Kerstin at the gym?'

'Only Graham, the gym instructor. None of us liked being anywhere near him, which is why we reported him to the management. His hands stray where they shouldn't and he looks at people in a leering way. I can't remember any exact incidents to share with you. It's not something I kept a note of.'

'Is there anything else you can think of that might help our investigation? It doesn't matter how insignificant it might seem.'

The woman shook her head.

'I'll leave you with my card. Should you remember anything, please call me straight away. Do you live alone?'

'No, I have a partner but he left for work just before you got here. Are we safe in our home?'

'With what has happened to your friends, we would suggest that you stay somewhere else for a few nights if you have that option, otherwise we can organise drive-bys every so often throughout the night.'

'We don't have anywhere else to stay and, to be honest, a hotel would be out of the question. My earnings just about cover the rent. I'd really appreciate it if someone could drive-by the house regularly. We also have CCTV and I get notifications on my phone every time someone comes onto the drive. It's set up facing the back garden too. I'll turn the notifications on.'

'Have you checked your smoke detectors lately?'

'Yes. As soon as I heard about Glen, I checked them and they all worked fine. Do you really think we're in danger?'

Gina bit the side of her mouth and continued, 'I think we need to be on our guard. If your CCTV sends you any alerts or you hear anything in the night, don't dismiss it. Call the police straight away and get out of the house.'

Heather swallowed and Gina was sure she could see the woman trembling slightly as she exhaled. 'That's a lot to take in.' She let out a nervous laugh and shook her head.

Gina flinched as a key turned in the front door. 'Forgot my laptop like an idiot. Need it for the quote,' called the man as he stomped into the kitchen.

As he entered, he stood and stared at Gina. His hair was now grey and his face was now a little reddened around the nose area. He'd also filled out around the middle but she'd recognise him anywhere.

'I want her out of my house, right now.' Stephen marched over to Gina and pointed in the direction of the door. 'I'll get justice for my brother one day.' Gina's heart thudded hard, like it was going to burst from her chest. She couldn't let him see how terrified she was. It was like Terry had just walked into the room and the way he shouted; it was just like that night Terry had come home and gripped her around the neck. Just before she nudged him down the stairs. She wanted to say something but it was like her throat was swelling up.

Jacob got off the stool and Gina could tell that Jacob recognised him too. 'Mr Smithson, we are here making enquiries about a murder.'

'I... we...' He walked over to Heather and grabbed her wrist. She flinched as he dragged her over to the other side of the kitchen island. 'We have nothing to say to you. Do you have a search warrant?'

'No,' Jacob replied.

'Get out of our house, then. This woman dared to go over to my mother's and accuse my dead brother of being a wife beater. Upset an old lady, didn't you, Gina? There are other things aren't there, Gina? Things I can never talk about but hey, that's how life goes sometimes.'

Gina knew exactly what he meant by that. Briggs had helped her out in the past by warning Stephen off and threatening to plant evidence on him if he ever bothered Gina again. It was meant to protect her but it seems that Stephen and Hetty couldn't help themselves. All they had to do was let the past stay in the past. One thing was for sure, Stephen would never bring that up and she wouldn't either, both of them fearful of the potential consequences. This was all about Terry's final minutes and whether Gina did everything she could to save his life.

'See them out, Heather.'

Heather looked slightly wobbly as she stared at him.

'Heather, do it!' Stephen slammed his fist onto the worktop and she flinched. 'Oh, Gina, don't forget to give Pete Bloxwich a call. He's waiting. We're all waiting for your side of the story.'

Heather looked slightly shaken as she brushed her clothes down. 'Sorry about that.' She held her hand out, guiding them towards the front door.

'Don't apologise to her,' Stephen shouted from the kitchen.

'We'll get those drive-bys organised then.' Gina felt her vision prickling and all she could think about was getting out fast but Heather was stalling.

'No,' Stephen yelled. 'We don't need you or your help. You're not sending police over to spy on us. Don't you dare!'

As they reached the door, Heather bent over to pick up the post from the mat, revealing her back as her top rode up. A large purple bruise filled the left side of her back.

'Have you hurt yourself?'

The woman grabbed the post and pulled her top down. 'I fell.'

'It looks nasty. Have you had it checked out?'

Heather replied in a hushed voice. 'No and I'm fine. I'm just a klutz, that's all. I hurt myself at the gym. Fell off the treadmill.' The injury Gina was looking at wasn't caused by falling off any treadmill. It looked like a punch to the kidney.

Stephen banged the cupboards in the kitchen.

'Please, you should go.' She opened the door and the two detectives stepped out.

'You have my number. If you need to call me for anything, then please do.' Gina stalled for a few seconds, making eye contact with Heather. The woman went to speak but was cut off by Stephen.

'Heather.'

'Got to go.' She closed the door on them.

As they walked back to the car, Gina felt her heart rate calming a little but she could barely swallow. It was as if her throat had completely dried up. Inhaling the cold air, she felt her throat loosening up again, causing her to gasp. She hurried to the car and sat in the driver's seat, Jacob beside her.

'What was all that about, guv? I know Smithson, he was a suspect in a previous case and he's your ex-brother-in-law. Horrible piece of work from what I can remember.'

'It's nothing.'

'He mentioned the reporter, Bloxwich.'

'Yes, he wants to do some sort of article on Terry's death and Stephen has been obliging. He keeps pestering me to talk about what happened and I just want to move on from the past but it seems that every time I try to do that, something comes up. You know my husband, Terry, fell to his death, down a flight of stairs?'

'Yes. Sorry all that had to be brought up again today. It must have been hard in there.'

'It's okay, but it was a shock to see Stephen.'

'Why would Bloxwich want to write about all that?'

Gina shrugged. 'It's just Terry's family, they want to do some sort of memorial piece and he asked me for some words... for the piece. It's a shame. It would be best for all if they could just move on. It was such a long time ago. I've moved on and when they do things like this, it brings everything back.' She couldn't tell Jacob any more than that and whether he believed her about the memorial piece was another matter.

'The man's still got a temper on him.'

'He certainly has. Did you see that bruise on Heather's back?'

'I couldn't miss it.'

'I'm not going to say anything else on the matter but I will say, both Terry and Stephen were violent and had terrible tempers. I'm worried for Heather and what he might do to her. I really hope she calls me.'

'Sorry, guv. This must be really hard for you.'

She stared out of the window at the houses on the opposite side of the road. 'I'm a survivor, Jacob, and I'll survive this case and I'll survive Stephen's temper. When I tell Briggs about today, about Stephen being a part of the case now, I'll be back-seated which means I won't be senior investigating officer. I'm going to beg to be a part of the case and with what I can bring to it, I can see me being able to interview and investigate anyone but Stephen and Heather – conflict of interests, and all that. I'm going to recommend that you be SIO because I know we can still work closely together.'

'Thanks, guv. Obviously, I feel more than ready to step up in that respect. I won't let you down and we'll still be a team.'

'I know you won't. What you have in that house, should he become more prominent in the investigation, is a violent misogynist. Please spare a lot of thoughts for Heather throughout the investigation. I'll be with you all the way. Right, when we get back, we need to get Aiden Marsh in again. There was obviously a relationship going on between him and Faith. We have to consider that maybe he was angry at how Glen was treating Faith and he knew that Faith wouldn't be around that night. Maybe Faith and Aiden planned this together. What still confuses me is, why target Kerstin's household after?'

'Maybe to throw the scent off themselves.'

'It's a tall order, attempting to burn down a house with a family in it just to cast suspicion away from them. They're both parents and there were children in the house.'

'Or,' Jacob continued, 'it's possible that we've underestimated just how desperate they felt their situation was.'

'That's something we have to bear in mind. Aiden and Faith have kept their relationship under wraps but are they a pair of murderers?' Gina felt a lump in her throat. If enough suspicion was cast on her, she might be taken off duty altogether, unable to even help on the periphery. She sighed. What Stephen and Pete had was nothing more than a hypothesis. All talk and no evidence. 'We also really need to speak to Sonya Baker. Before we go back and I speak to Briggs, we'll head to her place of work.'

'That sounds like a good idea. She might be in danger so we can't delay that conversation.'

As Gina pulled out of the road she thought back to the night that Terry had died, more specifically, the moment he was taking his last breath. The words she whispered in his ear came back. If Stephen knew what she'd said, he'd probably kill her on the spot.

TWENTY-FOUR

Jacob buzzed at the factory door, then introduced himself and Gina through the intercom. A young man came and opened up. 'Come through. It's not often we get a visit from the police.'

'Thank you. We've come to speak to Sonya Baker, she's an employee here.'

'Take a seat. I'll go and find her.'

They sat in the cathedral-like reception area where shiny metal car parts were displayed in glass boxes, lit up by spotlights. Gina sunk into the comfortable sofa, trying to process the last visit.

'Did you manage to get a message to O'Connor about bringing Aiden Marsh in?' Gina asked.

'Yes. He confirmed that he was on it. He also messaged back to say that Kerstin Godwin and her family were now at her mother's so at least they're safe for now.'

'That's good news. Any updates from forensics yet?'

'Nothing new. Mr Chapman's post-mortem is taking place soon. Do you think we can make it?'

'I need to speak to Briggs. Would you be able to go with Wyre?'

'Yes.' He grabbed his phone and scrolled down his emails, looking for the appointment. 'It's at three so as soon as we're finished here, I'll have a catch up and get ready to head over there. Think I'll skip lunch.'

The man came back to his post with a woman.

'Hi, I'm Sonya. You wanted to speak to me?'

'Yes, and we're really sorry to interrupt you while you're working but it is important. Is there anywhere we can go, to talk in private?'

'Colin, is the conference room free?'

The man clicked his mouse a couple of times and nodded. 'It's free for the next forty-five minutes then I have to prepare it for a sales meeting.'

'Thanks. Follow me.'

Gina and Jacob followed Sonya through the wide corridors. Pictures showing the business's history and its founders filled the walls. Then at the end of the corridor, Sonya punched a code into a pad to open the door that opened up to the grandest conference room Gina had ever seen. The table must have had thirty leather chairs around it and a large cinema screen filled the one wall. Jugs of water had been strategically placed on the table at regular intervals, next to upside down glasses.

'Take a seat. I know what this is about. It's to do with Faith's husband, isn't it? I have heard and it's such bad news.'

Gina noticed that Sonya looked a little pale with a redness under her eyes. Her brown hair was roughly pinned back and her shirt was a little creased. Sonya nervously sniffed, took a tissue and began fiddling with the corner. 'Yes, we'd just like to ask you a few questions. How well do you know the Chapmans?'

'I know Faith from the gym, that's all. My ex is friends with her husband, that's how we met. As for me and Faith, we go to the gym with Kerstin and Heather too. We have drinks together after our workouts, we talk on the phone, I sometimes help Kerstin and Faith by having their kids and they do the same for me with my son, Erik. Don't know what I'd do without them.'

'How many children do you have?'

'Just the one. Erik is four.'

'Is he at school now?'

She nodded. 'He started this year and he loves it. He's in the same year as Kerstin's boy, Dominic, and Faith's little boy, Harvey.'

'So you could say you have a close bond and help each other out?'

'Yes, I guess we need to. Sometimes I've picked their kids up from school or they've helped me by collecting Erik.' The tissue was now piling up in little bits on the shiny table. Sonya grabbed a water jug from beside her and filled up a glass before taking a few sips. 'Want some?'

'I'm fine, thank you.' Gina could tell the woman was getting more nervous by the second. 'Can you tell me what Mr and Mrs Chapman's relationship was like?'

Sonya began to squirm in her seat. 'I don't really know anything.'

'You must have spoken at the gym or at the school gates. Did she ever speak about him or did you see him ever bring the children to school?'

'No, I mean, I've never seen Glen at the school. It was always Faith doing the running around even though she works full-time for their company.' Her shoulders dropped.

Gina and Jacob waited in silence for Sonya to continue.

'Okay, I don't know if I should say anything but Faith was seeing someone, a neighbour called Aiden. She's only seen him a couple of times. I've seen him at the school dropping his son off and he seems really nice. I can see why she likes him especially as Glen is so...'

'So what?'

'I shouldn't say. It really is none of my business.'

'Sonya, someone set fire to their house killing Mr Chapman and we really need to find out who did this.'

Sonya rubbed her eyes and fidgeted to get comfortable. That was when Gina could unmistakably smell stale wine on the woman. Maybe the stress was getting to all of the friends.

'He was mean to her, putting her down and things like that.

She had him on loudspeaker at the gym once when she was outside, talking to him on the phone but I overheard what was being said. She said she was coming home because she was tired but he said and I'll never forget these words, "You'll never get rid of that lard arse if you leave early all the time." I heard her crying after. I also heard from Kerstin that when they've all got together for a night out, he constantly mentions other women and puts her down in the same sentence. Whenever she tries to talk or express an opinion, he shuts her up by telling her that what she's saying is stupid. I've noticed that too, when I've been out with them all.'

'Did you all go out together often?'

'I suppose we do. We go to a wine bar in the middle of Birmingham about three or four times a month. Since I became single again, I really wanted to get out more and it was kind of them to still invite me.'

'Have you known them all for long?'

'I've known them for a couple of years, except Heather. She's newer to the group but I have met her before. We just lost touch over the years but it has been great to meet up with her again. Stephen introduced her to us as his new girlfriend and well, she just became one of us.'

'So, just to clarify, your partners knew each other first and you all met through them?'

'Yes. I mean I'm not with mine now but I stayed friends with the group and my ex, Justin, moved on, preferring to be with his new woman and their new friends.'

'Can we take his full name and address?' Her focus on the case seemed to be shifting. They'd been linking the gym friends but their husbands and partners knew each other before the women's friendships had taken off. Heather was also new to the group. Instead of looking at the four women, they needed to see if they could come up with any links between the four men. But that was yet another avenue to explore. She still hadn't finished with Faith and her lover, Aiden, who had both lied about their relationship.

Sonya wrote Justin's address on a pad. 'He lives in Evesham now.' She passed the slip of paper to Jacob.

'How well did Glen, Cameron, Stephen and Justin know each other?'

'Oh, really well.'

'How?'

'They'd known each other for years, through work. Glen owned the plumbers' merchants. Stephen and Justin are in the building trade and sometimes buy supplies from him. Cameron works in the pipe supply chain doing something, I'm not sure what. His company supplies to Glen's outlets. You don't think it's anything to do with their work?'

Gina waited for Jacob to catch up on the notes. 'We're investigating all possibilities at the moment. How well do you know Kerstin and Cameron?'

'Fairly well. Again, I've looked after their kids while they've gone out and, as I say, done the school run for them now and again. Kerstin and I chat at the gym but I've never really spoken to Cameron much. He comes across as nice enough, always polite and friendly. He seems like a lovely family man.'

'As you know, we've had an attack on two of your friends in as many nights and these attacks have happened to friends you're close to. Do you have somewhere else you can stay while we investigate?'

'You think whoever is doing this is coming for me next?' Sonya's throat clicked, like she'd swallowed too hard. Her left foot was bouncing on the floor. She grabbed another tissue and began twisting it between her fingers.

'We're just trying to keep everyone safe.'

'I, err, I don't know. I have a couple of friends. Maybe Erik and I could stay with them for a few days. Do you really think this is needed?'

Gina knew she'd scared Sonya with that suggestion. The woman was already a bag of nerves before they started. Something told her that Sonya was holding something back from them.

'Is there something you know that you're not telling us?'

Sonya stopped tapping her foot and the room descended into silence for a few uncomfortable seconds. 'Like what?'

'I don't know. You seem really nervous, like there's something else you want to say.'

'Well I don't want to say anything else. You've just told me that my son and I might be in danger from a killer arsonist and that I need to leave my home for a few days. Isn't that enough to make anyone nervous?'

'You seemed nervous before.'

'I'm so sorry. My friend's husband has just been burned to death and it looks like it wasn't an accident. Of course I'm nervous and I'm upset for her. I'm gutted for their children, Harvey and Kiara... it's all so sad and, yes, I'm scared, I'm worried and I'm nervous. This has really shaken me and my friends. I don't want anyone else to get hurt.' Tears spilled from her cheeks.

'Yes, I'm sorry. I can see that this is traumatic for you. Do you have anyone who can be with you or can we call anyone for you?'

She shook her head and used the remaining half a tissue to wipe her eyes. 'No, I really should get on with my work. I have so much to do today. I'll be fine honestly. I'll pack a few things up later and I'll stay with a friend so you don't need to worry about me but can you keep me updated?'

'Of course we will. We have your number so we'll call you.'

The door clicked and Colin came in. He pushed a trolley laden with cakes and sandwiches through the door, ready to set up for the meeting.

'I really have to get back to work now. Besides, in less than ten minutes this room will be full of people.' Sonya checked her watch.

'Thank you for speaking to us. We'll be in touch.' Gina gave Sonya a card.

As they left the building, a wall of frosty air hit Gina. She did her coat up and shivered. 'I don't know what to make of her. Without a doubt, she knows more than she's letting on.'

'I agree. That's another thing we need to get to the bottom of.

We need to get back to the station if I'm to make the post-mortem, guv.'

'Yes, and I'll have a word with Briggs about Stephen then we can catch up on everything.' She glanced back at the building as they got into the car. As Gina pulled out of the car park, she glanced in the mirror. 'Sonya is running across the car park, coat half off. Didn't she just say how much work she had to do? We need to do a bit of digging on her. She knows something and we have to find out what.'

TWENTY-FIVE

Sonya could barely catch her breath. After turning into her street and pulling up, she messaged her manager, apologising for leaving abruptly. It was no good, she couldn't carry on with her day as if nothing had happened and now the police were onto her. Her nerves had been impossible to control. For a moment, she thought she might vomit in front of them. How would she have explained that reaction? Her head felt fuzzy and her hands tingled. She checked her phone for any updates – nothing.

She stared at her house. Once it had felt like home, back when she, Justin and Erik were a cosy little family but then he had left her for that woman. Life would never be the same again. She thought things couldn't get any worse, but they did. What she was now going through was worse than anything she'd ever experienced. Her life was over in every way.

She left her car and started the forty-minute walk to the Angel Arms. Maybe the answer wasn't in the bottom of a bottle but it would give her a bit of thinking time. Besides, she needed the alcohol to calm her nerves. She'd just have a couple of drinks. She knew that all the alcohol in the world wouldn't solve anything but it would take the sting out of the searing emotional pain that she needed to numb.

Hurrying along the path, she turned and walked for the next half an hour before finally reaching Cleevesford centre, heading straight through the door of the pub.

'What can I get you?'

'Hi, Elle, can I have a double vodka and Coke?'

'Has it been a rough one?'

'Rough?'

'You look like you've seen a ghost?'

'Tough day at work.'

'How's that lovely lad of yours?' There was something in Elle's tone, maybe it was accusatory or inquisitive.

Sonya glared at Elle for a few seconds in the hope that she would give something away. 'Why do you want to know?'

The woman shrugged and smiled. 'Just being polite.'

Not knowing who to trust was the worst thing ever. Sonya glanced around the pub. A toothless man grinned at her. A couple caught her eye and she whispered in his ear. Did they know things about her? If they did, their whisperings were cruel. 'Scrap that drink.'

'I've just poured it.' Elle placed it on the bar.

Without hesitation, Sonya hurried from the bar, leaving the drink and as she left, she almost bumped into Graham, the gym instructor. She went to push past him but he blocked her every move.

'You and your friends are going to pay for what you're doing to me. Mark my words.'

A tear rolled down her cheek as she nudged past. Standing in the car park, she took several deep breaths until she was dizzy and ran, almost slipping on a puddle in her useless boots as she stepped back onto the high street.

The off-licence, that's what she needed. As the lights changed to red, she darted across the road, into the shop and bought three bottles of the cheapest wine going. She was going where she should have gone in the first place – home. She would stay in, drink wine and wait for another message. Her heart pined for a message. A crash of thunder preceded the downpour.

Darkness started to fall as she walked through the estate sopping wet, wine bottles clanging in the carrier bag. As she passed the play park, she heard heavy footsteps behind her. A figure darted down a cut through as she turned. No more walking. She had to get home. Her jog turned to a run. A searing pain cut through her side but she didn't stop. Her house was in sight and whoever was out there wanted to scare her.

As she entered her hallway in the dark, she slammed the door closed and leaned against it as she got her breath back. This is how she would stay all night. She'd drink, wait for messages and watch out for intruders.

Her phone beeped. She read the start of the message. This was the lifeline she was promised.

I said I'd contact you and here's the deal...

As she read the rest, she slid to the floor, sobbing in a heap. She unscrewed a bottle of wine and took a swig, quickly followed by another. The words in the earlier message rang through her head. 'You're all I had and you weren't there. You're going to fry and your son will die.'

Who wasn't she there for? There was a clue in that statement and however much it whirled around her head, she was no closer to who had Erik. Were they hurting him? She imagined her little boy, alone and scared, and how she might never find out where he was. She wondered if whoever had him was hurting him, punishing Sonya for something she wasn't even aware that she did. She spotted Erik's stuffed elephant, the one he had as a baby called Jumbo and she clung to it, holding Jumbo close to her heart as the tears flowed. Full helpless tears that were getting her nowhere. There was only one way out of this mess. Time to sort out her predicament once and for all.

TWENTY-SIX

Gina sat opposite Briggs in his office. One of his strip lights was out so the office was in half darkness, forcing Gina to scrunch her eyes. Rain thrashed against the window and she wished that all she had to do was stare out of a window and not face what she had to say next. 'I have to report a conflict of interests.' Nothing like coming straight out with it.

'What? In the case?'

Gina nodded and rubbed her tired eyes. She'd thought about nothing but this conversation while driving back. While Jacob had spoken about what would happen next and the post-mortem, her mind had been on how to tell Briggs. With it not being the first time Stephen had cropped up in a case, she knew she was now even more of a burden to him and the team. 'It's Stephen. He's only become a part of the investigation.'

'How?'

'He's partner to one of the women in the group of friends and he was also good friends with the victim, Glen Chapman. They both met through their work and have been friends for years.'

'Damn. You know I can't keep you as SIO on the case?'

She couldn't fight this one. 'Yes, sir. I do. I'd go as far as saying Jacob should be SIO.'

'Agreed. Do you know if he wants to run with the case?'

'He's desperate to be SIO so that would be a yes.'

Briggs ran his fingers through his hair from front to back and stared out of the window for a few seconds. 'I'll ask him when he returns and then we'll announce it to the team.'

Swallowing, Gina knew she had to fight to stay on the case. 'I need to be a part of this. Please don't take me out of it completely.'

'There's a lot going on, Gina. With Pete Bloxwich and Stephen already threatening to turn public opinion against you with their "theories", leaving you on the case could be damaging for the department.'

'But—' Briggs held his hand up.

'I know how much this job means to you and I know how good you are. We need you on the case but you cannot front it. If I feel that at any point we are being compromised as a department, I have to put that department first. Do you understand what that means?'

Her shoulders dropped. 'I do, totally.'

'You can't interview Stephen or his partner. If he has to come to the station, you have to be away from him. You can listen to the interviews after, when he's left but I'm demanding that you have no contact with him or his family. As for the other witnesses, please continue to interview them with Jacob. I want you and him working closely together on the case.'

'Thank you so much. I won't let you down, I promise.'

He placed his hand on the desk and she placed hers over his, knowing that she probably only had this chance because he'd do anything for her. Any other DCI would have taken her completely off the case.

'I'm sure seeing Stephen again wasn't a pleasant experience.'

'It was a shock.'

'Do you want to talk about it?'

'No, I just want to interview Aiden Marsh and get on with things. That will give me enough to work on at home later.'

'If you want to come to mine, I've got an M&S meal for two in.'

She didn't want to be alone and Briggs had a way of grounding and reassuring her. He was what she needed. 'Can I let you know?'

He smiled. 'Of course. Now go and see what Aiden Marsh has to say. O'Connor's joining you, isn't he?'

'Yes, with Jacob and Wyre attending the post-mortem he said he'd sit in.'

'Great. Find out why he was lying about his relationship with Faith. Jacob and Wyre are heading to Faith's parents straight after the post-mortem. You'll be able to compare notes after.'

She was going to do exactly that.

TWENTY-SEVEN

'Mr Marsh, thank you for coming in. The time is sixteen forty-five and it's Monday the fifteenth of November. DI Gina Harte present.'

'And DC O'Connor,' O'Connor said for the tape.

'We're just going to ask you a few follow-up questions relating to the murder of Glen Chapman.'

Aiden's dark curls looked tangled on top of his head after coming in from the downpour. 'I told you all I know when you came to my house. Sorry, do you know how long this will take as I have to pick my son up from the childminder soon?'

'Do you need to make a call?' Gina waited for him to reply.

Aiden leaned back a little and loosened his puffed-up coat. 'No, I should be okay as long as it doesn't take too long.'

'Can you talk us through your relationship with Faith?'

'It's like I said, we sometimes meet at soft play and Elias likes to play with Harvey.'

'We have witnesses who say your relationship was more than that. One saw you with Faith, kissing her by the golf course. Another stated that you met her at a hotel in Stratford about a month ago.'

The man swallowed and glanced at Gina, then at O'Connor.

O'Connor finished scribbling and loosened his tie. The fan heater had over-warmed the room. Gina leaned over towards the wall and turned it off, leaving the room silent.

'They're lying.'

'Mr Marsh, you really don't want to get into trouble for obstructing a murder investigation. I'll remind you that perverting the course of justice is a serious offence and can carry a custodial sentence.'

'Perverting the course of justice?'

'Yes. We're not here to judge your relationships, we just need to know the truth. A man has been murdered. It's serious, as is withholding information or giving false information. Do you understand?'

He placed his elbow on the table and leaned his head in his hand as he stared at its grain for a few seconds. The nerves next to his eyes twitched away. 'Yes. I don't want to get into any trouble.' He scrunched his nose.

Gina closed the folder full of notes and sat up straight. 'I think the best thing you can do is tell us the truth.'

'I love her.' His voice was now shaky.

'Faith Chapman?'

'Yes. All I wanted her to do was leave him so that I could look after her and treat her right. It hurts me to hear him shouting at her and speaking down to her. We've been seeing each other for about three months. I did meet her at the golf course. It was during one of her gym sessions. She could barely get away from Glen as he seemed to monitor her every move. I told her that this wasn't healthy. He'd call her all the time, demanding to know where she was and threatening to get someone to check that she was telling the truth. She was only really allowed to go to the gym alone so I knew it would be okay to see her there. As for the hotel, we arranged it as she knew Glen would be in a meeting for a few hours that day. It wasn't what you think. It's not about sex; I wanted to talk to her again about her leaving him. I said I'd rent a house for us so we could get out of the area. She said it was more complicated than that. She couldn't leave her children and he'd never let her leave with them. He said if she ever tried to leave with the children, he'd kill her. Of course, Faith would never leave them and I get that. I would never leave Elias. Things were complicated.'

'Would you say it would suit you to have Mr Chapman off the scene? With him out of the way, you and Faith could be together and there wouldn't be threats hanging over her.'

'No. No way at all. I didn't like the man, in fact I hated him, but kill him? I would never do that. I haven't got it in me to hurt anyone.' Aiden grimaced and began nervously scratching his neck. 'I was with my son when the fire happened. I would never have left him alone.'

'You could easily have sneaked out, set fire to the Chapmans' house and still be back for when your son came downstairs.' Gina needed to push him. If he did it, she might get a confession.

'Don't you think my son would recognise me if he saw me outside? He would have said, I saw Daddy walk into that bin, not a person. He knows my shape and my build.'

Gina had to agree with him there.

'He'd also have heard the door go and there's no way he wouldn't have said something when you spoke to him. I love Faith and I hated Glen but I'm no killer. I find solutions to problems, real-life solutions. I'd have helped Faith get legal representation to make sure she got custody of her children. I'd have helped her build a case against him. He had so many shouting fits at her, in front of so many people, that there were witnesses galore. There's no way he would have got full-time custody with that temper. She couldn't see a way out though. It was all too much for her.'

'Are you saying that Mrs Chapman may have decided to take the law into her own hands?'

'No, you're twisting things. She wouldn't do that either. She wouldn't risk going to prison and being parted from her children. She isn't a violent person either. There's no way she would have hurt anyone, even her controlling abusive husband.'

Gina took a sip of water and thought hard about what he was

saying. She believed that when people were pushed to their limits, they would do all kinds of things that were out of character. She only had to look at herself to know that. As far as the investigation went, everyone was a suspect until there was a reason to eliminate them. What she had on Aiden was coincidental, not concrete. He had motive and, maybe at a push, opportunity but there wasn't enough to present a case to the CPS.

'I'm not just saying these things,' he continued. 'I wouldn't do anything that risked me being parted from my son. You have to believe me.'

'Do you know a Kerstin and Cameron Godwin?'

He scrunched his brow. 'No, don't think I've ever heard those names before. Wait, I think Faith has mentioned a friend called Kerstin. She might be one of the women she speaks to at the school gates or goes to the gym with. Has she got red hair?'

'So you've met Kerstin?'

'Not officially. If she is the woman with the red hair who Faith talks to, I've seen her around. She's a parent at the school my son goes to. But I don't know the first thing about her.'

'Do you know where she lives?'

'Definitely not.'

'Do these names mean anything to you? Justin Baker and Stephen Smithson?'

'No, never heard of them.'

'How about Garth Shaw?'

'No.'

'Graham Pollard'

'Oh yes, the gym creep that Faith mentioned.'

'Do you know him?'

'Sorry, I don't. I couldn't even tell you what he looks like.'

The interview was coming to an end. Aiden was beginning to fidget and check his watch. 'I really need to collect my son now. He'll want his tea. If you need to speak to me again, I can come back later or tomorrow or you can come to my house. Can I leave?'

There was nothing she could do to keep Aiden any longer.

'Yes, and thank you for coming in. We'll be in touch. Interview suspended at seventeen thirty.'

O'Connor stopped the tape and stood. 'I'll see you out, Mr Marsh.'

Aiden knotted his scarf and nodded. 'Thank you.'

As Gina listened to O'Connor walking the man down the corridor, Briggs appeared at the door. 'Your thoughts?'

'He lied but I don't think he did it. Obviously we need to know what Faith says but more investigation is needed.'

'The techies have produced an activity log of Graham Pollard's computer. There's some interesting things on it that you might want to see.'

'I'm on my way.' She stood, taking her glass of water with her. Whatever was on Pollard's computer, she had to see it now. It would either prove his innocence or make him their prime suspect.

TWENTY-EIGHT

The little boy yawns. It's dark and he's been asleep all day. He flinches as he hears a pained moaning sound followed by a bang. He wonders if the monster has woken up and is coming up the stairs so he pulls the quilt over his face and gasps for breath under the quilt. The noise has stopped. Maybe he's safe for now. He peers out and spots the jar of sweets. He's so hungry that his belly is making horrible groaning noises so he reaches over in the lamp-light and grabs the jar. Within minutes, he's eaten half of them and now he feels a bit sick. Something isn't right. He's never really had a headache and he often hears his mum saying that she has one. This is how it must feel.

Rubbing his eyes, he tries to focus but the light is low and his eyes are gritty. Wiping the sleep away doesn't help. Maybe he's coming down with a cold because his throat is also a bit scratchy and dry. Another drink has been placed on the television stand. He takes a sip. The fruity flavour takes the staleness out of his mouth so he has another swig. This isn't fun anymore. He wants to go home.

'You're awake.'

He flinches as he turns to see his friend sitting in the dark corner of the room. 'Yes. When can I go home? My mummy will wonder where I am.'

'We haven't finished our story yet. When I've told you everything, I'll answer that question. Do you want to hear more?'

He nods, keen to hear the rest and keen to keep his friend for longer this time. It's getting lonely in the attic. 'Are you going to tell me about Ziggy the dinosaur?'

'Yes. You need to know the rest. Why don't you take your drink and get back into bed while I carry on with the story.'

He smiles and gets comfortable. He's always loved stories and he loves this one. He wants to know what happened after the party, when all the jelly and ice cream had been eaten up.

His friend speaks in a low voice. 'Right, where were we? Ah, I remember. I'm going to take you back a little so you know what was going on in Ziggy's life. Ziggy hadn't been happy for a long time, but things could change, couldn't they? No longer did Ziggy have to put up with people who were horrible which is why—'

'What did they do to Ziggy?' He almost doesn't want to hear the answer but he cares and he wants to know what happened.

'It was when Ziggy was at school, the other dinosaurs said that the little dinosaur would always be a no one and they all made Ziggy sad with their bullying. Ziggy felt like no one cared. The little dinosaur could do things but they all kept saying that Ziggy was awful at everything so the dinosaur decided to prove them all wrong. One day, Ziggy made a great big unicorn cake and showed it to them. They all laughed and said it was rubbish, but they all ate it, every last crumb. They said the cake was horrible and that Ziggy was smelly and weak. Really mean things.'

He could feel a tear in the corner of his eye. It was so sad that Ziggy had been hurt like that.

'But that was behind Ziggy and it wasn't the worst thing that had happened. Ziggy decided to start a new life, which is why the little dinosaur went to the party with Topsy to celebrate. Later that day, when it was dark, Ziggy stepped outside for a breath of fresh air. Topsy hadn't been seen for a while and Ziggy thought that

Topsy had gone outside to cool down from all the dancing because it was very hot. That's when the little dinosaur heard a step coming from the darkness.'

'Was it Topsy?'

'No. When Ziggy turned, two big dinosaurs roared with their teeth out and they ran at the little dinosaur. They were bigger and stronger. Even Ziggy's mean friends had never roared like this.'

He grips his blanket, almost scared of the next part of the story.

'Drink your juice, matey. Remember what I said about it making you big and strong.'

He does as he's told because he's a good boy and it's nice. A fuzziness washes through him and his arms feel floppy. 'I'm scared,' he mumbles. 'Did the big dinosaurs hurt Ziggy?' His last word is nothing more than a whisper. 'I feel funny.'

'It's okay. Don't fight it. It won't hurt.' What won't hurt? he wants to ask but it's too late. Tiredness has taken over.

TWENTY-NINE

Gina hurried to the incident room where O'Connor was staring at his computer screen. Briggs followed her and they both sat either side of him as he scrolled through the activity log.

'What have we got?'

'I'm just reading through it, guv.' O'Connor reached for a large cookie out of a lunchbox. 'Mrs O made these, help yourself. Triple chocolate chip.'

As Gina scanned through the words on the screen, she decided not to have a cookie while looking at such disturbing online chat.

O'Connor crunched and continued to talk as he ate. 'As you can see, Graham Pollard was into some extreme stuff, mostly gender hatred. It does appear that he was using his home computer at the time of the murder but if we look at what he was typing onto this forum, we open up a whole new avenue of investigation. He not only names the four female gym friends, he outs their addresses for this sick community to see.'

'Can you tell us more about the community?'

Briggs and Gina waited for O'Connor to turn a page in his notebook.

'I made some notes earlier after seeing them mentioned on the system. On social media they come across as quite innocent.

Mostly they talk about male suicide rates and prostate cancer. They then mention how these issues aren't taken as seriously as women's issues. This is where the conversation stops, which is odd as people seem to be commenting but these comments gain no momentum. I would say that the group members are then contacted in a private message and drawn into this very private forum. I created an account to get a better look. Most of what they discuss is extreme. They're a women-hating group, blaming women for everything from losing their jobs, to women earning more, and men not being able to take their rightful places in society. They hate feminists and plan troll attacks on social media with very specific attacks against feminist speakers. You know how it goes.'

'I wish I didn't but yes, I do.' Gina knew enough about how these people operated. 'So, he outed their addresses. That opens up a whole new can of worms putting the women as targets back in the spotlight.'

'It looks that way.'

'Can we identify any of the people in this forum on the night the addresses went out?'

'The good thing is, there weren't many online at the time but the bad news is, most of them are using a virtual private network.'

Gina took a cookie, giving in to hunger. 'Good old VPNs. That's all we need. A group of women haters who now have the addresses of women who upset one of their members by reporting him for sexual abuse. Were they all using a VPN?'

'That's where we have some good news. We have the name and address of one member who calls himself VenMan.' O'Connor rubbed his bald head.

'VenMan, Pollard used him as his alibi. Wouldn't he be at his computer too? Have we checked out his IP address?'

'Oh, I must say, look at the times this particular conversation took place, when the addresses were released. Two hours before the Chapmans' house was set alight.'

'Giving them enough time to spread the word. We need to work out who everyone else is.'

'That's going to be near impossible.'

'Can we identify VenMan?'

'Yes, I'm sorry, guv. He's come up in a previous investigation. He was online at the time of the murder, chatting away. That's unless someone was chatting for him, using his login.'

'So, who is he?'

'Stephen Smithson.'

Gina dropped the cookie and felt the colour drain from her face as she read the conversation where Stephen had accused women of being murdering bitches deserving of all the bad that can come to them. 'Damn.'

'You alright, guv. Have another.'

She pushed the plastic box away. 'Thank you but I've just lost my appetite.' She needed a plan and quick. If she brought him in, she was definitely off the case and he was online at the time. His hatred was obvious but that wasn't enough to bring him in. 'O'Connor, keep monitoring this group. Add more to the fake profile so that it looks more convincing. We don't need them throwing you out, we need to infiltrate the community. Do it with the help of IT. Can't have any of these whack jobs tracing your profile back to us. Just observe them and chip in here and there. We need to get deeper into this rabbit hole and flush out whoever killed Mr Chapman. Obviously this is only one line of enquiry but it's one I don't want put on the back-burner. These people are dangerous, simmering away, and who knows what they're capable of in the real world.' Gina stopped reading when she came across a barrage of rape jokes. She wasn't at all surprised to find out that this was a community that Stephen was so deeply a part of. Gina sat back. 'Also, can you go back further? Read some of the other threads and see if any of the people in this one give anything away. I'd say, go back a month and let me know if you find anything significant.'

'I think I'm going to need all these cookies.' O'Connor put the lid back on the plastic box. 'It's going to be a long and challenging couple of days.'

Minutes later, Gina was packing up to leave for the evening when she heard Wyre's voice coming from the incident room. She left her office and hurried to see her. She and Jacob were updating the board.

'Any news?'

Jacob turned and smiled. 'We were just catching up with your interview. The one with Aiden Marsh.'

'And?'

Wyre put the pen down after making a few notes under Aiden's name. 'Faith's statement pretty much matches what he said to you. She says she really likes Aiden but she never killed her husband.'

'So nothing further to report there at the moment. We still can't fully prove that she never left the hotel on the night of the murder.'

'Ah, there is something.' Jacob smiled.

'Go on.'

'Her parents state that she definitely didn't leave the house last night so there's no way that she could have been the person that Kerstin Godwin saw outside her door. Her mother set the burglar alarm and nothing was tampered with during the night. She also said she suffers with insomnia and was reading in the lounge half the night and Faith never left her room.'

'It's not looking likely that it was Faith Chapman. It would have saved us a lot of hassle if both she and Mr Marsh had told us the truth in the first place. Although Aiden Marsh is still staying on the maybe list for now. How did the post-mortem go?'

Wyre pulled a face. 'The pathologist confirmed that he had died of smoke inhalation. We spoke to Bernard and Keith too in the hope of a forensics update. Bernard said there were no batteries in the smoke alarm.'

Gina took a step back and allowed her mind to whirr away. 'We don't know who removed them. Had Mr Chapman taken them out to replace or was the whole evening set up? Did someone remove the batteries knowing that the house was going to be set fire to? Just throwing a few theories around. Could Aiden and Faith have got someone else to do the deed? Maybe she removed the batteries. Again, there is no evidence for this but we have to bear it in mind as a possibility. However, that doesn't explain why someone would want to attack the Godwins. No one has mentioned that either of them had any enemies. We're missing something big here.' Gina stared at the board, taking in the photo of Glen and then the notes on Faith followed by the photos of the candle in the jar and the burnt-out house. 'The candle. This is really personal. These candles are often used for remembrance or to mark the death of someone. Who is our killer mourning?'

Jacob bit the inside of his cheek as he thought. 'I don't think we've unravelled that information yet but there was another update from Bernard.'

'Great. We need a break.'

'The fingerprints pulled on the lighter did not belong to the Chapmans. The bad news is, we do not have a match to anything on the system. The owner of these prints has never been in trouble with the police.'

Gina sighed. 'We know Pollard's are on file. Stephen Smithson's are too. That rules them out from using that lighter. Although, we can't confirm that this was the lighter used to start the fire. So many possibilities, still. Have the drive-bys been organised or have all the people at risk left their homes for now?'

Jacob took his phone out of his pocket and checked an email. 'Sonya Baker confirmed that she wouldn't be staying at her house. The Godwins won't be either and Heather Walton and Stephen are remaining at home and Stephen said he didn't want us interfering and he sounded really angry.'

'That sounds about right. At least the others won't be at home but they won't be able to go on like this forever so we have to move quickly with this investigation. Let's get a good night's sleep and get back on it tomorrow. Have you been updated by O'Connor about the *Boyz R Takin it Back* online forum?'

Wyre and Jacob nodded.

'Let's hope that gives us more to work on. We need more research on that front. We know Stephen Smithson is a part of that community but there are other members that we have yet to identify. Work closely with O'Connor. We know that the members released the addresses of the four women. I'm just relieved that they're not at home. I'll call them to update them. They have to know what danger they're in and just because Stephen and Graham Pollard were online at the time, it still doesn't mean they had no involvement. Dig deep. Right, I'm heading home to work. Any updates, call me straight away.'

'Will do,' Wyre replied as she opened a can of pop.

'We need to nail this person before they kill again.'

THIRTY

The petrol sloshes in the can so I place it down. It sinks into the mud as I take a few deep breaths. Never did I ever think that I'd have to pull up in the middle of the night on a country road, syphoning petrol from my own car but life is a test and it's definitely testing me to my limits. I can still taste petrol in my mouth even though I've had a mint or two.

I pull the small bottle of vodka from my pocket as I can't do what I have to do without a top-up. It's the only way I can go through with this. The warm liquid trickles down my throat. There's no putting off what I have to do. I'll pay for my wrongs in the end but when a person has no choice, they do what they have to do.

Something I've done in my past has led me to this but however hard I try, I can't think. How could I possibly deserve this? I've never hurt anyone, ever. Okay, I've had a few arguments and I think I pushed my sister over when I was twelve but haven't we all done things we're not proud of? Burning houses down is the worst thing I've done. That's a real bad thing. Everything else was nothing.

Why me? That's all I keep asking myself.

I can't put this off any longer. The message was loud and clear.

Lifting the petrol can, the spout, the lighter and the candle in the jar, I creep across the road, leaving my holdall where it is for now. After I've done the deed, I'll run back into the bushes and hide while I get my things together. No one can see me here, in the dark corner where I lurk. I'm alone. It's like I don't exist. I zip up my hoodie and feel the biting cold air on my face. As I reach the bench, my hands tremble that badly I can barely light the candle. I watch it flicker warmly in the jar and wish I was at home drinking a strong spirit over ice while looking into a soothing fire, but I'm not.

My breaths come in short bursts leaving white puffs of mist in the air. I gently pour the petrol into the spout and through the letter box. It falls onto the mat below, barely making a sound. I don't hear any sign of movement so I hurry, pulling the lighter from my pocket. My gloved fingers feel fat and cold and I can't seem to strike the rag to post it so I remove them. Eventually, I succeed and it catches. The flames quickly whoosh up the material and I drop the rag through the slot just before it reaches my fingers then I run back to my bush, out of sight from peering eyes.

I stand there, my gaze fixed on the dancing flames and the alarm sounds. That wasn't meant to happen. I can't be here. I grab the bag and run so fast, I feel as though my heart will give way. Over the lane, across a small field, I hop over a stile and come out the other end. I double over gasping as I spot my car in the distance and I vomit unexpectedly. The vodka burns more coming up than it did going down. I choke and gag until I have nothing left to expel.

All I have to do now is get home and hope for the best. This has to be the end here.

I stagger back to the car and get in, throwing my holdall onto the passenger seat. Sirens sound in the distance so I have to get out of here, now. 'I hate you,' I murmur to myself.

Gina woke to the sound of her phone buzzing but she couldn't see it anywhere. She lifted the blanket and stared at the unfamiliar living room and spotted the last of the embers in the fire. She must have fallen asleep on Briggs's sofa after dinner. Jessie the Labrador plodded towards Gina on her arthritic legs and began to lick her face. She patted the dog and returned to untangling the blankets to find her phone. As she grabbed it, it began to ring again.

'Jacob. What's happened?' He wouldn't be calling her at three in the morning for nothing. She heard creaking on the stairs and Briggs appeared in nothing but his shorts at the bottom. His hair sticking up and his eyes half closed.

'There's been another fire, guv. Firefighters are still at the scene and forensics are on their way over now.'

'Whose house?'

'Kerstin and Cameron Godwins.'

'Thank goodness they weren't staying at the house.'

'She left but Mr Godwin didn't. One of the team called Kerstin to tell her what had happened. It seems that Cameron didn't go with her. He changed his mind and stayed at home. As far as we know, he was in the house. There's something else.'

'What?'

'The firefighters reported that there was another candle outside the house. A tea light in a jar.'

'I'm on my way.' Jessie began to wag her tail and barked.

'I thought you had a cat.'

Gina glanced up at Briggs who was now heading towards the kitchen and filling up the kettle. 'I'm looking after my neighbour's dog. I'll meet you there.'

Jacob ended the call.

'So fill me in.' Briggs handed Gina a strong black coffee.

'Another fire, this time at the Godwins' house. The husband was at home, alone.' She took a sip. 'I best get ready and head over there.'

'Anything I can get you? Some toast, maybe.'

She shook her head as she headed to his bathroom to get tidied up.

Within forty minutes, she arrived at the Godwins' house and the fire was out. The acrid smell of the aftermath turned her stomach. She glanced at the building, watching how everyone worked the scene, everyone in thick yellow protective gear, dog handlers and a hose being reeled back into the fire engine. The house looked much worse than the Chapmans' did. Maybe with it being a lot smaller, the fire took more of it. Several neighbours had been shepherded behind the cordon. Gina heard one man asking if he could go back into his house.

PC Smith stood at the join in the cordon and noted Gina's details down and time of arrival before letting her through. She spotted Jacob and hurried towards him. Billowy tendrils of smoke drifted through the air, one catching Gina's nose. She instantly coughed as she inhaled, coating her throat with bitterness.

'Morning, guv. They've just confirmed the body of a male inside so we're working on it being Cameron Godwin. They said he was barely identifiable so I think we're going to have to get confirmation from his dental records. He was wearing a wedding ring with K&C inscribed on it.'

She pursed her lips and nodded at Jacob. 'He wasn't meant to be there. Why didn't he just leave with his family for a few nights? Did we have drive-bys checking on the property?'

'Not many. There was going to be no one in the house and the department is already stretched. An officer passed about one thirty and reported that the house was in darkness.'

A car skidded up the road and stopped beyond the band of people milling around or displaced from their homes. A car door banged and Kerstin burst through the cordon in her nightdress and coat. Gina hurried back and intercepted her but the woman pushed her aside with such strength that she almost knocked Gina over. 'Mrs Godwin, it's too dangerous to go any further.'

'I don't care, I need to see him.'

'Please, Mrs Godwin.' Gina reached out to hold her arm and Kerstin fell to the floor like a dead weight and sobbed. Gina kneeled on the floor beside her while she let it all out. That's when she spotted Pete Bloxwich with a photographer taking a photo of Kerstin.

'Cam was in there.' Her long, red-tangled hair fluttered in the chilly breeze and she began to shiver. Gina nodded at a paramedic who ran over with a foil blanket. Gina placed it over the woman's shoulders, helped her up and led her away from the house. 'Please tell me they were wrong and you've pulled him out. He can't be dead.'

'I'm sorry.' Gina bowed her head as Kerstin snivelled.

'I told him he shouldn't stay there alone. If only I'd gone on at him more.' She sobbed and hiccupped at the same time. 'He kept saying that they'd already tried to burn the house down the night before, that they wouldn't be back and he wasn't coming to stay with my mother and stepdad. We argued. My last words to him were that I hated him for being such a selfish prick. He died tonight and those were my last words to him.' She broke down and sat on the kerb as the firefighters nodded for forensics to enter.

Gina spotted the knocked over candle on the grass and Bernard picked it up and bagged it.

'Your husband would have known how much you loved him.'

'But I told him I hated him. I don't hate him. Why would I say that?' The woman's face glistened with tears and mucous. Gina pulled out a packet of tissues from her pocket and offered her one. 'I should have insisted that he leave the house.'

'And would that have worked?'

Kerstin shook her head. 'No.'

'This isn't your fault, Kerstin, but we need to find this person. Can you think of anyone who would want to harm you or your husband?'

She took a deep breath and wiped her face with the tissue. 'I've already told you. No one would want to hurt Cameron, he was a good guy. Always kind to everyone and got on with everyone. I don't have any enemies as far as I'm aware. I've already told you about Graham from the gym.' She paused. 'How am I going to tell the children that their father is dead and they've lost their home?' The tears came again.

PC Kapoor pulled up and nudged through the ever-increasing crowd to get to Gina. 'Guv.' The short woman tilted her head in sympathy.

'Would you please sit with Mrs Godwin while I speak to Bernard?'

PC Kapoor swapped places with Gina. Bernard waved her over.

'I can't believe we have another one.' Gina met him at the end of the garden just outside the gate.

He began tucking his beard into his beard cover. 'I know. Only two nights between them. We're only just being allowed in but I'm not holding out any hope of getting much from this scene. The fire and water will have destroyed so much. Like with the last scene, accelerant was used. That was confirmed with the chief firefighter when I arrived. They could smell it and the way the fire travelled through the house, from the front door outwards, backs that up.'

They both glanced at the house. Black, sooty water dripped from everywhere and the hall carpet squelched as a firefighter walked back and forth. 'The house is a right mess. I hate fire scenes.'

'Just do your best. It's possible that the garden holds more evidence. There's the candle for a start. How about footprints in the garden? It's quite a muddy garden.' Gina remained hopeful.

'We'll be taking casts but just about everyone has trampled on it while putting the fire out.'

Gina glanced around. 'I wonder which direction the killer came in. Did they drive or did they arrive on foot?' There were people everywhere. Families, teenagers, journalists. The streets were full and that meant any precious evidence that they may have come across would definitely be of no use now, not in such a large crowd.

'Guv, there's a young man in the house two doors away who's asked to speak to the person in charge so I thought I'd come and get you.' Jacob wiped his runny eyes, the smoke making them sore.

'I'll come with you. Call me if you find anything.' She nodded to Bernard and followed Jacob. 'You know you're the senior investigating officer now?'

'We're a team, guv. Let's go and speak to him.'

THIRTY-TWO

'I'm DS Driscoll and this is DI Harte. You're...'

'Harry. My mum's house is that one there.' He pointed. 'She's on holiday and I said I'd stop here to look after the place. She doesn't like it being empty when she goes away.' The young man was probably no older than twenty-five and his long hair passed his shoulders.

Gina hesitated, waiting for Jacob to begin questioning but he pulled out his notepad and glanced her way. She cleared her throat, trying not to cough and wishing that she had a bottle of water to take the acrid taste from her throat. 'Can you talk us through your evening and tell us what you saw?' She was grateful to still be on the case and leading with the questioning of the witness.

He pulled his parka-style coat across his thin frame. 'I was listening to my headphones in bed because I couldn't sleep. My bedroom faces this road. I sat up in bed to have a cigarette. My mum doesn't like me smoking in the house but it's so cold out. I didn't want to go in the garden so I pushed the window open. Wait, I know what time that was as I posted on Twitter that I couldn't sleep.' He pulled his phone out. 'It was ten past two.' He showed them the tweet containing a sad comedic photo of himself sitting in bed, wide awake.

'What happened after that?'

'I saw someone running into the bushes while I was blowing smoke out of the window so I watched in the dark for a second. I didn't fully close my window as some of the smoke blew back in and I had to get rid of the stink. I got back into bed, not really worrying about the person in the bushes too much. I knew our burglar alarm was set and no one had tried to get into the house. After that, I lay there with my headphones on checking Twitter, replying to fellow night owls and then I browsed Instagram and TikTok as I still couldn't sleep. That's when I heard the crackling sound. Soon after I could smell smoke. At first, I thought it was coming from our house. When I looked out of the window, I saw the glow coming from the neighbour's house. I ran out but the flames had already taken over. I knew there was no way I could get in without being burned alive so I called the fire brigade immediately. Then they turned up.'

'Thank you for that. Can we go back to the person you saw in the bushes. Can you describe them?'

'They were wearing some kind of jacket or hoodie. All dressed in black or dark colours. Maybe even navy blue but I couldn't tell.' Gina gazed up and down the road, looking for the street lamps and there were none directly in front of the Godwins' house. 'Oh, I saw something glint around their wrist, when it caught the light. Maybe they were wearing a bracelet or a watch.'

'How tall would you say they were?'

Harry shrugged. 'It's hard to tell from upstairs but I'd go with average. They didn't look particularly tall.'

'And how about their build?'

'I'd go with slim, definitely slim. They managed to dive into the bushes and bend with ease, so I'd say agile or young maybe. I'm not sure if I'm just guessing now. I could only see an outline and a glint around the wrist.'

'Could you show us where you saw this person?' They all

turned to the line of trees and bushes opposite the row of houses. There were a combination of tall oaks and mixed evergreens and branches were entangled around a fence that had long since fallen apart due to rot.

He began walking across the road and led them to the spot. 'It was about here.'

Gina scrunched her brow as she tried to focus. Jacob took a tiny torch from his pocket and passed it to her. She aimed the light and observed what was around. There were a couple of gaps in the conifers that someone could have hidden beneath or behind. The fencing was also missing behind the branches, giving anyone an easy way onto the field. A police officer with a dog was working the area and his Alsatian stopped and barked. Gina bent over and shone the torch through. That's when she saw the miniature empty bottle of vodka and a lid beside it. The damp leaves looked trodden down.

She turned to face Harry. 'What's beyond these trees if you carry on through the gap?'

'Just a playing field. The kids play football on it. At the other end, there's another estate.'

'Thank you, you've been really helpful, Harry,' Jacob said. The young man smiled as if really pleased that he'd helped.

Gina turned back to Jacob. 'Call a member of the forensics team and dog handlers over here. I think we've found the entry route.'

THIRTY-THREE

Sonya clocked in a little early. With every step she wobbled a little. It wouldn't take a genius to work out that she wasn't totally sober but she had to hide it. It had been a couple of hours since she'd downed the rest of the wine and she'd been sick. It should have been out of her. No one could notice how out of it she was and no one could question her. She almost fell as she entered the corridor. It was swaying as the sickness inside her was building up. She wanted to turn right back and get out of work. There's no way she would be able to concentrate. All she could do was stare at her screen and pretend. Stopping, she held a hand over her mouth then she hiccupped and burped. Acting normal was now too much to ask.

She pulled her phone from her bag and despite staring at it non-stop all night, there had not been another message. She was still in the dark. The last message she'd received from Justin was nothing. So what if he was going to his solicitor today because she wouldn't let him see Erik. So-bloody-what! All she wanted to do was see Erik. Her eyes watered up a little.

'Sonya, you don't look so good.' Colin approached and stopped in front of her. 'You seriously look sick.'

'I am sick. I think I have some sort of flu or bug,' she managed to mumble. 'I can't be here.'

He got a little closer. 'Is there anything I can get you? Water, maybe.'

She shook her head and he sniffed a couple of times.

'Have you been drinking? You reek of stale wine.'

She didn't answer.

'Look, if your manager catches you here in this state, you'll get a warning or maybe even suspended for turning up at work in this state.'

A tear rolled down her cheek. 'Please don't say anything. I can't lose my job.'

'I know, I know. You have a son to support. I know things have been hard for you with your divorce but you really need to pull it together.'

She stared up the corridor, keeping her focus on one spot. She didn't feel too bad if she did that. Maybe it was the drink sloshing in her stomach or maybe it was the churning anxiety that was causing her heart to bang in her chest.

'Look, go home. I'll tell your manager you threw up and had to leave. He won't want you here if you've got a bug anyway. Just get out of here before he comes in and sort yourself out. Come back tomorrow and all will be fine.'

She forced a smile. 'You're a good person, Colin. Thank you.'

'Oh and get an Uber home. Don't you get in that car.'

'Thanks, I won't.' Turning, she made her way back to the entrance and out into the car park. She went to unlock her car and then changed her mind. Colin was right about the Uber. She'd already wrongly driven to work in the state she was in. She was going to call a taxi and leave her car. She pulled her phone out again and began to search for the number of the firm she'd used before when she'd gone for a night out and just as she was about to press, another message arrived.

Get home. You will receive a call on your landline in ten minutes.
Miss it and you'll never see your son again.

Blood whooshed to her head and prickles filled her eyes, threatening to cloud her vision. Inhaling sharply she shook her head, needing the fuzziness to go away. It was as if she'd instantly sobered. She unlocked her car, got in and turned the ignition on. She now had eight minutes to save her son. She over-revved her engine, clumsily trying to find the bite and reversed out of the space without even looking in her rear-view mirror. As she did, she clipped the edge of Colin's new car. She then hopped the car towards the exit and waited to pull out onto the main road but the rush hour traffic kept coming. There was a gap, a small one but she was going.

Six minutes.

She pulled out, almost causing the car behind to crash into her. The driver tooted their horn. She didn't care. She continued to the traffic island, again, the traffic was dense. With shaky hands she gripped the steering wheel and revved up the engine, ready to pull out.

Four minutes.

She was never going to make it. She began to hyperventilate as she slammed the accelerator down and went, causing traffic behind her to skid and stop.

Three minutes.

Down the next road, then another. Only one island and then her street.

One minute.

A learner stalled in front of her. She crashed the car out of the way. If she abandoned her car in the street and ran straight into the house, she could still make it. She had to make it. Who cared about blocking traffic? Her son would die. As she turned into her street she crashed head-on into a police car, then a queue of traffic filled the road.

Another message came through.

You missed the call! You killed your son.

It disappeared as quickly as she read it. Then another message came through. As she opened it, the phone slipped out of her hand and into the passenger footwell. She watched as the text disappeared. She would never know what the message said.

Beyond hysterical, she couldn't move as the police officer with the thick Brummie accent snatched her keys from the ignition. She pushed the woman out of the way with the car door and began running towards her house. 'Erik,' she called out. It can't be too late. They would message again. They had to give her another chance. She was brought down by the officer who began reading her rights to her as they both fell to the floor. Something about dangerous driving but it didn't matter. Nothing mattered. She lay there with her nose touching a melting ice puddle next to a drain. It was over. She'd failed. All she could do now was cry for Erik. Tears spilled down her cheeks and she wailed as she expressed the pain that no parent should ever have to endure. All she saw in her mind was the smile of her beautiful and loving little boy.

THIRTY-FOUR

Gina stood beside Jacob at the head of the incident room as he summarised where they were. 'The candles in jars were left at both crime scenes. The exact same jars and candles were used. Finger-prints have been taken from the miniature vodka bottle found outside the Godwins' house, and they were a match for the prints on the lighter that was recovered from the last scene. Officers and police dogs followed a trail of footprints from where the vodka bottle was found, over the field, all the way to the estate at the other side. A clear mucky print was left on the stile at the other side of the field. We believe our perpetrator was shoe size seven. Anything to add?'

'I'm going to catch up with the door-to-door team at lunchtime, see if anyone else saw this person.' O'Connor bit into his greasy bacon sandwich, spilling a bit of brown sauce on his shirt as he chewed loudly.

Jacob smiled. 'Guv, you have a few questions?'

Gina nodded in appreciation. 'Anything else come from the *Boyz R Takin it Back* forum?'

O'Connor swallowed his mouthful. 'Nothing yet, guv. We still can't identify the others on that thread and there hasn't been so much activity but I'll keep checking. I actually have an account now so I've signed up to alerts on various threads.'

'Well, thank you for going through them all and keep looking. I'll also take your login details so that I can have a look when I'm home later.'

Wyre did her top button up and fidgeted. 'That reporter, Pete Bloxwich, keeps calling. I've said the usual, contact Annie in corporate communications or wait to be told of a press release, but he was insistent that you owed him a story. He said you'd know what he meant.'

Gina exhaled and rolled her eyes. 'He's a nightmare. Keep telling him the same thing if he calls.' She knew that wouldn't distract him for long and he'd start emailing or calling her again. He'd love to know how her personal life had crept into the investigation and, for a second, she wondered if Stephen had told him to stir things up even more. 'Also, could you please visit Kerstin Godwin and get a follow-up statement?'

'Yes, guv.' Wyre made a note.

'I spoke to her at the scene. If she tells you anything at all that will help with the case then please call me straight away. We also need to double confirm that she couldn't have been there at the time the fire was started. We need to handle that sensitively though and I know you'll be able to do that.' Gina's phone beeped. It was as she suspected, Pete Bloxwich.

Could investigating Stephen be a conflict of interests on your part? Sounds to me like you're trying to set him up. He wasn't happy about you being in his house. Gina, Gina... You just can't help yourself? I'll be keeping my beady little eyeballs on you.

Your favourite journalist, Pete.

She threw her phone into her pocket hoping that the team couldn't see the worry etched on her face. The term beady little eyeballs had her grimacing. 'O'Connor? When Cameron Godwin's post-mortem time comes from Bernard, could you please attend and feedback anything of relevance to me straight away?'

O'Connor licked a dollop of sauce from his lip and nodded.

PC Kapoor ran in, silencing everyone in the room as she stood there, catching her breath. 'I've just arrested Sonya Baker for dangerous driving and she failed the breathalyser too. We have her downstairs sobering up but she keeps saying that someone has abducted her son and they've threatened to kill him. And there's more.'

'What?' Gina felt her heart thrumming.

'Her fingerprints match those we took from the lighter.' Kapoor leaned on the door frame.

'And they'll match up to the ones on the vodka bottle then. I think we have our killer.' Gina scrunched her brow. 'Can we locate her son?'

'No, guv. We've called the school and the boy's father. He didn't go to school yesterday, nor today and his father hasn't spoken to him for days.'

Now they not only had two murders, they had a missing child and the mother was claiming that she thought he'd been killed.

'She's in a terrible state, guv. I thought she was just drunk at first but it's more than that. She was so panicky when I arrested her, I had to call an ambulance. They gave her something to calm her. She said she's okay to speak and didn't need to go to hospital but that could change at any time. An officer is sitting with her as we didn't want her left alone. She's not in a cell, we have put her in the family room. We can deal with the drink and dangerous driving later as it seems there's bigger things at stake.'

'Put everything we have on this. We have her in custody and we have evidence that she murdered the two men. If she's confessing to killing them, the boy's whereabouts is our biggest concern right now. Use every resource, every officer and fast track all forensics. I need to speak to Sonya and we need to find the lad.'

Gina swallowed knowing that they might not find the boy alive if Sonya was telling the truth. A chill danced around the back of her neck and she shivered.

THIRTY-FIVE

He lies there, half awake and half asleep thinking about his friend and Ziggy the dinosaur, then he flinches. The monster downstairs is making that horrible wailing noise and there is a thudding up the first flight of stairs, then the next. His little heart beats so fast, he feels like he might stop breathing. Is he still asleep? He's not sure. He can't tell whether he's dreaming this or it's real. He's so tired all the time and he doesn't know why. His dreams have been weird too.

He saw the monster with his milky eyes and the warts on his face, except in his dream, the warts were bigger and he roared like a nasty dinosaur. Was he one of the bad dinosaurs that was hurting Ziggy?

His friend starts to wail and yell outside the locked door, then things are thrown and he imagines those items crashing apart as they hit the walls. Shaking, he hopes his friend won't come in, not today. He wishes he was back home with Mummy. All he wants is a hug and he wants to see Daddy too. He didn't see Daddy at the weekend. Daddy would wonder where he was. Maybe Daddy would come to pick him up.

The door crashes open so Erik pulls the quilt over his head and holds his breath.

'It's okay, it's okay, I promise. You're going to go to sleep. This won't hurt.'

He doesn't want to go to sleep so he stays under the blanket.

'Please, I won't hurt you. I promise. Drink the juice.'

He lets go of his blanket and his friend pulls it from his eyes while stroking his hair. There's no escape from what's to come and his little body quivers and he cries so hard, he almost chokes on his sobs. He has to trust his friend. There's no way someone so nice to him would hurt him. He is being helped from the man monster who is creaking and cracking on all fours as he enters the room, his empty eyes, staring as dribble strings from his mouth and a loud cry fills the stairway. It's over. He will never see Mummy and Daddy again, not now the monster is here. He drinks the juice. It's all he has and he wants to escape. The monster yells, exposing a mouth with only two rotten teeth, and it's all over.

THIRTY-SIX

Gina ran down the corridor with Jacob on her tail, and they entered the room with the couch and the sunny yellow walls. Sonya sat with her knees under her chin as she hugged them. Tears had wet her standard issue joggers and her dark baggy eyes were now red and puffy. The officer sat beside her, holding a box of tissues.

'They abducted and killed my son. They said they'd kill him. I didn't want to hurt anyone, you have to believe me.'

Wyre knocked and placed the recorder on the table at the back of the room. She then left with the officer. Jacob plugged in the recorder and grabbed a statement book and began filling it in before pressing record. 'I'm DS Driscoll,' he said for the tape.

'And I'm DI Harte. Can you please confirm your name?' Gina pulled up a chair and sat opposite the woman. She checked that the camera in the corner of the room was flashing red to show it was recording.

'Sonya Baker. They killed my baby.' Tears continued to spill and she rocked back and forth, wailing.

'I know this is hard for you but we want to find Erik too. Can you start from the beginning?'

'Someone has my son. They took him last Saturday when I was at the park with him.'

'What time would this have been?'

'About ten in the morning.'

'Which park?'

'The one at the back of my house. It's where I've always taken Erik. I just turned away for a second and he was gone. Then I got a message.' She wiped her eyes.

'What did that message say?'

'I have your son. Come back to the park at ten tonight and look under the roundabout. Tell anyone and Erik dies.' The woman stopped rocking and stared at her knees before letting her feet drop to the floor.

'Do you have this message?'

'It was a Snapchat. It disappeared. All the messages are sent through Snapchat.' She bit the skin on her thumb.

'Did you go back to the park at ten?'

She nodded and wiped her eyes.

'And what did you find?'

'A lighter and a candle in a jar. Then I got another message telling me to take a can of petrol in the early hours to Faith's house and burn it down with that lighter. They said I had to light the candle and leave it on the bird table.' She began to shake and wiped a tear running down her cheek.

'Please go on.'

'I killed Glen. I did it to save my son's life and I failed.' She stood and bashed her fist on the wall as she let out a scream. 'I waited and waited for whoever was doing this to me to message again and return my son. I did what they wanted but all I got was another message saying that I had to act normal and wait for them to message again. Again, I was reminded that if I brought any attention on myself, Erik would die. They said they'd burn him alive. I waited and waited. I went to the gym with my friends and pretended nothing was going on. Still no message about Erik. Then I got another message with an instruction to be at the park again on

Monday night at ten.' Sonya opened her mouth to speak, then stopped.

'Monday night? So, Sonya, it wasn't you who attempted to set light to the Godwins' house in the early hours of Monday morning?'

She shook her head and grimaced, then continued her story. 'On Monday night, I left early and hung out in the bushes. I wanted to know who was doing this to me but they must have guessed. They hit me over the head.' Sonya pulled back her hair to reveal a bruise.

'What happened after that?'

'I was dazed for maybe a few seconds and then they'd gone. Another two candles in jars were next to me. About an hour later, I got yet another message telling me that if I pulled a stunt like that again, they would make sure Erik was in a lot of pain when he died. My heart was broken. All I could think about was my little boy and what would happen to him. Then the next message said that Cameron, Kerstin's husband, was alone that night and I had to do the same again.' She paused. 'I would have done anything to save Erik. I'd kill for him. Tell me of one parent that wouldn't have done the same. I killed them but someone made me and I don't know who that someone was, but when I find out I'm going to kill them. I want them to suffer like I have.'

Gina swallowed and tried not to think about Terry. 'Did you say two candles in jars?'

'Yes.'

'Where is the other one?'

'At my house, in the dining room.'

For Gina, everything Sonya was telling her confirmed that the husbands were the targets. In front of her, she had yet another victim, one that had committed the unthinkable and one she would have to deal with later after a talk to the Crown Prosecution Service. This was probably the most complex case she'd ever had to deal with. Murder committed under duress. She thought of her own daughter and granddaughter and she knew she'd do anything it took to protect them. She had done the unthinkable to protect herself and Hannah.

They were dealing with one calculating person who knew exactly how to get what they wanted. In her mind, this person was also getting other people to do their dirty work. Could they really have killed an innocent child? A flame of hope flickered.

'What happened today, Sonya?'

She took a few fast breaths and furrowed her brows. 'I was at work. They gave me ten minutes to get home or they were going to kill Erik. They said they were going to call on my landline and if I didn't answer...' She sniffed and wiped her eyes. 'I didn't make it. I crashed and your officer arrested me. Erik died because I didn't make it home. I want my son! I want Erik. They killed him.' She slumped to the ground and let out a primal yell before shaking uncontrollably as she gasped for breath. She could barely breathe as she tried to catch her breath.

'Call first aid.' Gina reached down, stopping Sonya's head from catching the side of the table as she fainted. Closing her eyes and taking a deep breath, Gina could barely contain her own tremble. Jacob left the room and seconds later came back with an officer. They left him to it. 'Damn, that poor little boy. Who could do this to her and her child?' Gina kicked the skirting board and paced a few times until she calmed down. Her neck was prickling and her cheeks burned.

'I've never been so disappointed at solving a murder case. Why? Because we've barely scraped the surface and the person pulling all the strings is still out there. What an evil game to play. We need to talk to the boy's father, Mr Baker, search Sonya's house and speak to Heather Walton again. Dammit! I can't speak to Heather because Stephen will be there. You'll have to speak to Heather. Let's get uniform to search the park behind Sonya's house and speak to any of the residents that live close by. See if they saw anything that morning or on Saturday or Monday evening. We also need to speak to Erik's teacher, maybe someone suspicious was seen hanging around. There's a link and we have to find it. Get digging on them all. Something links them and we don't know what. Don't let the ball drop on the disgruntled employee, Garth Shaw, or the gym employee, Graham Pollard, although knowing that the men are targets probably puts Pollard at the back of the suspect queue. We still don't have a motive though so an open mind is a must. That poor boy.'

The police officer came out and he pressed his lips together before speaking. 'She's not good. I've called her an ambulance. She's definitely in shock. When she came around, she just kept repeating her son's name, sobbing and ignoring me. It's as if I wasn't there.'

Gina sighed. That wasn't good as they probably wouldn't get much more out of her that day. 'Make sure an officer is posted outside her door at all times when she gets to the hospital and she needs to be in a private room. As soon as she's able, we'll need to speak to her again. She's also had charges brought against her and all we have is her word on the abduction. We'll be searching her house. I want that last candle in the jar, maybe the perp left a print on it. Who knows? The worrying thing is, it looks like there was meant to be another victim. We have her phone. Monitor it. Whoever messaged might send another and that would back up her version of events too. Maybe they didn't follow through with their threat to kill Sonya's son. They needed her to burn one more house down and they won't know she's in custody. We need to get to her house now. If the person who's abducted Erik was the last person to call her house, the number may just come up. In fact, get someone to contact the phone company and get the records too. Grab your coat, we have her keys. This is a matter of life and death and time is against us.'

THIRTY-SEVEN

Gina hurried to get the key in the lock of Sonya's door. Gloves on, she stepped in first and Jacob stayed close. PC Smith guarded the entrance and PC Kapoor led the team inside. Before Gina gave out any instructions, she ran to the phone and pressed one-four-seven-one to see if the last number was stored. The others waited in anticipation, hoping that there would be a number. Gina's shoulders slumped. 'No one has phoned Sonya today. The last call was two days ago. Can we call O'Connor? We need him to put this number into her phone, see if we can identify who the caller was?' Gina listened again and noted the number down.

Jacob dialled and his colleague answered immediately. He relayed the number and waited. 'It's her ex-husband, listed as Justin in her phone.'

'No one called today. What kind of sicko tells a woman that she has ten minutes to get home or they will kill her son and then they haven't even called? That's good though. The threat was empty, they were trying to control her; show her who's in charge. We have to work on the fact that Erik is still alive but being held against his will.' Gina looked around the room and spotted a framed professional photo of a little boy with short shaved hair and a missing tooth. She felt her stomach gripe as she took in his happy face. 'We'll take that photo and share it with all departments so that we can keep an eye out for him. We can't share the details with the press yet or his safety could be jeopardised.' She sighed and stared out of the window at the terraced houses opposite. 'Sharing Erik's photo with the media could find out if he's been seen with anyone or spotted anywhere but it could also put him in danger if the abductor gets desperate. It's tough to call but we need to see if the perp contacts Sonya again. We can't wait, especially as a child's life is at stake. Right, PC Kapoor, can you take two officers upstairs and begin searching. We'll search downstairs and the garden. We're mostly looking for evidence of the arson attacks and anything to suggest where Erik may be. Diaries with addresses in, tablets, laptops or any other digital devices will need to be handed in to the techies. Notes that have been made, even on a scrap of paper.'

The young PC nodded and led the others upstairs. Gina darted straight to the dining room with an evidence bag. 'We didn't find any fingerprints on either of the glass candleholders before but who knows, we might get lucky.' She lifted it carefully and dropped it straight into an evidence bag, ready for processing. As the team began rummaging through drawers and cupboards, Gina kneeled in front of the toy boxes next to the round kitchen table and began sliding the drawers open. There were plenty of plastic toys, mostly figures from Disney films and lots of Lego bricks and coloured pencils. Stuffed animals filled another drawer. Gina picked up the stuffed green dinosaur and held it. It smelled like malted biscuit. She tried to swallow her sadness down. The tag rubbed against her arm and she read the message on it.

Happy fourth birthday, Erik, from Mummy's Motivation Lady friends. Sending lots of hugs and kisses. XXX

Gina placed the dinosaur back in the drawer. It was lovely that the friends had done something for his birthday. She then dug a little deeper and found a box full of dinosaurs; she knew they were all the rage at the moment. Kids were collecting them like mad, even Gracie had several. She wondered if whoever was holding him was trying to make him comfortable or were they purposely hurting him. The candles in jars meant something deep. The instigator of all this hurt was trying to say something. Had someone close to them died and could it be the fault of the men that were being targeted? The candles could be for remembrance, they are trying to say that the dead person's memory still lives on... but who died and when?

Leaving the dining room, Gina met Jacob in the kitchen. 'Anything?'

He shook his head. 'Only a shedload of empty wine bottles and wrappers. I can understand why she hasn't kept it together.'

Gina stepped in and leaned against the kitchen sink. 'The instigator of all this is blaming the victims for the death of someone. They want this person to be remembered and whatever happened is something to do with Glen Chapman and Cameron Godwin. There was a third candle so there is someone else in danger. Glen, Cameron, Stephen and Justin all knew each other through work. I'd like to work on the theory that either Stephen or Justin are the third target.'

'Justin has been visited by an officer and he's being brought to the station as we speak.'

Biting her lip, Gina shook her head. 'And Stephen refuses to have anything to do with us, mostly because of me.'

'We can't force people to accept our help,' Jacob replied. Gina wondered if she really cared about Stephen's safety. He was, after all, putting her through her own personal version of hell at the moment but at the end of the day, she had to do her job without prejudice and the danger to him had to be considered. He would be told by Jacob, keeping her out of it, and they could all take it from there. 'Another thing, find out if Stephen or Justin are set to be alone for any reason over the next few days. Whoever has targeted our victims has not hurt the partners or the children. I'm not sure if this is the case but the aborted attempt at the Godwins' could have been to get Kerstin and the children out of the house and they knew that Cameron had stayed on alone. They are being watched closely.'

Jacob's phone rang. 'O'Connor, what have you got?'

Gina watched how Jacob scrunched his brow then the call ended with him open-mouthed. 'A Snapchat message has been sent to Sonya's phone. "I know you have her in custody so I'm signing off now. Sonya will never see Erik again."'

'Let's get back. We have to speak to Justin Baker now.' Gina placed her trembling hands in her pockets. The next decision she had to make could see little Erik's life in her hands and that thought killed a part of her inside.

THIRTY-EIGHT

Sonya's out of the picture. This is my life. This is my plan, and it's down to me to make sure that justice is served. I picture Erik's face just before... I can't think about that right now but the thought of him won't leave me. The fear, how he reached out to me and held me like he knew that something big was happening.

I watch from beyond. Sitting at the other end of the park. From round this corner, I can just about see all I need to see. Faith stands up to help Harvey into the little wooden house, then she goes back to staring at her phone, blankly. Little Kiara is happily sitting at her feet, playing with some bright plastic toys while she dribbles melted chocolate biscuit down her chin.

Glancing back at Harvey, I see that he's wrapped up nicely in his winter coat. The fake fur-lined hood almost covers the top of his eyes. He's looking down.

Faith's phone rings and she steps away from Kiara and walks towards the park gate. She thinks just because they are seemingly alone, her children are safe. Too many people don't treat their little ones like the precious cargo that they are. It's okay for Faith. If Harvey or Kiara go, she can have another child. She's young and healthy. She'll move on. I try not to think about how I've affected Sonya. There will always be casualties and that's all she is. There are bigger things at play and they must play out. We all have to suffer the consequences of our actions and I know I will have to suffer mine soon too. There's no escaping that, which is why I need to get everything sorted without any more hitches. Sonya was perfect, she responded perfectly but I pushed her too far. If only I hadn't sent her that message but I needed to make her pay. I only hope Faith will be the same in that respect. What parent wouldn't do anything to save their child? If they wouldn't do anything, they don't deserve to be parents.

Harvey soon gets bored of the wooden house and he's exploring further. Jumping on the roundabout, he uses his one foot to gather momentum but he doesn't spin for more than a few seconds. 'Mummy, push me,' he calls out. His mum ignores him. In fact, she opens the gate and goes out of the park. She's becoming animated and teary, even raises her voice for a few seconds. I wonder who she's talking to on her phone. One of her motivation lady friends or maybe a lover; everyone but her stupid husband knew she had one.

The girl is wandering, she goes to a little bouncy elephant and tries to climb on. She's too small and can't do it on her own. 'Harvey,' she calls, but the boy ignores her, so she keeps trying. This is where I hope she doesn't slip. A crying child would ruin my plan.

Girl or boy? I have a choice.

Harvey glances back to see that his mother is still talking away and I see that he will take his chance on turning the corner. He wants to play on the swings, I know he does and I'm waiting for him. Come on, Harvey, you know the swings are the best thing in the park.

'Mummy, going on swings.'

Faith holds a thumb up to the little boy but she doesn't even look back. In my view, she doesn't deserve him. I need another chance to get things right. I have let Erik down but this time, it's going to be different. I get another chance and I will make it work. There's a place I've secured, where we can go. There's just one loose end I need to tie-up after this and I'm gone. New identity in place. New home.

'Hey, Harvey.' Now that he's out of his mother's sight, I make my move. 'Do you want a go on the swing? I'll push you.'

'Yay,' he says, trusting me implicitly. Why wouldn't he? He smiles at me and it helps that he's not afraid. I sneak a look at Faith. She's still on the phone.

Harvey hops on the swing and I push him a little. 'Mummy doesn't want to play.'

'Well, Mummy is busy talking on the phone when she should be pushing you on the swing.'

'I'm hungry.'

'I have some sweets in the car, it's just through that cut in the bushes. We can get them and bring some back for Mummy and your sister.' I smile widely and he giggles.

'Can I have some sweets?'

'Of course you can. Here, have this.' I give him the cute little plastic dinosaur with my gloved hands and he smiles. 'Come on, let's go and get them.'

My waiting and watching has paid off. Now that Sonya is out of the picture, I need someone else to complete my tasks. And this someone else has just given me the gift of a little boy. I'd say that was a double win. My heart bangs as I lead him through the leafless brambles, protecting his delicate skin. 'I tell you what... why don't you have a drink too. You must be really thirsty.'

He nods and flashes me a cheeky grin.

I pass him the bottle of orange juice and he guzzles it.

'Hop in the car. I have a surprise for you.'

'But Mummy says I shouldn't go anywhere with strangers.'

I ruffle his fair hair. 'It's okay, I'm not a stranger. We'll be back in five minutes.' He yawns and gets into the back seat where I already have a car seat fitted. I can see his eyelids starting to close as I clip the safety straps together.

'I'm tired.'

'It's okay, just have a little nap and we'll get there quicker.'

Through the line of trees, I hear Faith yelling out the boy's name so I hop into the driver's seat without putting on my seat belt and I drive away.

I glance back at the sleeping boy and almost crash when I realise that he doesn't have the dinosaur. He must have dropped it while getting into the car. Damn, that's my first stupid mistake.

Before I head onto the main road, I send the message I already have prepared. Faith will do what I say.

THIRTY-NINE

Justin leaned over the interview table with his head in his calloused hands. His padded lumberjack-style coat gaped open to reveal a bobbly old jumper. 'Please, you have to find my son. If only Sonya had said something to me, I could have helped but no, she shut me out like she always does, even when my son had been abducted. When I catch the bastard behind all this, he's going to know what pain is!' Gina knew this was going to be a tough interview. Jacob took a sip of his drink as the man continued to speak. 'He's dead, isn't he? They've killed Erik.' The man's breaths were deep and fast.

'We hope not and we are doing everything we can, Mr Baker.' There was nothing Gina could say to help and she hated the hurt that the abductor was causing. Justin was totally broken, angry and helpless and there wasn't a thing she could say that would make anything better.

'You're not. Look at you both. You call this doing all you can? You're here talking to me when you could be out looking for him. He's been gone for over three days now. Three whole days. Two of my friends are dead. I just want him back. He's only four, he's never hurt anyone. Please tell me he's not dead. I can't believe my little boy could be dead.'

Gina cleared her throat. 'We believe that the person who has your son wanted to hurt the victims and has been using your son to get what they wanted.' A band of pain spread across her forehead, tight like it was wedged in a vice.

'Well deduced! It's great that I have you lot on the case with gems like that,' he replied with a hint of sarcasm. 'Now they've got what they wanted, he's of no use to them. Can I do a TV appeal? Someone must have seen my boy.' The man tapped his foot on the floor as his brain processed everything. 'We can show his photo to everyone. Someone will come forward and I will get him back.' His brown-eyed stare was wide as if he had just come up with the idea that would solve everything. With held in breath, he waited for the answer.

'Under any other circumstances, I would say yes, that would be a good idea but I'd advise you to say nothing to the press as this could put Erik in more danger.'

The man slammed his hand on the table and kicked the leg. 'How can he be in more danger? Someone abducted my son and forced my ex-wife to kill two of my friends and they threatened to kill Erik. Now you have Sonya and you tell me there was another intended victim. So she failed and my son is in immediate danger or already dead. Why can't I do an appeal?' He kicked the table leg again and seethed through his teeth.

Gina took a deep breath. 'Okay, we believe that you could be the intended third victim.' There was no way to sugar-coat that information. 'If the person who has your son sees you making an appeal, it might just be enough to push them into hurting Erik to get at you. We can't risk that happening. As tempting as that idea might seem, please stay away from the press. It could make things worse. We also need to ask you a few more questions.'

'Ask whatever you have to. I'll answer anything.'

'Tell me how you know Glen Chapman?' Gina tilted her head and spoke gently.

The man's eyes started to glass over and he slumped in the chair, hunched over with his chin tucked into the top of his jumper. 'I met Glen about twelve years ago when he was training to be a plumber. I was a trainee plasterer at the time and we saw each other on site. We became mates and started going out together for a few beers, things like that.'

'Tell me a bit more about Mr Chapman?'

Justin shrugged and exhaled as he frowned. 'He could sometimes rub people up the wrong way when he was drunk. I remember he got in a few scraps when we were out, mostly because he was drunk but it never amounted to much. No one got really hurt. We'd go out clubbing and had the odd weekender in Spain, that sort of thing. We've kept in touch since. I met Sonya, had a kid and he met Faith and had a family. We didn't see each other as much but we still met up occasionally. Sonya really got on with Faith and, from our friendship, they became friends. They'd go to the gym together and go for coffees, lunches and play dates with the kids, that sort of thing.'

'How about Cameron Godwin and Stephen Smithson?'

'Stephen has always been in and out of the building trade. I always said he couldn't stick the same job for more than a couple of months. We all joked about that with him. It's normally the same with girlfriends but he seems different with Heather.' Gina mulled over that statement. After seeing how worried Heather looked when Gina mentioned her bruising, she doubted that Stephen had changed at all. He'd just found someone who would put up with him and not say anything. 'He met Heather and moved in with her recently after his tenancy ended on his flat.' He stopped talking and scrunched his brow. 'As for Cam, he always worked in the sale of supplies so was always around. Both Cam and Stephen were friends of mine since I was an apprentice. None of it matters now. Cam's gone. Glen's gone. When me and Sonya split, I left them behind. She'd become really good friends with the wives so I decided to move on. Leaving her with my friends. She was never grateful of that sacrifice. I haven't seen much of the lads since.'

'Why did you split up?'

'What's that got to do with anything? We're here to find whoever has my son.' He leaned back and folded his arms.

'Please answer the question. The more we know, the more chance we have of finding Erik.'

'Right.' He rubbed his crew cut hair, then his dark stubble. 'I'm not proud of it but I met someone else. Me and Sonya weren't getting on. I moved out and went to live with Charlene.'

'Does Charlene know any of your friends?'

'Not really, I introduced them once when I saw the lads out having a beer. They came into the same pub we were drinking in. I met Charlene while building her extension. I didn't plan to break up my family and leave my wife but what we had wasn't fun for Sonya or me. All we did was bicker. It wasn't good for Erik either. Life's short so I left her for Charlene, but I never left my son. I've had him every weekend since I left except for this one. I'm getting sick of this. None of what you're asking has anything to do with Erik.'

'No, but it all has something to do with you and your two murdered friends. Can you remember any significant incidents over the course of your friendship? Deaths, accidents, anything like that.' Gina was hoping he would say something that would explain the candles in jars.

The man scrunched his bulbous nose and started to play with the zip on his jumper. Gina saw his Adam's apple bob as he swallowed and the vein on the side of his head began to pulse. 'No.'

He took too long to answer. 'Not one thing over all those years?'

He shook his head. 'I said no.' He stared directly into Gina's eyes. 'Right, onto my questions. What are you doing to get my son back? If he is still alive, he'll be scared and missing me and his mother. He might be injured. Who knows what this psycho has done to him.'

Gina discreetly exhaled. As he stared, she'd held her breath. In front of her was a man who knew something significant had happened in his life and he knew that possibly had a bearing on the case. 'As I said, we have teams out questioning everyone who knows Sonya and your son. We're conducting door-to-door enquiries and as soon as we can speak to your wife again, we will.'

'Where are you keeping her?'

'She's been treated for shock at the hospital. She may be in there a day or two as she fainted at the station earlier today. She also has a wound on her head that needs looking at. We'd also advise that you and your partner move out for a few days, as I said we believe that you are in danger.'

'Fine, we'll stay at a hotel.'

'We'll need you to tell us where you're staying when you've found somewhere so please call in later.'

'It'll be the Cleevesford Cleaver. I do a fair few jobs there and it's local. I need to see Sonya.'

'You won't be able to do that as she's in custody.'

'My son is missing and Sonya is in shock. I may have left her but I'm not a monster. She's the mother of my child so try stopping me. I've had it with you lot and this is a waste of time.' He stood and barged out of the door, leaving it swinging behind him.

Gina twisted her torso to look at Jacob. 'Call Kapoor, I think she's headed over to relieve the officer who was guarding Sonya's room and we'll need a couple of extra officers there too, just in case anything kicks off. And warn the ward not to let him in if he beats them to it. Did you see his reaction when I asked about significant incidents of his past? I know his son is missing and I can make a lot of allowances for his reactions but that wasn't normal. What isn't he telling us? As we're none the wiser, we need to make sure someone is guarding his house just in case there is an attack on it. We also need to make sure they don't go back to stay there like Cameron Godwin did. Someone knew he'd gone back alone. They're being watched closely so *we* need to watch them closely and watch for whoever's watching them.'

'What about Stephen Smithson's place.'

'I know he said he didn't want any type of protection but arrange for a car to be on the street all night; just a discreet one set back a little. Someone is next but we don't know who. We're still only assuming that it will be Stephen or Justin but the pattern so far points at them.' For a second, Gina succumbed to a fleeting thought. If whoever was doing this took Stephen out next, a lot of her problems would be solved. But if he died, that would make Hetty come after her harder. She willed those thoughts away. She would do her job regardless and if that meant protecting the person she hated the most in the world, then so be it. 'We have to do everything we can to find Erik and put an end to all this.'

FORTY

Jacob drove to St John's Junior School in Cleevesford as Gina checked her phone.

Nestled between two of the new estates the school was fairly new too. Several rows of red tiles circled the playground and a bright green hopscotch grid had been painted on the tarmac. At the one end was a large fenced off field but to the side, there was a row of brambles and an even taller wooden fence. Gina's phone rang. Withheld number. As Jacob turned off the engine, she stepped into the damp air. 'Hello.'

'Is this DI Harte?' The woman sounded nervous and muffled, like she was talking through a cloth.

'Yes, how can I help you?'

Jacob's brows furrowed as he got closer. He went to speak but Gina held her index finger over her mouth to hush him.

'I, err, I didn't know who to call but you said I could call you. He hit me again. I don't know what to do.'

'Is that you, Heather?'

The woman ended the call.

'Damn.'

'Who was it?'

'I think it was Heather Walton, Stephen's girlfriend, but the voice was muffled so I can't be sure. The number was withheld too. You need to pop around to see her after the briefing, make out that it's a routine visit about the case. If I could go, I would.'

'First of all, are you sure it was her?'

'Not one hundred per cent. If Stephen is there, be discreet. I don't want him hurting her again. If she's alone, remind her that she can press charges against him. Also, Stephen needs to be told the level of danger they're in. I don't think he's taking it seriously just because they have CCTV and an alarm. I don't want Heather harmed any more in all this.'

'Okay, and I'll call you when I've been around, let you know how it goes.'

As they walked through the frosted puddles in the car park, Gina couldn't help thinking about Erik. She hoped more than anything that he was still alive. She then wondered how everything would affect him and what would ultimately happen to Sonya. Pete Bloxwich didn't matter. All her dirty laundry could be aired if it meant getting Erik back. She wondered how he was or had been kept. Thinking of him in the past tense made her muscles clench and she shook. 'It's hard to keep a four-year-old still let alone quiet. Surely a neighbour has heard or seen him, unless he's being kept somewhere rural.'

'What?' Jacob continued to hurry, taking big strides. Gina had started jogging to keep up. She tied the belt around her winter coat, trying to keep the cold out. She hoped Erik wasn't cold. Her thoughts turned to horrible places like damp cellars. Then, her thoughts worsened. None of them were saying it much, but Erik could have been killed. No, she had to keep focusing on him being alive.

'I wonder how the abductor is treating him. Young children, they take a lot of work and patience. I remember Hannah at that age and Gracie is only a little older now. They're full of energy and loud. All these scenarios keep whirring away in my head. Have they hit him, locked him up in a cellar, maybe they've even drugged him to keep him quiet? All that sounds awful. Then I wonder if they have killed him.' She paused. 'We have to keep hopeful but I can't stop thinking about what Sonya said. The messenger said if she didn't do what they told her, Erik would die. Not only would he die, they would burn him to death. I can't even begin to imagine how I'd feel in her situation and what I'd do. No, I can. I'd do anything to make sure my child was safe.' Gina swallowed and bit her lip. She knew she'd die or kill to protect her daughter and granddaughter.

'But, guv, with the abduction, they got Sonya to do their dirty work. We have to pin our hopes on this person not having it in them.'

'You're right and there have been no more reports of any fires but the clock is ticking.' She paused. 'Why fire? Everything has been planned to the nth degree and the perp has chosen to kill them by setting fire to their homes. It's also someone close as they had access to their homes. My mind keeps coming back to Mrs Chapman. But then it asks, why Cameron Godwin? She had motive for her husband along with her lover, Aiden, but there's no motive that we know of for Mr Godwin's murder.'

'The answer is there somewhere, we just have to find it.'

'And we have to find it before another murder takes place. No one is safe while this person is still walking free.'

They entered the large magnolia painted reception that had been adorned with the children's finest artwork. Bright finger paintings of dogs, houses and elephants filled the walls, as did craftwork, like sewing. The smell of school hit Gina, it was like fish pie mixed with sweaty feet and milk. Not strong but just enough to cause Gina to scrunch her nose.

A short man with a bald head looked up. 'Have you come to collect your child from trampoline club?' He scrunched his brow as if trying to recognise them.

'No sorry, I'm DI Harte, this is DS Driscoll. We're here to see Ms Bannister. An officer called earlier. She's expecting us.'

'Ahh, let me see. Yes, she's in room 1B. I'll show you through.' The man tucked his tie in, emphasising his large round belly and led the way along a corridor. Gina glanced at the tiny chairs and the open-doored mini toilets and she swallowed. Erik was that small. He was the youngest a child could be to start school. She could only imagine what both Sonya and Justin were going through. 'There she is, feeding the school rabbit. Just head through.'

The man left them and they approached the tall, thin woman wearing a pink chunky knit cardigan. 'Ms Bannister.'

'Yes, hello. You're from Cleevesford Police, aren't you? They wouldn't tell me what it was about. Come through.'

After entering the classroom, Gina pulled the door to and joined the other two sitting on the miniature chairs around a tiny table. 'We're here to speak to you about one of your pupil's, Erik Baker.' Jacob had a hand on the floor to steady himself.

'Erik. He's been off this week. Is he okay?'

'I can't say much as we're in the middle of an ongoing investigation. May we ask you a few questions?'

'Of course. I'm worried now. He's such a lovely lad. Should I be worried?'

Gina swallowed. She wished she could tell the teacher what had happened but again, they didn't want to put Erik in any more danger than he was already in and a teacher would have to warn parents, who would soon gossip. She first had to see if the teacher had anything to say. If there was a chance that other children could be in danger, then she'd have to say something. This whole case was like a piece of frayed string that was being pulled tighter and tighter, one pull too far and the whole thing could snap. 'Could you tell us what Erik is like?'

'He's a bright and inquisitive little boy. He adores stories and is very participative in lessons. As far as mixing is concerned, he gets on well with the other children. He's a delight to teach, always happy and likes to help too. He gave up his break time to help me clean the rabbit out last week.' The teacher smiled warmly.

'Who normally brings him to school?'

'Always Mrs Baker. I've only seen Mr Baker once and that's

when they came on our open evening to see the school. They looked like they weren't getting on. She sighed a lot and he stomped around with folded arms.' Gina could just imagine them both like that if they weren't getting on.

'When she drops him off, is she ever with anyone else?'

'Yes, she seems to always be with Harvey's mum, err.' She flicks through her notebook. 'Faith Chapman, oh and Mrs Godwin.' The teacher pressed her lips together for a few seconds. 'I heard on the news about what happened to their husbands. I must say, it was a concern for the school. We've had a memo go around. Some of the parents have been worried. Are these attacks connected to our pupils or parents?'

Gina gave a sympathetic smile. 'Not as far as we know, but we're looking into every line of enquiry. It's definitely worth telling the parents to report anything or anyone suspicious but we have reason to believe the attacks aren't random.'

The chair that Ms Bannister sat on squeaked as she shifted her position. 'Sometimes, the three mums take it in turns to pick the children up. Each one has registered that either of the other two can pick their children up so they must be good friends.'

'Have you seen anything unusual around the school, maybe anyone hanging around who shouldn't be?'

'There was one thing and it does involve Erik.'

Gina undid her coat as she waited for the teacher to continue and Jacob's pen made a swish sound across his notebook as he wrote.

'It was two weeks ago today. The children went out for morning break as they always do and when they came back in, Erik was holding a plastic dinosaur. I know he didn't go out with one. He was trying to stuff it in his rucksack, which always hangs on his peg at the other end of the classroom, so I asked him about it. He said someone gave it to him when he was playing in the bramble bushes. The whole edge is all fenced off to keep the children safe. I asked how he got it, thinking that maybe he'd borrowed it from another child. He said that someone called him over to the fence and they gave him their dinosaur. I asked if he knew who the person was and he said he couldn't see them through the gap in the fence but they said they were his friend. I did report this at the time but never heard anything.'

'Who did you report it to?'

'The head teacher. I don't think it was reported to the police but the dinosaur was taken from Erik and his mother was told. I don't think it was taken seriously at the time as we thought it might be another child who gave him the toy. Erik did say his friend gave it to him and he has lots of friends at the school. We have a mountain of things to do and we put it down to the harmless passing of a toy between the kids. It didn't sound or seem sinister at the time.'

'Do you have CCTV covering that area?'

'Yes, we do, and we looked at it just for peace of mind.'

'Could you see anything?'

Ms Bannister shook her head. 'No, only shrubs and trees. Erik also walks out of the camera's line of sight along the fence.'

Gina thought back to all the dinosaur toys in Erik's toy boxes. She couldn't help but think that this person already knew that Erik loved dinosaurs. The stuffed toy had been from Sonya's friends. Whoever gave it to him may have been on the other side of the fence, grooming Erik for later. She imagined someone pushing the toy through the gaps or throwing it over. If it wasn't one of the other kids, this person knew exactly how to get him where they wanted him. As Erik described this person as a friend, did he know them and did he willingly walk away with them at the park on Saturday, all for another dinosaur?

FORTY-ONE

Arriving back at the incident room, Gina threw her damp coat over a chair and nodded to Wyre, O'Connor and PC Smith who were ready and waiting. PC Kapoor was still at the hospital, guarding Sonya Baker. Briggs entered with a huge cup of coffee and stood at the front of the room, waiting for everyone to stop talking before he spoke. 'Right, let's see what we've got. We suspect that Erik Baker is in imminent danger if not already dead. We hope it's not the latter and we will work as if he is being held against his will. The last bit of information we have is that the person holding him was going to set him alight. We have to take this threat seriously. There have been no more reports of any fires so I'm hoping that we still have time. As far as we are concerned, Erik is still alive, he's still being held, and every resource we need is at our disposal. We have more PCs coming on board and PCs Smith and Kapoor are going to coordinate them.' PC Smith nodded, then Briggs continued. 'Harte, what have you got?'

Gina stood beside him. 'Jacob and I have just come back from the school. Erik's teacher confirmed that two weeks ago someone gave Erik a plastic dinosaur, which didn't arouse too much suspicion at the time but no one knows who he got it from. All he said was that a friend gave it to him. When we went to Sonya's house earlier to obtain the candle and book her electronic devices in, I saw Erik's toy boxes and one was full of dinosaurs. I'd say that someone knows this little boy well enough to know what his favourite toys are. It's someone close to him or someone he trusts and knows well.'

'If they know him, is it less likely that they'll hurt him and the threats are empty?' Wyre ate the last of her grapes in a small plastic box as she waited for an answer.

'I'd hope that was the case but we also have someone who's running desperate. It's hard to predict how people will react and his safety is our prime concern.'

Briggs shifted his weight from one foot to the other. 'Can you talk us through our suspects?'

Gina took a deep breath. She wished it felt like they were getting closer. 'I wish I could. Everyone claims that the victims really didn't have any enemies. We interviewed Mr Baker in the hope that he could maybe shed light on a big incident that links their pasts, maybe a death or a tragedy – to link the candles – but he didn't say anything. I also felt that he wasn't giving us the full story. As well as Erik being missing, we still have reason to believe that there will be another victim soon and there's a high chance that it could be either Justin Baker or Stephen Smithson.' She saw Briggs clench his teeth at the mention of Stephen's name.

'What's the plan for them?'

Jacob flicked through his notes. 'Mr Baker and his girlfriend will be staying at Cleevesford Cleaver for a few days and Stephen Smithson is refusing to move, so he and Heather Walton are staying put. I'm going to speak to him and Heather after this briefing where I will fully warn them of the dangers of staying at home. If they choose to remain, we will be stationing a car on their street all night but there's nothing else we can do.'

'Do we have any reason to believe that Justin, his girlfriend, Heather or Stephen have anything to do with Erik's abduction?'

Gina decided not to reply and left Jacob to talk. In her mind,

Stephen would be to blame for everything. It was best that she stayed quiet.

'We don't have any evidence in which to further question them or search their properties. At the moment, they are potential victims but that doesn't rule them out. As DI Harte and I said, we believe Erik knew his abductor and they all knew him. That puts them in the frame but as yet we still don't have a motive that links both murders.'

Briggs glanced at the board again. 'How are we doing with that online forum, the *Boyz R Takin it Back?*'

O'Connor raised an eyebrow. 'It's a sick place to be but since the release of the addresses, nothing else that could be linked to the case has come up. We still haven't identified any of the participants except Stephen. I'll keep digging though. We could do with knowing who the other participants on that thread were. The tech team haven't been able to identify the others either. It's proving really hard.'

'Thanks, O'Connor. Do we have an update on forensics and Cameron Godwin's post-mortem?' Briggs asked Jacob.

Gina took a deep breath, relieved that the conversation had moved away from Stephen. She fully intended to log in to that site when she got home. 'Yes, sir. Nothing else that hasn't already been mentioned from either fire scene. Cameron's post-mortem is tomorrow at eleven in the morning.'

O'Connor half raised his hand and spoke. 'Mrs Godwin called earlier. She demanded to see her husband's body even though we explained that he'd suffered a lot of burns. I've managed to put her off for now.'

Gina rubbed her cold hands together. 'Well done on that. It can't be a nice sight. Those candles mean something and someone in this group of friends knows exactly what they mean.'

Briggs nodded. 'Sounds like we have a plan. Who's going to be at the post-mortem in the morning?'

Jacob glanced at the schedule in the email that he'd sent out. 'Wyre and O'Connor?'

They both nodded.

'I'll give you an update on where we are with the press. We are not releasing any information on Erik's abduction. We don't want to alarm the person who has him and further endanger him. Someone out there has him and hasn't as yet got their own hands dirty when it actually comes to killing anyone. They used his mother to do that for them. No mention of anything to the press. One last thing, look at everyone involved again. There has to be something in their pasts, something that links them that is more than meeting at the pub or gym or work. Right, let's get on with it. Find that boy.'

'Great.' Gina exhaled. 'When you all go home tonight, please read through all the case notes again. Look at the crime scene photos, listen to all the interviews. There's a little boy out there. He's probably scared. He might be hurt and we have no idea where he's being kept. No one is off duty tonight. Keep your phones on and be prepared to come back in.' Gina pointed to the boy's photo on the board and continued with a crackle in her voice. 'Erik is our number one concern. We have to get him back.' Again, not a person spoke, as if the boy might already be dead.

Nick, the desk sergeant, ran in. 'Have you all seen the news?'

Gina pulled out her phone and went online to check. She played the report as Pete Bloxwich reported from outside Cleevesford Police Station. All she could hear was Justin Baker's voice begging anyone who had seen his son to call the police straight away. Her heart sank to the point she almost threw up. She leaned on the wall and stood still until the wooziness subsided. 'If Erik wasn't already dead, he is now!'

FORTY-TWO

Gina sat in her office nervously biting the end of her pen as she watched the local news on her phone. Justin's plea for his son's safe return was filled with emotion, then anger as he ended with the words, 'When I find you, I'm going to rip your head off.' That was the last thing they all needed. An angry abductor who can now see no way out at all and they still had no clues or ideas as to where Erik was being held. The park where he went missing had been searched and so had the surrounding areas. The neighbours had been interviewed and no useful CCTV had been obtained from any of the nearby houses. And now their phone lines were going every five minutes every time someone saw an adult with a young child. Their resources were about to be needlessly pushed to the limit, all because Justin Baker couldn't wait to tell the press. The worst thing about it was that Pete Bloxwich had managed to stop and question him outside the station and Gina could tell that the reporter had relished every moment. Pete didn't care about Erik's safe return, he only cared about getting ahead of the next reporter.

Her phone rang. 'Jacob, how did it go with Heather?'

'Well, Stephen was there so I didn't say anything about the phone call, I thought it could potentially make things worse for her. He is moaning like mad about having a car stationed on their road overnight but Heather actually spoke up and said she was glad as she was terrified that someone would come and set them alight. When I left, PC Smith was setting that up outside. I asked them the same questions that we asked Mr Baker, about any incident he could think of that could explain the candles. Stephen just said he'd only lost his brother and that you knew all about that, that's when he lost it and told me to leave. He's really got it in for you.'

'You know how it is when someone dies unexpectedly, people look for anyone to blame and that's all he's doing by dredging up Terry. Well, you tried and we're doing all we can to keep them safe. Are you on your way back or heading home to work?'

'I'm heading home, guv. I'll update my notes as soon as I get back and I'm going to carry on working after my dinner. Let's hope between us or with uniform being out there speaking to everyone, we get a breakthrough.' He paused. 'I hate this case. The thought of a scared child, in danger, makes my skin crawl. I can't stop thinking about him.'

'Me neither.' She swallowed down the invisible mass in her throat. 'The fact that the news has been shared with the press now is making my stomach sick and I hate that all we have is hope right now.'

'Let's keep that hope alive and keep looking for anything that might help.'

'Definitely.' Gina ended the call and put her head in her hands. Defeated, that's how she felt. She was virtually running the case but her name wasn't heading it up. In ordinary circumstances, she would have been there at Stephen and Heather's with her colleague. She could have scrutinised their expressions. It was like she was working in dim light, the whole picture not being visible. She lifted the tiny amount of notes they had on Kerstin Godwin and Faith Chapman. Neither had a motive for both murders and Kerstin had said how happy her marriage was. Faith had no reason to kill Cameron and if they worked together somehow to do what they did to Sonya... no, nothing was adding up. The women were friends and not one of them had a horrible word to say about the others. Did Heather ever get the chance to leave the house under Stephen's watchful eye? She was the newest member of the friendship group. Sonya and Heather knew each other from years ago but hadn't kept in touch. Gina grabbed her pen and snapped it out of frustration, then she threw it into the bin on top of her half-eaten petrol station sandwich.

Her phone went again. 'Smith, have you set up?'

'Yes, guv. I'm now stationed on Stephen and Heather's road. No one is coming here in the night to burn down their house with me on guard.'

'Good. If you see anything suspicious, call it in first, then call me.'

'Will do. Anyway my fish and chips have arrived so I'll speak to you in a bit.' He finished the call.

Gina leaned back in her chair, swivelling around to look out of the window. The car park was now full of reporters. She stood and peered out through the slats in the blind, pulling two apart for a better view. That's when her eyes locked on Pete's. Not content with what he already had and with the further dangers he'd bestowed upon Erik, he was out there, waiting for more. Gina stared back at him. He wasn't going to win. He couldn't win and she would never talk to him. She swallowed as she thought about the one-sided feature he'd inevitably produce and the mud it would sling in her direction. She'd have to leave her job, while her past was dredged up again. Even though no one could prove what she did to Terry, the doubt would be cast. That 'did she/didn't she' question would always hang over her head in the public sphere if he planted that seed. All the police haters would have a field day with it. Social media would blow up until she'd get run out of the job and life she loved so much. All this started because Hannah no longer wanted Hetty and Stephen to see Gracie.

Her phone beeped and she saw the email heading pop up.

The article is going to be on my editor's desk in two days with or without your side of the story.

Her breath quickened and her heart began to beat heavily in her chest. All she could hear was the sound of blood pumping through her temples. She placed her cold hands on her burning cheeks and wondered if she might topple right back into her chair but she held on to the windowsill. Pete held his phone up and smiled before turning away.

Her finger hovered over the email and she opened it. She had to know what was in it.

Gina,

The Herald are looking for more stories like this so I know the paper will lap it up. Everyone's interested in potentially dangerous coppers.

I will be publishing my article with or without your statement. I mean, how good is that? I can tell them what Hetty said. I can tell them what Stephen has said and the public can decide. You may never have been a suspect and Terry's death may have been ruled an accident but you were there. You saw the end of his life and with the fact that you're choosing not to speak, the public will be on their side. They won't know of the times he beat poor little you to a pulp because you won't tell them.

I don't know what happened but I believe Terry's mother and brother. I also believe that the public will believe them when they tell of how cold you were at his funeral; that you've never mourned him like a widow would. You get people involved in your dirty work too. Does the department know that you're sleeping with your boss? Oh, you have so many secrets and I just love exposing a secret or two. I'm like a little honeybee, travelling from plant to plant, gath-

*ering nectar and those people, my readers, they love a bit of honey.
They're all waiting for their sweet fix and I won't disappoint them.*

*Anyway, you still have time to tell me your side. Don't let them win.
Call me.*

Goodbye for now and my phone is always on.

Your favourite reporter, Pete.

Gina ran from her office and into the ladies' toilets. As she
turned on the cold tap, she splashed water all over her face. There
was literally nothing she could do. What does a person do when
another has them in a corner? Do they cower and wait for their
world to fall apart around them or do they stand up and fight? She
stood straight and stared at her rough, tired reflection. Her hair had
mostly fallen from the tucked up knot at the back of her nape and
her under eyes looked almost grey. She grabbed the waste bin and
hit the wall with it, letting out a roar. She had to fight and the best
thing she could do was find something on Pete. She wasn't above
fighting fire with fire and everyone had secrets, right? Even Pete
Bloxwich. It didn't even matter if she came to the wrong conclu-
sions about what she found, she'd leak everything and everything
with a spin on it to all his rival papers. The only thing holding her
back was she had nothing on him. Not yet. They were now at war.
She was going home and she was going to stay up all night going
over the case and investigating Pete at the same time. She stared at
her reflection again, her own stare boring into her own mind. *Gina
Harte, you are no quitter.* The best way to defend is to attack. Best
way to attack this particular stinging bee was with a mallet and that
wouldn't be hard, after all, this despicable man had put Erik's life
in danger too.

FORTY-THREE

Sonya lay in the hospital bed, half in a dream world. She didn't want to leave as she was with Erik and they were happy. There had been a lot of shouting going on earlier and it sounded like Justin. She'd been dreaming about Justin, that they were together again with Erik. They were all on holiday in Cornwall.

Why had Justin been shouting? He was always angry and he hated that Erik wanted to stay with her in the week, citing that as Charlene worked from home, Erik would be best off with them but Sonya had fought. She needed her son and he wasn't going to make her feel guilty for being a working mother who needed childcare in her life. She didn't want the new girlfriend to become his primary carer and start calling her mummy. Justin had left them, not the other way around. If she'd run off with another man and left their home, Justin would be the one taking Erik to school and having him all week. A flash of a nightmare interrupted her inner argument.

'Mummy, he's killing me. Mummy, save me.' The sound of Erik's pleas rang through her fuzzy head.

She wanted to lift this fog, to wake up but she couldn't move. Sedatives, that's what she'd had and everything felt odd, disjointed and weird. This sleep was not normal and she couldn't wake properly. She knew she'd heard Justin's voice though, that had to be real. He'd come to the hospital.

As one dream led to another, she thought of the only person that could do this to her. It had to be Justin. His coming around and demanding to see Erik was out of character. He was framing her for murder so that he and Charlene could have Erik all to themselves. Or was it Charlene? A memory flooded her dreamy state. One of the arguments she'd had with Charlene when they dropped Erik back one Sunday. She claimed that she could do a better job with Erik and that he was happier when he was with them. It was no secret that Charlene couldn't have children. That was the only reason she stole Justin away from her. That woman wanted the package of her man and child.

'Are you okay?' The young police officer stood over her.

Sonya tried to move but something chained her wrist to the bed frame.

'Sorry about the cuffs. Can I get you anything? A nurse, maybe?'

'N-n-no. I just w-w-want my son. It's Charlene, Justin's girl-friend. She has him. It has to be her. It all makes sense now.'

FORTY-FOUR

'Guv,' Kapoor shrieked down the phone. 'Sonya Baker has been murmuring incoherently all evening but something worried me so I thought I should call. She said that Justin's girlfriend has Erik. I don't know if she means it or if she has him but she seemed agitated. It was after Justin tried to muscle his way in to see her. There was a bit of commotion and shouting in the ward. She must have heard him. I don't know if she's confused or something has clicked.'

Gina sat back in her office chair. 'What happened when she got to the hospital?'

'She wouldn't stop crying, then she started hitting out and trying to run and punch anyone who came near her. She accepted a sedative in the end for her own safety as well as everyone here.'

'Stay with her and if she says anything else, let me know straight away. In the meantime, I'll head over to the bed and breakfast that Justin and Charlene are staying at and check on them. I'll ask why Sonya would make such a claim and see what their reactions are.'

After the call ended, Gina's mind began to whirr. Had she missed something all along? Maybe the last candle was for

Stephen, and Justin and Charlene had set Sonya up. Why? It still wasn't making sense. Had something happened between the friends, something none of them would speak about? Something so bad that murder was preferable to the truth coming out?

She grabbed her car keys and spotted Wyre packing up. 'Fancy a trip to the Cleevesford Cleaver with me?' Gina filled Wyre in on the conversation she'd just had with PC Kapoor.

'I'll just grab my coat.'

Gina drove past the high street and down a couple of roads then parked outside the Cleevesford Cleaver, the old building that used to be a butcher's shop many years ago. Even though it had been recently revamped, it still looked like a dreary old bed and breakfast and the fact that it was dark, didn't help. Gina hammered on the door and called Justin's number. He didn't answer but she could hear a phone ringing from inside. 'He's in there and not answering.' At least they knew which room he was in now. Gina knocked again and one of the other guests came out, letting them in. Gina rang his number again and followed the sound. It led her to the first room. Gina banged as hard as she could. Wyre stood by her side. As the door opened, Gina saw the teary eyes of a young woman. 'May we come in? It's DI Harte and DC Wyre.' She held her identification up.

The woman opened the door wide and let them in. Her braided black hair fell down to her bottom and her dark cheeks glistened with tears. There was no sign of Justin in the room.

'Where is Mr Baker?'

The woman shrugged.

'Are you Charlene?'

'Yes.'

'Can you tell us where Justin is?'

The woman shook her head. 'I told him not to go out, especially with this person going around killing people but he just shouted and was acting all funny, then he left. I tried to call him, that's when I saw he'd left his phone.'

'What do you mean by acting funny?'

'Nervous, I guess. But I get that. Someone has his son. We're both feeling rotten right now. Is there any news about Erik?'

Gina shook her head. 'Sorry. I wish there was. Did you and Justin talk about the media and what happened this evening?'

'Yes.' She sat on the double bed and frowned. 'He kept shouting, saying that he couldn't leave it to you, the police, to get his son back.'

'Do you know if he left to meet someone, maybe you've checked his phone?' Gina hoped that Charlene had taken a look.

'It's password protected and you need his thumbprint too. I don't know where he went but he was so agitated which I can understand. His son is missing. I get that, but I thought we were a team. It was like I didn't know him.'

'In what way.'

'He just told me it was all none of my business. I love Erik, a lot, and I do care. We haven't been together long but I've bonded with the lad and Justin can't see that I'm feeling it too.' She paused. 'I can't believe what Sonya did. What will happen to Erik when you find him?'

Gina shrugged.

'He will come to live with me and Justin, won't he? I mean, Sonya will go to prison for what she did.'

Gina couldn't help but think that Charlene had this all worked out. Her gaze kept darting around the room, then back at Gina and Wyre. 'What is your relationship with Sonya like?'

'The woman's deranged. Last time we dropped Erik back, she called me a floozy. I get why she'd be angry but their marriage was over. He left her to be with me because they weren't happy together. She should never have said something like that in front of Erik.'

'How are you and Erik?'

'I adore him. He's the loveliest little boy. I read him a lot of stories and play dinosaurs with him. Those are his favourite things, that and sweets. He has such a sweet tooth.'

Gina thought of the stranger at the school who gave Erik a dinosaur and the present in his toy box from Sonya's friends. Everyone knew about his dinosaur obsession but something wasn't sitting right. 'When did Justin leave?'

'About half an hour ago?'

'Has he been at home a lot lately, maybe these last few days?'

Charlene scrunched her brows. 'No, he's been coming and going a lot and late sometimes. He kept saying that he needs time to think.'

'To think?'

'Yes, about how to get Erik living with us full time. It's been playing on his mind. He says that Sonya drinks too much, that she's always neglecting him to go out with friends or go to the gym. He says that Erik would be best off with us. That I could take him to school and pick him up and that Sonya could have him at the weekends. He misses his son when he's not around. I'm the one who soothes him when he's lying around depressed. No one sees that side of Justin.'

'How about on the early hours of Sunday, Monday, and this morning? Can you confirm Justin's whereabouts for those times?'

'I take sleeping tablets, have done for years. If he was out at those times, I wouldn't know.'

'Can anyone vouch for your whereabouts during those times?'

'Justin, because he was with me.'

Gina glanced at Wyre who was scrunching her brows. 'Charlene, we will need you to come to the station to make a formal statement.'

'No way. You're joking, aren't you? It's that cow, isn't it? Sonya. Just because she doesn't like me, she's trying to say that I took Erik and made her do those awful things. The woman's mad. I wouldn't be surprised if no one took Erik and she is behind all this. He'll just miraculously turn up, unharmed. She'll stop at nothing to get her own way.'

'And what is her own way?' Gina stepped back and waited for Charlene to answer.

'To keep Erik away from Justin forever.' She paused and looked up at them. 'What if I don't want to come to the station? I want to wait here just in case Justin returns.'

'Charlene, a little boy has been abducted and his life is under threat. It wouldn't look good if you were to refuse to help with our enquiries.'

The woman sighed and stood. 'Fine.'

'May we take this?' Gina pointed to Justin's phone. 'With Mr Baker missing and with what has happened to his friends, I'd say it's urgent that we find him for his own safety.' There were many reasons Gina wanted to locate Justin but most of all she wanted to know why he'd left the bed and breakfast and where he was on the night of Glen Chapman and Cameron Godwin's murders.

'Yes, of course. He has another phone though, his work phone. He took that with him but I heard him swearing because as he left, the charge was about to go.'

'We'll need that number from you. Does Mr Baker have any other premises at all, another house, caravan, office where he works from?'

'No... oh wait. He has a lock-up that he keeps all his tools in. He rented it when he moved out of Sonya's as I didn't have room in my house with all the work I'm having done.'

'And where is that?'

'On a farm just outside Studley. Boulder's Farm.'

Gina knew that it would take Justin about fifteen minutes to get there from the bed and breakfast. She stepped outside the room with Wyre while Charlene got her coat and bag together. 'Call O'Connor and tell him to organise someone to collect Charlene now and take her to the station. We have to head to Boulder's Farm straight away and meet uniform. Make sure we have a team there. Call Jacob and the fire department too. With our perp's track record, we need them on standby. We need to get there now. Also, if Justin has his son and he feels that we're closing in on him, he could run with the boy and that's the last thing we want.' Gina bit her lip as the cogs in her head turned. 'Maybe that's why he left his phone. No traces.'

FORTY-FIVE

Harvey whimpers in the dark where he'd woken up. The light of the moon helps him to see a little. He doesn't know how he got here. He remembered getting into the car but it wasn't with a stranger. Mummy was on the phone and they were at the park. He'd been playing but he wanted to go on the swings. When he got into the car he started to get tired which doesn't happen to him a lot. It was after he had the drink. He tries to murmur the word Mummy but his throat is dry and gravelly. He heard his friend talking about going away, somewhere far. It was going to be an adventure; a game, that was all. Harvey likes games but this one wasn't fun, not right now. A tear escapes from his eye and he sniffles a little. His tummy hurts too and he feels a bit sick, like the time he had a bug. An icky feeling gathers in his throat so he swallows. Maybe he's a bit dizzy, like he's on a boat – swaying back and forth.

The shadows of a tree look like spooky fingers that reach across the ceiling. He flinches as a branch hits the window above. An animal screams... or maybe it's a person. His heart is banging so hard he's struggling to hear. He reaches out on the floor, searching for the plastic dinosaur with his fingers and he grabs something.

Holding it up to the ceiling window, he can see from its outline that it's a dinosaur but it's not the dinosaur he was given. This one has a long neck, his had spikes on its back. Is it another dinosaur for him? Maybe he shouldn't take it; it might not be. Mummy says not to take things that don't belong to him. He places it back down and begins to reach for more things. His finger prods something sticky and he smells it. Chocolate. He wipes his finger on the soft blanket. Mummy said he should always wash his hands before he eats so he shouldn't lick his finger.

A loud bang and noise comes from beneath but he daren't shout or scream. Shaking, he reaches for the blanket and pulls it over his little body on the floor bed. That's when he feels something next to him, in bed. He slowly turns and his fingers touch skin, cold skin. The area around the thing next to him is wet and smells of wee. He moves away and his heart starts to hum so badly, he wants to shout, but he can't; not until he knows what's making that noise.

Remaining still, he holds his breath and closes his eyes. *Be a brave boy, Harvey.* He has to look. A cloud passes the moon and the room becomes a little lighter. That's when he sees his friend Erik and Erik isn't moving. He shakes Erik but still, nothing. Harvey can't help but scream. Once again, the moon is covered by big clouds and he's plunged into darkness. He jumps up out of the bed and runs around the room, feeling for a door. There's a handle. He presses it down and slams into the door because the door doesn't open. It's locked. He is trapped. He bangs and bangs. 'Mummy, I'm scared. Mummy.' The person who is making the noise stops. Harvey runs to the corner of the room and slides under what feels like a large chair, peering out from the bottom. They're coming; step by step until the footsteps reach the top step. A lock turns in the door and it creaks open, then the clouds pass the moon and he sees exactly who it is. They're going to do to him what they did to Erik. He shivers and closes his eyes, hoping that they don't see him. That's when he feels the hand pulling his arm. He screams like he's never screamed before but it's not going to help. Nothing will help. This person is too strong and he can't escape their grip.

No one is coming. He shouldn't have got into that car.

FORTY-SIX

Gina snaked through the dark roads with a convoy of police cars following behind as they all headed to Boulder's Farm. The trees either side were thrashing in the gale force winds that had been forecast. A branch came from nowhere and slapped her windscreen. Wyre let out an instinctive scream as she directed them.

'Next left, guv.'

Gina turned in slowly, the car hopping over the potholes as she drove further to the open-gated entrance. Boulder's Farm wasn't a farm anymore. From what she'd read, it hadn't been a farm for over twenty years but had kept the name. A large sign advertised vacant lock-up units available for the best rates going. She drove past the gate and spotted the large spread out bungalow to her right. 'I'm going to knock.' She turned off her headlights and stepped out of the car. 'Tell everyone else to turn off their lights and wait for further instructions.'

As Wyre coordinated the team, Gina ran against the gale. Gritty debris caught one of her eyes and she rubbed it in instead of rubbing it away. What was left of her tied up hair came loose. As she turned to look for the front door, a few strands ended up in her mouth. She knocked and waited. A plastic carrier bag flew past and caught on the picket fence.

'Hello.' A man who looked to be in his seventies scratched his white hair and pulled his pyjama bottoms up his chest as a gust of wind whistled through his hallway. 'What's going on 'ere?'

'Sorry, are you the owner of Boulder's Farm?'

'Yes. Oh God, has someone been growing weed in one of the lock-ups? I've had that before. Don't want any trouble. If you need to nick 'em, nick 'em. I didn't know anything about it. I keep myself to myself.'

'It's not about weed. We're investigating a missing boy and we have reason to believe he may be on your premises. He may be in one of your lock-ups and his life may be in danger. Can you tell me if your client, Mr Baker, has been here this evening?'

'Look, I don't keep a check of who comes and goes. They pay their rent, they get their keys and I leave them alone. I did vet him and he said he needed to store his tools and building stuff here. I saw the news. Sad about his boy.'

'Do you have CCTV?'

'At the prices I charge. You're having a laugh. No. I offer a basic service. Security is up to them, I just give 'em a key and that's the end of it. That's why I'm so cheap.'

'Is it okay if we take a look around?'

'Yes, go ahead.'

'Which lock-up does he rent?'

'Let me see.' The man flinched and held his back as he turned to open a diary. He grabbed a flyer and a red pen, circling something. 'See this map. This is where we are now and this is where Mr Baker's lock-up is. It's number thirty-two. You head straight up and take a left at the top. It's the one on the end.' He shivered. 'It's a cold one tonight.'

Gina took the map. 'Thank you.' As she hurried back up the path, rain began to pelt down. She gave the signal to the convoy to follow her before getting back into the car. Her stab vest was intact, she had everything she needed. Bolt cutters in the boot should they need to use them to enter. The PCs were on hand with the battering rams too. If Erik was in there, they were getting him out. She swallowed. 'Do you think Justin would take his own son hostage?'

'Who knows what will happen. We have to be prepared for everything.' Wyre bit her lip and stared out of the window as they approached slowly with only sidelights on.

As Gina reached the end of the first road, instead of turning left, she got out of the car and signalled for all the cars behind to stop. She was going to take the rest of the journey on foot. They couldn't be seen approaching. All engines off, she led the way, with Wyre close behind. Several uniform followed in line, keeping as close to the buildings as possible. She spotted Jacob at the back. The outbuildings weren't in a single storey line as Gina imagined they would be. There was a row of attached low-level units followed by a miniature barn-like building and next to that, their target building, it was a single storey with a dormer sticking out of the top. The loose felt from the roof flapped like a trapped bird.

Gina swore under her breath as she stepped into an icy puddle that reached her shin. Shaking her freezing cold foot, she stepped out. Her heart was now beginning to hum and bang. As she got nearer, she could see that there were no low-level windows and there was only one door. A blast of wind whipped around them, whooshing a tornado of leaves around their heads. A cold rain shower splattered down. 'His car isn't here,' she said as Wyre caught up.

'Maybe he left and Erik is in there alone.'

Gina hurried towards the building.

A PC came up behind her holding a pair of bolt cutters and a battering ram. 'Shall we take the door down?'

'Wait.' Gina placed her ear to the soaking wet wooden door and listened. She couldn't hear a thing. She ran around the building, there wasn't another way in. 'Yes, but just bear in mind that there might be a scared boy in there.'

The officer slammed the door once, then again. It finally gave in with a huge creak and crack as a part of the door snapped. 'We're in.'

Gina pushed the door open. 'Mr Baker. Erik.' She shone her torch in each of the corners of the room and could see nothing but toolboxes, bags, old bricks and pipes. An old bath stood at one end. The lock-up was full of items that had been stripped out of houses. Sinks, cupboards, block paving, slabs. A cement mixer blocked the ladders that led to the boarded off roof area. Gina grabbed them and hoisted herself up, taking one step at a time. One of the rungs cracked and she slipped. For a second, she stopped breathing as she imagined her head slamming into the cement mixer. She took a moment to compose herself before continuing. 'Erik. It's the police. My name's Gina. We've come to help you.' She called in the gentlest voice she could muster, the one she used when she spoke to Gracie. As she reached the top, she was almost startled by a face and she let out a yelp.

'You okay up there, guv?' Wyre called.

She shook her head and exhaled. 'Yes, it's just an old scare-crow. There is no sign of Erik here at all.'

As she began to come back down, Jacob burst into the lock-up. 'Guv, you have to get out here now.' She rushed down, almost slipping as she navigated everything beneath, then she ran back out of the building.

The old man from the bungalow pulled up. 'You lot need to get over to the east wing. Someone's set one of my units alight. I saw it from my back window.'

She ran down the road and got into her car with Wyre just about making it before she pulled off. She hopped the car over the bumps all the way along the road and took a left at the end. That's when they saw the unit on fire. On the floor was a candle in a jar, flickering away. A miniature version of the inferno that was taking hold next to it. Gina left the car door open and took off her stab vest as she ran, dropping it to the ground. This time there was a window and through it, she could just about see the flames licking what she thought could be an arm. She tried the door and it was open. 'It's Erik, I'm going in.' She nodded at a group of officers. 'Whoever did this must be on foot, go chase them, find them, now.' Those were the last words she said as she entered and called Erik's name. On the floor lay a melting plastic dinosaur.

FORTY-SEVEN

Gina wanted to cry but that wasn't an option. As the flames came for her, she held her breath and ran as fast as she could to the body and tried to drag it. It was too heavy. She couldn't hold her breath any longer. She sharply inhaled a lungful of smoke. Within seconds a fully protected firefighter entered and shoved her towards the door, taking over.

'Over here, guv.'

A paramedic ran over. 'Are you hurt?' She coughed a few times and held up her arm.

Her shirt was a little blackened and her hair was giving off a singed smell. 'No, I'm okay.'

'Your face, it's slightly burnt.'

'I'm okay.' It barely hurt. Either it wasn't that bad or she was running on adrenaline. 'I'll deal with it later.' She watched with anticipation as a firefighter dragged Justin Baker under the arms out of the building. No wonder she struggled to drag the body. He placed the man on the ground and they covered him with a fire blanket, extinguishing the flames that still flickered away on his arm. A paramedic ran over to help. 'Is he okay?' Gina took a few steps forward for a look.

'Keep back.'

The man lay still, no coughing, no moving.

'We have a pulse.'

Another paramedic ran over and they began treating him.

Gina glanced at the jar and candle. The rain had now extinguished it. 'Wyre, there's a sticker on the jar this time. It's a label and it has something printed on it.' She flashed her torch at it and read. '"One more to go." There's another victim and what have they done with Erik?' Glancing into the distance, she saw flickering torches in the woodland as officers tried to chase down whoever was out there, running from the carnage that they had caused. She knew Sonya had burnt the last two houses down, but who had burnt this one? Sonya was in hospital and the door had a PC guarding it. One thing was for sure, they had eliminated Justin Baker. 'Does he have a phone on him?'

The paramedic shook his head. Gina knew that his phone was probably in the wreck of the building, damaged.

Had the perp done their own dirty work this time or had they blackmailed someone else into doing it? There was another person Gina could eliminate from starting the fire and that was Charlene but she wasn't eliminated as the potential abductor. There would be plenty of time to interview her later.

'That was close, guv. You could have set yourself on fire going in like that.' Wyre stood beside her.

'I saw the melting toy dinosaur and I thought it was Erik. I couldn't let him burn like that. I had to go in. Can Justin Baker talk yet?'

'He's not even conscious. They're just preparing to take him to hospital.'

'He was lucky, so lucky.'

'That he was.'

'That's two witnesses we can't speak to at the moment. One is in hospital on a cocktail of sedatives and the other is unconscious. If we hadn't gone to see Charlene, we wouldn't have come here. Whoever set this up thought they'd kill him and they failed. They still have Erik.' Gina smiled and looked up at the dark skies. Rain splattered her face and she let out a smile. 'It wasn't Erik. He's still alive. He has to be.' She paused and wiped her face with her arm. 'One more to go – I have no doubts as to who that is. Call Smith right away and let him know what's happening. He needs to be extra vigilant while he's watching Stephen tonight. They're going for him next.'

FORTY-EIGHT

Gina grabbed a tea towel from the kitchen and patted her hair as she hurried through to the incident room. Everyone that had gone home to work that night was back. A pizza gave off steam in the middle of the table and Jacob and O'Connor grabbed a slice. Gina threw the towel onto a desk. 'Thank you all for being here. It's going to be a long night. Jacob, can you fill me in on how the chase went? Someone lit that fire at Boulder's Farm while we were there and no cars left that road as we were blocking it. They had to have arrived on foot.' Gina pointed to the map that had been pinned to the wall and Boulder's Farm had been circled. 'There are two routes out of here that the fire starter could have taken. Here, from the lock-up, over the stile and through this walking trail in the woodland. The other would be along the river. There's a bridge about a quarter of a mile down that leads to a road. They could have been parked there. I know units were called in to block off the exits as soon as we saw the fire but whoever started this had a head start. They were probably already at their car as the fire took hold enough for us to see it, especially if they were fit. They could have been at their car in a matter of a few minutes and gone. These roads are all rural. There are no cameras, no way of knowing who passed and when. I know there are officers calling in on some of the properties that were close to these two stopping places. How is that going?'

Jacob swallowed the pizza in his mouth. 'It's still going. I've told the team to call me if they find anything out.'

'O'Connor, have you interviewed Charlene and put her in the picture?'

He tapped his nails on the desk. 'Yes, and she claims to have known nothing about what was going on. She's absolutely devastated to hear about Justin's attack and keeps asking if she can see him.'

'Have we located Justin's work phone, the one Charlene said he had?'

O'Connor shook his head. 'No, there is a possibility it will turn up in the fire debris so we may know more when forensics have finished processing the scene. It wasn't on his person.' He grabbed another slice of pizza.

'But we have his number?'

'No, not at the moment. We'll follow up and get it from Charlene.'

'Okay, when you do get it, speak to the phone company and try to find out who he's been speaking to or messaging. The same for Sonya. We need to chase them up as we could have the answers right in front of us. Can you do that?'

O'Connor nodded. 'Yes, guv. It feels that no one can get the information we need soon enough.'

The phone rang and Jacob grabbed it. He nodded a few times and stood straight. He smiled at Gina. 'The owner of a cottage close to the bridge by the river saw someone.'

'We need to get over there, now. O'Connor, keep on with the phones and processing anything that comes in from uniform. Wyre, give Bernard a call, see if forensics have found the phone or indeed anything else that can help us. I also know there are officers out there in the woodland searching for anything that might lead us to the perp, chase them up, and see if they've come across anything. Also, find out if the dogs have arrived and ask if they've picked anything up. I know a helicopter was dispatched but I also know it came too late. One more thing, I think we can safely assume that Stephen Smithson is the next intended victim. PC Smith is parked up on the street at the moment. Because I know Stephen from the past, I can't be seen there. If you need a detective on site, Jacob is SIO so call him straight away. That doesn't mean I'm outside the investigation. I want to be kept up to date with everything. Have we had an update from Smith?'

Wyre nodded. 'Yes, no activity so far. The house is quiet and no one has been anywhere near it. An officer who joined Smith said he walked around the back and said the back gate was secured. He also said that Stephen and Heather have placed barbed wire along the fence to stop anyone jumping over. No one is getting into that garden tonight. Oh, one of the neighbours has said Smith and the other officer can use his spare room to watch the house. They didn't say anything about the investigation but they have taken up his offer. They're also setting up a video camera to record anyone who tries to approach the house.'

'That's very kind of the neighbour. Jacob, should Wyre join them?'

Jacob stood and smiled. Although he'd been assigned the role of SIO, Gina was grateful that he'd still allowed her to take charge. 'Yes, that would be great. We need a detective on site and I think the guv and I should head to speak to the witness.'

'I'll head over now.' Wyre grabbed her coat.

'Do you want to take some pizza?' O'Connor held the box up with his chunky fingers.

'No, thank you.' She smiled.

'Right, keep the system updated at every stage. We all need to know what's going on at all times and sharing of updated information is key. Let's get to the bottom of this and make sure no one else gets hurt and, most of all, we need to bring Erik home.' Gina bit her bottom lip and frowned. Bringing Erik home seemed like such a distant thought. She looked out of the window and wondered how scared he would be in this storm. Thunder clashed and lightning lit up the night sky. She shivered. 'Let's not waste any more time.'

FORTY-NINE

Lightning flashed over the hills followed by another crash of thunder. The rain fell so hard, Gina was sure the river would be bubbling up. They had all been warned that the flood risk was as high as it could be. She pulled up just in front of a gurgling drain.

Jacob rubbed his eyes. 'I don't think uniform will be searching these woods for much longer. It said on the news that the river was close to bursting its banks.'

'Everything is against us tonight. Let's go and see what the witness has to say.' Gina stepped out into the rain, her hair still sodden from being drenched earlier. Every time she inhaled, she could still smell smoke. She touched her nose and flinched. The sting was kicking in now. She was a mess. This investigation was a mess. Her life was a mess.

They walked down the uneven path to find a tree battering the roof of an old thatched cottage. The security light came on, exposing the white building. Empty hanging baskets clanged together in the wind. Jacob pressed the bell. A thin woman with sleek, grey hair answered. Her hook-like nose sat above her thin lips. 'Police?'

'Yes, I'm DS Driscoll and this is DI Harte.' Gina held her identification up and smiled as the woman let them in. Water dripped from both her and Jacob and pooled on the flagstone floor. They removed their coats and shoes and left them by the door. The woman opened a small cupboard and took out a couple of towels. 'Here. You look like you need these.'

'Thank you.' Gina took the towel and patted her hair as she followed the woman down several steps into the sitting room.

All the furniture had been elevated. 'The things you have to do when you live by a river. This room tends to get a little flooded.' The tiled floor was a cold grey and the fire was still burning away – for now. The woman threw another log onto the hearth. 'It should warm up a bit more in a minute. It doesn't take long for the logs to catch. I know the sofa is a bit higher than usual but you can still just about sit without needing a stepladder.'

Gina stood on her toes and sat on the cottage suite, comfort not one of its main features but she guessed that the woman didn't invest much in soft furnishings in a room that flooded regularly. 'Thank you. What's your name, sorry?'

'Ally.'

Gina smiled. 'Ally, I know you spoke to an officer a short while back and you said you saw someone this evening. Can you tell us from the beginning what you saw?'

'Yes, I'd just finished putting the sandbags out the back as I'd heard we were in for a downpour. I saw lights from a car but it wasn't passing, it was pulling over. The next house is quite a way down so I thought it was someone coming here. I'll admit to being a bit worried. I don't get many unplanned visits, and I definitely don't get any at night. I panicked, ran back to the house and turned off the lights. I watched from the kitchen, which faces out the front. I kept back so they wouldn't see me, in the darkness of the kitchen.'

'Then what happened?'

'The person got out of the car. The central locking beeped and flashed and they walked off into the woods. I ran upstairs and carried on watching them. I mean, who would be out walking alone in the woods in the dark when the river is set to burst. I watched them head down the gravel path at the side of my house and they carried on. I was just grateful they weren't coming to mine.'

'What time was this?'

'I would say about eight, maybe eight-fifteen.'

That would be about the right time for the perp to arrive at the lock-up and meet Justin. 'Can you describe this person?'

'It was quite dark. They had a rucksack. I remember thinking at this point that they must be stupid, going out walking with a storm coming.' The wind howled down the chimney and the fire flickered.

Gina swallowed. 'How about the person's build or height?'

Ally shrugged. 'I couldn't tell. Well-built maybe. They weren't skinny but then again, they could have been wearing layers. It is cold.'

'How about the car? Did you see what make or type it was?'

'I'd say a hatchback and it was dark in colour but I don't know what make. I'm not very good with cars.'

They had a dark hatchback and possibly a well-built person with a rucksack. It was something but Gina had hoped for more, much more.

'Wait.' The woman smiled and held up a long thin finger. 'I run an Instagram page called Ally's Badger.' She laughed. 'The name is silly I know, but it gets me a lot of followers and it's all meant in good fun.'

Gina furrowed her brows, wondering what was coming next.

'I have a visiting badger I call Brigadoon Stripy. I have a lot of motion sensitive cameras around the garden. I edit the footage and post photos and videos onto my social media for my followers. Nearly one hundred thousand people follow me.'

Gina hoped that they would be able to see something on one of the cameras. 'Can we see this evening's footage?'

'Of course and you may even see Brigadoon Stripy.'

On a normal day, Gina would love to watch online badger videos, but she was more interested in whoever pulled up and walked over the bridge. 'Great.' Gina followed Ally through the low-ceiling rooms into a windowless study full of computer equipment. Two shiny monitors were spread across the wall-to-wall purpose-built desk.

Ally turned the computer on, grabbed her glasses and sat at the desk. 'Right, camera one is in the backyard, you won't see the path or the car on that one. Camera two, side passage. That's no good to you either, it's the wrong side. Camera three, the feeding station to the right of the house that borders the path. Stripy seems to prefer this to the backyard for some reason. He must live close by because this is his favourite spot. I have a camera four. This tapes him from above. Camera three might give you the person's shoes but camera four will give you a bird's-eye view with any luck.'

'Can we see camera three's footage first?'

'Yes, let me just get it up. I haven't even looked at this yet. There, as you can see Stripy hasn't visited yet. I leave dog food and mealworms out. They're still there at this point.' Slowly, a badger appears and begins snuffling away in the bowl. Ally clicks on the timeline to a few minutes ahead.

The badger scurries off and a few seconds away, Gina and Jacob clearly see the mud splattered white trainers passing by. Gina points. 'What time was that?'

'Eight twelve.'

Jacob leans over for a better look. 'Can we skip to eight twelve on camera four?'

Biting her nails, Gina waits as Ally starts playing the footage a little before that time. The badger appears. The badger eats. The badger scurries away and their perp passes by. The shape she saw was definitely that of a heavy-busted woman. 'Can we get a copy of this footage on a stick or a hard drive? We will return the hard drive.'

'Yes, it'll take a few minutes. I'll set it running now.' Ally popped an external hard drive into the computer and began to transfer the footage.

Gina hoped it wouldn't be long. She wanted to get this footage back, get it blown up and take a good look to see if they could identify the person in the footage. She bit her nails as they waited in silence, watching the onscreen progress bar going as slowly as it could. She thought of Sonya and what the perp had done to her. It had to be happening again. Her stomach began to flutter as the realisation of who it was on the screen kicked in. She only hoped that another child wasn't in danger. She glanced at Jacob and knew from the worried look on his face that he suspected the same person that she did.

He pulled his phone from his pocket. 'I'm just going to pop out to make a call.'

'There, all done.' Ally carefully ejected the hard drive and passed it to Gina. 'I keep a backup and I keep a backup of the backup so if you need it again for any reason. I have it on the cloud too.'

'Thank you so much, Ally. You've been a real help. An officer will come to take a formal statement soon.' Gina hurried towards the door and the woman followed as she and Jacob put their shoes and coats back on.

'Don't forget to check out Ally's Badger on Instagram.'

'I won't. I'll definitely take a look. Keep up the good work. Stripy is adorable.'

The woman beamed a huge smile as they left, running towards the car in the pouring rain. Thunder blasted again.

As Gina turned the engine, she glanced back. The woman had gone.

Jacob grabbed a cherry drop from the centre console. 'We're heading straight to Faith Chapman's mother's house, now. Not only did that figure match her shape, she has a dark blue Volvo.'

'I hope this will be the end of it and Erik will be found but I suspect the opposite is happening here.' She almost wanted to cry. 'I think whoever has Erik, now has one of Faith's children.'

FIFTY

Gina pulled up alongside the three-storey town house on the modern estate. 'That must be Faith Chapman's mother holding one of the kids.' She glanced at the time, it was quarter past midnight, way past their bedtimes. Something definitely wasn't right but Gina was relieved to see one of the children. Maybe she was wrong about the possibility of another abduction.

'And look who else is there.' Jacob watched through the windscreen as rain dripped down.

'Aiden Marsh, and that's his son, Elias. Where's Faith?' Gina used the wipers and they both glanced up at the house. All the lights were on but she couldn't see Faith through any of the windows. 'Right, let's go in. I want to know what's going on. Call for backup. With a missing child, we need to search the property. I can't rule out Erik being here, not yet. We have reason to believe that Faith was at the lock-up tonight and attempted to murder Justin Baker. We need to search the house to secure any evidence of that and I want us looking for any connection to Erik while we're there. He is still our priority above and beyond anything else. Let's see what we can find out first though.' She thought again, of the tiny boy, alone somewhere, missing his mother. In her mind he wasn't dead. He couldn't be dead. She felt a whoosh of adrenalin dart through her body. Now wasn't the time to slow down, despite every bone in her body telling her she needed a break or maybe even some food.

Jacob grabbed his phone. 'I'll make the call, get some officers over to assist.'

'Thanks. We need a family liaison officer too. Can you see if Ellyn is available to come over? I'll go and knock while you do that.'

Jacob began talking and Gina left the car. Once again, she felt the full weight of the storm coming down. A gust caught the neighbour's wheelie bin, making it blow along the path and the gutters were bubbling over, leaving an eggy stench in the air. She pulled up her hood and ran along the tiny crazy-paved path, then knocked. Behind the door, she could hear a child crying, then Aiden Marsh eventually opened the door. 'Hello.' The startled expression on his face told her that he wasn't expecting to see the police tonight.

'Mr Marsh,' Gina said, acknowledging his presence. Jacob darted up the path and stood beside her. 'We need to speak to Mrs Chapman. May we come in?'

'Erm, it's not a good time.' Elias scurried along the hallway and wrapped his arms around his dad's leg.

'Mr Marsh, we are investigating a serious incident tonight and we have reason to believe that Faith Chapman was involved. This is where she is registered as staying at the moment. We will be searching the property to secure any evidence but we'd rather come in peacefully and speak to everyone in the house. We know what is happening.'

The man scooped up his son and opened the door. 'Sorry, yes, come in.'

Faith stood at the top of the stairs screaming as she pulled at her wet matted hair. 'Get them out. Get them out, now!' She sobbed and gasped for air before running into the bathroom and locking herself in. 'They can't be here.'

'I need to be with her.' Aiden ran upstairs leaving his son in the hall. Elias stared up at Gina as he clutched a dinosaur.

Gina stared at the toy. 'That's a lovely toy, Elias. Where did you get that from?'

The boy closed his mouth and shrugged.

Faith's mother walked into the hall, followed by her husband now holding the bawling girl. He took Elias's hand and led the two children into a small snug with a television fixed to the wall. 'Come on, Elias, you're a big boy. Can you turn the television on and help me take care of Kiara?'

Faith's mother pulled the door to on them. The tiny girl's sobs began to subside but Mrs Chapman's got louder. Aiden banged on the door, calling for her to let him in.

Gina followed the woman through to the kitchen. 'Sorry, what's your name?'

'Vera.'

'We need to know what's going on here, a little boy's safety and life is at stake so I don't want to waste time. His name is Erik and your daughter knows him. It's important that you tell me everything, now.'

'They have Erik too?'

Gina nodded knowing that both of their worst fears had just been confirmed. The abductor now had Harvey.

The woman slumped into a wooden chair and rubbed her pained-looking face. 'Someone has abducted Harvey. They made Faith do it. She had no choice.'

'Do what?'

'Set the fire...' Vera broke down. 'I shouldn't have said anything. They'll kill him now and it'll be because I told you. They said they'd kill him if she told anyone and she told me, and then Aiden. We've only just found out, when she came back in a state. Aiden arrived just before she did. She apparently called him and told him to come here too. It's as much of a shock to him as it is to us. Will this person kill Harvey? Please tell me it's an empty threat and he's okay.'

Deep down she didn't know if the abductor had already killed Erik and Harvey might be next, but she had to hope. That's all they had. She listened to Faith's desperate sobs from above and knew that anyone that could do this to a parent was capable of anything. No... she had to hang on to the fact that the abductor was still getting others to do their dirty work.

'Tell me what happened this evening so that we can do everything we can to get Harvey back.'

'Faith hasn't been herself all day. This morning Harvey was going on at her to take him to the park. He was really bored, I mean he doesn't fully understand what has been going on and was still asking when he could see Daddy. Don't blame her for not telling him. She needed to find the right time and she hasn't worked it out in her own head yet. Anyway, she came back without Harvey and she told me that he'd gone to play at Aiden's, with his little boy, and I thought no more of it. All afternoon, she'd been nervously pacing and staring at her phone. She went out again about teatime and when she came back, she shut herself in her room, refusing to come out. Not long after, about six this evening, she left the house without saying a word about what she was doing or where she was going. I was so worried but I thought maybe she just needed some space from me and Kiara; some time to think. I mean, she's lost her home and her husband. However horrible he was to her, he was still the father of her children and it was still a shock.'

'Which park was that?'

'The one on Beddow Close, just behind this estate. It's where we always take him.'

'Did she have anything with her when she left?'

Vera nodded and a tear slipped down her cheek. 'A rucksack, the same one that she came back with when she went out earlier. She didn't have it when she left earlier in the day.' Jacob scribbled a few notes down and Aiden continued banging and pleading with Faith to open the door. Kiara still cried even though Gina could hear her granddad and Elias trying to soothe her in the other room. She hoped that the other officers would arrive soon.

'Do you know what was in this rucksack?'

'No. I barely saw her, let alone what was in the bag. She just hurried out the door without saying a word. I've never seen her look so scared and yet determined at the same time. Now I know why.'

'So, when did she arrive back?'

'About nine forty-five. Aiden arrived about fifteen minutes earlier and we were both pacing the floor, wondering what was going on.'

'You know Aiden?'

Vera nodded and wiped her eye. 'I'd been trying to help Faith leave Glen. I know he was horrible to her and I knew she was seeing Aiden. I looked after the kids when she met him; only a couple of times though. He loves her... Aiden. Glen never loved her, he just treated her like she was his property. I never liked how he spoke to her or how he tried to control her and I caught him physically pushing her around. I confronted him once and he called me an interfering old bag. At the time, I told Faith but she told me I was exaggerating. When I heard that she was no longer happy with him, I was happy that she'd be leaving him. As for Faith, the gym and her motivation lady friends had become her sanctuary.'

'When Faith arrived home, how did she seem?'

Swallowing, Vera went to talk but then stopped as if she had choked on what she was about to say.

'You need to tell us.'

'She... she was frantic and crying. She smelled of smoke and was in a right state. Her skin was bleeding and she was covered in dirt, like she'd dragged herself through thorns and brambles. It looked like she'd been running for her life. I pulled a few twigs from her hair. She was soaking wet.' Someone knocked at the door.

'That'll be the officers,' Gina said as Jacob hurried to answer the door. 'Vera, I'm so sorry but we have to search your property. As Faith attempted to take the life of Justin Baker tonight, we need to secure any evidence.'

'She didn't intend to hurt anyone. She had no choice. They threatened to kill Harvey. I wish I'd have known what was going on. I'd have done it for her just like any mother would do. She was just protecting her child and I'd do anything for mine.'

'I know and I'm really sorry we have to do this. I can see how much your family is going through, right now.'

'What are you doing to catch the bastard behind this? My daughter is nothing more than a pawn in all this. You're taking the wrong person in.'

'I have no choice but I promise that we'll do all we can to find Harvey. He and Erik are our prime concern right now. I know this is hard for you and your family.'

Vera stood and slapped her hand on the patio doors, leaving a sweaty imprint on the glass. 'Hard, it's more than hard. I feel as though my heart is being ripped out. My family is falling apart.'

Ellyn, the family liaison officer, stepped into the room, her head tilted slightly in sympathy as she listened to what was going on. Gina moved aside and let her take over. Ellyn's brown hair was wild and fell just below her shoulders, it looked like she'd just got out of bed. She removed her thick coat, walked over to Vera before saying a few hushed words and leading her to a chair. Gina nodded and Ellyn took over. Jacob entered with an officer who he'd just briefed. They then began carefully looking through the kitchen drawers.

Gina pushed through. 'I'll go upstairs first. I need to speak to Faith. Jacob?'

'Yes.'

'Can you get someone to take a look at the park on Beddow Close? It's literally just at the end of this road. One of the PCs here could go.'

Jacob turned to an officer and spoke, the officer nodded and headed off to the park. He then stepped forward. 'Faith is still in the bathroom, guv. Locked in.'

'It's okay, give me five first before the officers come up.' She listened, Kiara was no longer making any noise. Faith had stopped screaming and Aiden had stopped banging. She glanced up the stairs, seeing the man resting his head on the door as he sat on the landing.

Jacob sneaked a look behind the door. 'The kids are asleep.'

Gina glanced around before going up the stairs. 'Close the door.' She waved her arms, gathering the three officers around as she spoke in a hushed tone. 'I want everything to be done as quietly as possible. There are two young children asleep in that room and I don't want them disturbed. They've already had enough of a traumatic evening. When all the bedrooms have been searched, we'll get the children in a bed so we can see what's in that room. Remember, gently and quietly.'

Each officer nodded. Gina beckoned Jacob to follow her. When she reached the top of the stairs, she sat on the carpet next to Aiden. 'Faith, please open the door. We want to help you find Harvey.'

'I didn't want to burn his lock-up down,' she sobbed. 'But someone abducted Harvey and they said if I didn't do it, they would kill him. They said they would pour petrol over my boy and set him on fire. They said if I told the police, they'd kill him.' She began to sob, hyperventilate and wail. 'I killed him. I shouldn't have told anyone.' She paused. 'My boy is dead.'

FIFTY-ONE

'Faith, please open the door so that we can talk. Please, our priority is Harvey's safety.' Gina tried to gently plead, hoping that Faith would open up. The last thing she wanted was to have to forcefully open the door but she knew full well that time was ticking and Harvey and Erik's lives were at stake. They needed Faith to talk, not to withdraw. Gina refused to believe that the children were dead despite all that had happened and the threats that had been made.

The whole landing went silent. Two officers shuffled past without making a sound and headed into the bedrooms to start searching. She heard drawers gently opening and closing. She listened as Ellyn spoke in a soothing voice to Vera but she could hear nothing more from behind the bathroom door. Aiden leaned against the wall, his head right back and his eyes glazed over. He began to bite his nails. 'Faith, my love, please open the door. We can't run or hide away from this.'

A few seconds later, the lock slid across and Faith pulled the door open, then she sat on the toilet seat with her head in her hands. Gina entered. It wasn't the best place to interview her but if the bathroom was a safe and comfortable space, then the bathroom it would be. Jacob followed and sat on the edge of the bath.

Faith placed her hand over her mouth and began to silently sob.

'We're so sorry, Faith, but I have to ask you a few questions, and then we're going to have to take you down to the station.' Gina felt a lump forming in her throat. The woman in front of her had committed an awful crime, which she'd be charged for, one that could easily have resulted in the death of a man, but she'd committed it under duress. She hadn't received an update since Justin had been taken in. He may have taken a turn for the worse or he may have improved. She hung on the last words she heard at the scene. They'd found a pulse. If he'd died, the officer that went with Justin to the hospital would have called straight away.

'I went to the lock-up at Boulder's Farm a few hours ago. I bought a petrol can and filled it up at Tesco petrol station on the way.' Faith tore a few sheets of toilet roll and blew her nose. 'I saw Justin waiting there and as soon as he went inside. I ran up to the lock-up and poured the petrol in his direction. He kept staring at me, asking what I was doing. I took a lighter out of the rucksack and set him alight and I left the burning candle. I did everything the abductor asked of me, then I ruined it by telling my mother and Aiden. You know that whoever's taken my son is going to kill him. I failed and Harvey will die.' Her mouth downturned and she pulled her legs up onto the seat and hugged them closely. 'He's probably dead, all because I spoke.'

'We don't know that, Faith. We'd like to hope that we can find him alive.'

'Hope, what is hope? It's a useless word. They said he would die if I told. I told. I just couldn't keep it in. I didn't want to hurt Justin, I mean he's always been nice to me. Why would I want to hurt him? I feel sick, so sick. I killed him and I killed my son.'

'You didn't kill him. He had a pulse when we left the scene. He's in hospital getting treated as we speak.' Gina led Jacob onto the landing, leaving Faith staring at her knees.

'What, guv?'

'Contact Briggs. We have to let the public know that a man died in a fire tonight. Let our abductor believe that Justin Baker is dead. Keep him segregated from everyone else at the hospital. If the perp believes he's dead, it might just buy some more time for the boys.'

Jacob nervously ran his fingers through his hair and snatched his phone from his pocket. 'I'll do it straight away.'

For once they'd use the media for their own gain. Gina only hoped that the abductor wasn't closely watching the house right now, knowing that the police were involved. She walked over to the other end of the landing and stared through the window. The street was in darkness and there wasn't a soul in sight. She hurried back to Faith. 'How does this person contact you?'

'Snapchat. The messages just disappear. I got one saying that they had Harvey and I had to do what they said and that more instructions would come later. Then I had another telling me to go back to the park where he was taken from and if I looked in the bushes, I would find a rucksack. It had a lighter, a candle and a jar in it. Then I got another saying that I had to be at a certain lock-up with a can of petrol this evening and that I had to set Justin alight if I wanted to see my son again. They said if I failed, they would set Harvey on fire. I did what they asked and now I've heard nothing. It's because I've failed.'

'They don't know you've failed. We need your phone.'

The woman clutched the gadget. 'No, it's the only connection I have to my son's abductor.'

'You have to trust us. We will all go to the station together, where you'll be formally questioned and be able to call a solicitor. You will be with someone at all times. If they message, you will know and we will work out how to respond or what to do.'

With trembling hands, Faith handed it over.

A PC entered. 'Guv, we can't get into the attic. There are stairs leading up but the room is locked.' Another officer ran up with the key and Gina heard Vera saying that she locks it as she doesn't like the children going up. 'It's full of junk and some of it's dangerous,' she called out. Gina took the key from the officer and walked up the stairs. Slowly she turned it and opened the door.

FIFTY-TWO

Gina stood at the open attic door, staring into darkness. She turned on the dim light and saw an old cot, piles of boxes and a cupboard full of blankets. An old television stood in the corner of the room. Rain pummelled down on the skylights and there was a chill in the air. Her phone rang. 'DI Harte.'

'I found something at the park where Harvey was taken, in fact on the road, just by the bushes.' It was the officer that left to check the area. 'I've called forensics but I'll send a photo through now.'

Gina waited the few seconds it took him then her phone beeped. Once opened, she could clearly see the photo of a plastic dinosaur lying on the kerb, then she glanced back at the attic floor and saw a box of toys. On the top of the pile was a yellow dinosaur. 'Whose is this?'

Vera hurried to Gina's side and clutched the toy. 'It's one of Harvey's toys. He must have left it up here when I was clearing up or putting something away.'

Gina grabbed it and hurried back downstairs to the bathroom on the first floor. Faith was now sitting on the stairs, her head lay on Aiden's shoulders. 'Faith, who gave Harvey this toy?'

She shrugged. 'I can't remember, he had it for his birthday a couple of months ago. It would have been from one of my gym friends and their partners.'

'You and your friends gave a similar toy to Erik for his birthday?'

Faith scrunched up her brow. 'What has this got to do with my missing son?'

Gina had no idea how to answer. Erik had a toy dinosaur. There was a toy dinosaur at the scene of Harvey's abduction. Aiden's son, Elias, was clutching a dinosaur when she arrived and now there was yet another plastic dinosaur. It was too much of a coincidence to ignore. The fact that a dinosaur had been left at a crime scene linked them to the case. 'We found one at the park you took Harvey to earlier today. Can I have a list of everyone who attended Harvey's birthday party?'

'It wasn't a huge list. There was Heather, Stephen, my husband, Aiden, Kerstin, Cameron, Sonya and the kids. I invited Justin but not Charlene because it would have been awkward for Sonya, so he didn't come. That was all. Oh, my parents were there too. I can't remember who gave him the toy. It could have been anyone there. Wait, I know it wasn't my parents. They bought him an iPad and Mum said that was all they would get him as it was so expensive.'

'And Erik's dinosaur, the one he had for his birthday. Who organised buying that?'

'Oh that, we decided to all chip in to buy that. It was a bigger one, a more expensive toy.'

'Who suggested buying it?'

She paused for a moment. 'Sonya. We asked what Erik was into and she told us that he wanted that dinosaur. It's a more deluxe version of the plastic ones they all collect.'

Gina exhaled. That line of questioning wasn't as helpful as she'd hoped. Aiden, Stephen, Heather and Kerstin were the only ones left in action who could know about the dinosaur connection. She nudged past Faith and Aiden on the stairs and beckoned Jacob to follow, where she whispered her thoughts into his ear. She pulled her phone from her pocket and stepped outside, calling O'Connor for an update.

'Hi, guv.'

'Anything happening at Heather and Stephen's?'

'No. They've been in bed for a couple of hours now. The lights are off and no one has left.'

'Have you been checking around the back?'

'An officer has been walking around about every twenty minutes. No one has left the road and the four-by-four is still on the drive. They're all locked in and no lights have come on since they went to bed.'

'Call Wyre and ask her to look into the backgrounds again of Heather and Kerstin and also Sonya, while she's at it.'

'Will do. Do you think it's one of them?'

'I know one of them knows something but I don't know how much. I still don't know whether they're nothing more than pawns in this abductor's game. Someone knows more than they're letting on. There's a big reason behind all this and I need to find it. I need links. I need to know why our abductor is insisting on having burning candles left behind at the scenes.'

'I'll call Wyre now.'

'Thank you. We'll be heading back to the station soon so any news, call me straight away.' Gina heard a man mentioning tea and biscuits in the room that O'Connor was watching from. 'I'll let you go. Speak later.'

Jacob hurried out with Faith's phone. 'Guv, there's been a message. I took a photo quickly before it disappeared.'

You failed, now your son will die!

Gina felt her heart sink. She had to save this little boy.

FIFTY-THREE

Harvey runs to the other side of the attic room and gets back under the covers next to Erik where he pulls them over his head. He shakes the other boy over and over again, needing to wake him. If Erik wakes up, he won't feel so alone. Their friend kept telling him about this dinosaur called Ziggy and he's not sure he wants to hear the rest of the story. It's too scary and his little heart still beats fast from when he'd been pulled from under the chair.

He peers over the covers and there is a bowl of chocolates in front of him.

'It's okay, they're yours.'

He doesn't want one. It's too late and his mummy never lets him eat chocolate at this time and he doesn't have his toothbrush. 'Erik, Erik,' he calls.

'Please, Harvey. We need to finish the story.' The person saying they're his friend holds an overstuffed bag and holdall. A painful sounding scream comes from the rooms below. 'Ignore that, it's nothing.'

Harvey doesn't know whether to be scared of the person in front of him or the person below. He doesn't know why he's here and all he wants is to go back to his grandparents' house and see his mum. Maybe his friend needs to finish the story, then he will get to go home.

'Shall we go back to the story?'

He nods and a tear slips down his cold cheek. All he wants is to be back in his own bed, wake up tomorrow and see his friends at school.

'Here, love. Don't cry.'

He takes the tissue that is passed to him.

'Ziggy is scared by the three big dinosaurs and she knows that they will hurt her. They roar and stamp, then they cut her with their big claws. She wants her best friend, the one that promised to stay at the party with her, but her friend is nowhere to be seen. She glances ahead and she sees another big dinosaur. This one is keeping watch to make sure no one is coming. They all hurt Ziggy, really bad, and it hurts more than she's ever been hurt in her life.'

Harvey doesn't want to hear the rest. It started off as a nice story about a dinosaur at a party, now Ziggy has been attacked and there is no one to help her.

'When they finished with Ziggy, they left her there sad and sore. All Ziggy wanted was her friend. She wanted a cuddle and for someone to tell her she was loved but when she called her friend on the phone, she still didn't answer. From then, Ziggy knew she was alone.' His friend began to cry and continued telling the story through a teary face. 'Ziggy felt like she had no friends after that. And as time went on, Ziggy was told she was poorly because of what happened. But then she came up with a plan to be happy. That's where you come into it, Harvey. You and Erik are going to make Ziggy happy because Ziggy loves you both so much.'

He didn't know what to say or what to do. Erik coughed and turned around, rubbing his eyes and murmuring. 'Harvey, it's cold,' he said with a croak as he pulled the blanket over himself.

'Erik!' Harvey hugged his friend.

'See, my lovelies. We are all well and happy. We are all going to be together, forever.'

Their friend continued telling the story of Ziggy and spoke of how it was all about them. Now the two little boys knew every-thing, they could see what needed to be done. After leaning over and whispering a few last words, Erik and Harvey nodded to each other. This person was right, they had to go away and they had to stick together.

'Right, boys. Here, have a drink and go to sleep. It's late. In a few hours we are going on one final big adventure. I need to sort something out first but I won't be long. You have each other now. Are you ready for an adventure?'

They drank their milk, nodded and lay down on the floor bed. Their friend placed another blanket over them. It was warm and soothing. The glow of the lamp soon sent them both into a deep slumber. 'Night, night, Erik,' Harvey whispered.

'Night, night, my children.'

FIFTY-FOUR

Gina had left Jacob with a uniformed officer in the family room at the station, sitting with Faith. She leaned back in her chair, her head pounding hard as she turned on her computer to look for updates. The drink she'd made an hour ago had now gone cold just like her hands and the tip of her burnt nose.

Still they were no further ahead and there was no sign of the two boys. Wyre was doing more background and family checks on their persons of interest and the worst thing was, the abductor knew that Faith had failed. Maybe they'd been at the lock-up, watching from another lock-up, or maybe they had walked past Faith's mother's house and saw the police arrive. There had to be something missing. A link still to find. She pulled out the login details for the *Boyz R Takin it Back* forum that O'Connor had used to set up an account and she entered the chat room.

Women bashing hatred spewed out in every sentence. Then she noticed that VenMan was currently active. There was a conversation on the go. She clicked into it and read the lead up.

VenMan
I gave it to the bitch good and proper tonight! When they can't give

you what you want, it makes you wonder why you bother. All that work, all that effort and the rewards... well let's just say. The juice ain't worth the squeeze.

BeeMan
Good man. Can't let them beat us, these feminazis. Need the good old days. You're doing it for us all. Got turned down again. She was obviously up herself. I guess us guys are best off going alone. Leave the trash out and get on with it. Forget the selfish sex. All they want is our money and to take our kids from us. Bloody used up hags.

VenMan
Yes. Best off alone, mate. But then a readily available shag is out of the question so they're good for something. You're probably a better man than me. No willpower. That's my prob.

BeeMan
You just can't resist the honeypot, but don't let that rule you. You are the boss and keep it that way. Anyway, tell us what happened. Got a pic?

VenMan
Of course I got a pic. Got it as a reminder to her to not speak to me like that again. Bitch will learn. Hmm... why should I show you my pic? How do I know who you are?

BeeMan
No one knows who any of us are, that's the beauty. It's a private forum. Only like-minded people can join. Just show me. My beady little eyeballs would love a glimpse at your honeypot and you, my friend, are going to give this honeybee a treat. Come on, man, I need my sweet fix! Let me see what you did. You know you want to show me or you wouldn't have said anything. It was you that mentioned it. She deserved it so let me see. I am on your side.

VenMan
Okay. Bitch was asleep when I took it so don't get thinking she's dead. Well she isn't dead yet LOL.

BeeMan
Your home life is not my business. If the bitch is dead, the bitch is dead. Brother – I'd trust you over her and if you say she deserved it, she deserved it.

VenMan
Yeah. Too many of them killing us, breaking us, taking our kids, walking all over us, taking our money and our independence. If they were all like my mum, the world would be a better place. We have to put an end to this. Photo uploading!

As the photo appeared, Gina felt herself heave. She instantly placed her hand over her mouth until the nausea subsided. She recognised the eye and cheek of the woman in the photo. Heather lay asleep with dried up blood dripping from her nose. It must have been when she tried to call Gina. When Jacob had gone over to see them. A bit of make-up would have covered it all up. Gina knew exactly how that worked, she'd used make-up to cover every bruise and cut that Terry had ever thrown at her. She was an expert at hiding abuse. Stephen was Terry, nothing more, nothing less.

BeeMan
Oh man, I've literally cum in my pants. That must have showed her.

VenMan
Another tip, BeeMan, if you stop going alone, don't settle for one. Have a few. All the benefits and no responsibility. If they want more, ditch them.

BeeMan
Yeah, marriage wasn't for me. I like you even more now!

She stared at the previous message and went back through her emails. Honeybees and eyeballs. Her heart dropped and she gasped for breath.

Her phone beeped.

I'm still waiting and you, Gina, are running out of time.
Pete. XXX

She could never tell anyone about the emails that Pete Bloxwich had sent to her or the messages. To tell them would be to open every can of worms going and she had to protect herself. If she told Pete that she knew what he was saying online, then he and Stephen would stop talking. She needed them both to continue. Everyone at the station knew who VenMan was, Stephen could be arrested based on what she had just seen and taken a screenshot of, but there was a chance he would give her a lot more to arrest him with and a stronger case to present to the CPS was always a better one. While Heather was now asleep, she was hopefully safe and Stephen would continue to freely speak. O'Connor was positioned across the road so if the lights went on and Stephen kicked off, he would be seen. No, she had to sit on this overnight, then Stephen would finally get his comeuppance. Only she knew who BeeMan was, he was hidden by a VPN but she was personally going to deal with him. She formed a fist with her hand and her knuckles went white.

Briggs entered after giving the slightest of knocks. 'You okay, you must be shattered?'

'No more than anyone else, sir.' She clicked the cross on the webpage and leaned back.

He slumped into the chair opposite her desk, rubbed his eyes and massaged his temples. 'Any news?'

She wondered if she should come clean with what she knew. 'No, nothing. I'm still watching Stephen online while O'Connor is watching the house. Don't worry, I won't be the one to confront him with anything. I'm merely collecting information for Jacob.'

'Anything on the personal front?'

She swallowed and bit the inside of her cheek before answering. She had told him just about every secret she had but this was hers and she would deal with Pete. 'No. I think you're right. Pete has nothing and he's just trying it on, seeing what he can dig up.' *Play it down.*

Briggs raised his eyebrows. 'You seem a lot surer of things now. Has something happened? Something you're not telling me about.'

She smiled. 'I just know he has nowhere to go with it. You were right all along.' She felt a flutter in her stomach. Pete Bloxwich could either accept that she had enough to bring him down and ruin his life or he could happily let them both fall together. That, she wasn't prepared for but he was a selfish little man who got off on intimidating people into saying enough to ruin their own lives. He'd met his match with Gina. It was all or nothing and she was willing to take the gamble. She went down with him or they both got to keep their secrets. She hated the fact that she couldn't outwardly expose who he was but there would be another time, another place and now she knew where he lurked, she was going to keep a close eye on him in the future.

'I know there's more.'

She should have known that she couldn't hide anything from Briggs. She turned her computer screen and clicked on the screenshots so that they filled the screen. After reading, Briggs sat back. 'We have enough here to arrest Stephen on. What are we waiting for?'

'There is something happening amongst the group of friends and someone knows something and that may well lead us to who's behind all this. If we bring Stephen in, he'll clam up, go no comment for the next day or two. We don't have a day or two. We need them out there, leading us to Erik and Harvey. O'Connor is watching them. He's not going anywhere.'

'Okay, but if we're no closer in the next few hours, I want Stephen brought in and not by you. O'Connor is there so he can bring him in. We know that this is his account and we can just about see that the person in that photo is Heather. That's all we need, but I agree with you. We need to find those children now so we can't waste any time. Do we know who he's talking to?'

She shook her head. 'No, the others are using a VPN. The tech team are working on it but we might never know who the others are.'

'What sickos.' Briggs stood, walked over to her and squeezed her shoulder.

'The world is full of them.' She placed a hand over his. Erik and Harvey still needed her to be on form – at least she hoped they did. 'What if the children are dead and we're too late.' She bowed her head. 'What if this time, we've lost them?'

'Come on, we are not sitting here like a pair of failures. The whole department is working their socks off. Forensics are pulling all-nighters too and they're liaising with the fire department. No one is resting at the moment. We all want to see those children brought back safely. We are going to find them and we are going to get whoever has them.'

'The abductor... they leave a candle. They are remembering some loss in their lives, something to do with the group of friends. The gym buddies and their partners. Has Wyre found anything in their backgrounds?'

'Nothing so far. We have the basics, addresses and names of family. Most are fairly local. Kerstin's parents are divorced and her father lives just outside Cleevesford. The only family tragedy that keeps coming up is Terry's death and that involves you.'

'All this, the children and the fires, and the candles, it's nothing to do with me. You know that, don't you?' Her heart felt as though it was bouncing in her chest. What a stupid thing to say.

'Calm down, Gina. You're not even in the frame. No one is saying anything but they do know the details of what happened to Terry. They have now seen everything in the files as a part of investigating Stephen and his past. I can assure you that they will be discreet. You also spoke to the attending officer at the scene of Terry's death. She asked how you got your black eye and you told her that Terry had hit you the day before. They know, Gina. I just wanted to make you aware of that, which is why I popped in to see you. I'm sorry they know. I know you are not that person anymore and you wouldn't want them to see you as a victim but they're on your side.'

She looked away, unable to disguise the redness of her face or how humiliated she felt. She would forever be known as Gina, the victim, and she hated that more than ever. 'Who knows?'

'Everyone involved in the case. Jacob has been handling that side well, trying to keep anyone from needing to ask you anything about Stephen. They all love you, you know. Those people out there, they're your family. I'm your family.'

She placed a hand over her mouth. 'I don't know how I feel about this. Can you leave me alone?' The hand she had over his fell and he nodded before heading to the door.

'You know where I am. I am always there for you.'

'Thanks, Chris.' She forced a smile and he left.

Now everyone knew about her past; they already knew how her husband died but now they knew he mistreated her. Jacob knew a little and some of them had maybe suspected something had happened but it was all out there now. They'd seen the interview notes where she'd opened up a bit to the officer. How she'd let slip about Terry's cruelty. She no longer felt like a survivor, she felt exposed and she wondered how much more would be exposed. That was down to how she handled Pete Bloxwich. First she had to get him to admit that he was BeeMan. She knew from his wording that it had to be him. She also knew what a horrible slimeball he was and him being involved in a forum like the *Boyz R Takin it Back* didn't surprise her at all. But there was something more pressing she had to do. Working out where Erik and Harvey were was her priority.

Wyre burst through the door. 'Guv, you have to come quick. Stephen has just left the house, crashed O'Connor's car off the road with his four-wheel-drive, crushing the side of it and he's driven off.'

'What about Heather?'

'There's no answer at the door.'

'I'm heading over there now.'

'But, guv, should you go to Heather and Stephen's house?'

'He's not there and Heather could be hurt. You and Jacob can go up to the door, I'll stay in the car, but I'm not sitting here staring into space. Are a team tracking Stephen's car or following him?'

'They lost him, guv. With all that's going on, we couldn't get anyone over there quickly enough. All units are on the lookout for him and we hope that he's picked up by ANPR. Everyone is on alert. Officers have arrived at Kerstin's mother's house, they're also guarding Sonya's even though she's not there. Poor Kapoor is still at the hospital guarding Sonya's room. There's something else.'

'What?'

'When the officers arrived to speak to Kerstin Godwin, her mother said that she wasn't in. She also said they argued and she walked out about ten last night and she didn't come home, leaving her with the two children. I don't know what the hell's going on.'

'Let's go. First to Heather's. We need to see if she's okay. Someone must know where Kerstin is and Heather has to have some idea where Stephen went. I mean, ramming O'Connor's car. He's up to something big... What if he has the children or has something to do with it? But why?' Gina grabbed her coat and turned her computer around to show Wyre the screenshots of Heather. 'We now have reason to believe that Heather is in that house and she's hurt so you can enter the house. I'll fill you in on the way. Call O'Connor. If she doesn't answer, he has to go in. Her life could be in danger.'

FIFTY-FIVE

It's time. I have to go. 'Come on, boys,' I call, but I can't move them. I shouldn't have given them that last drink. There was only a bit of crushed sleeping tablet in the mix. They shouldn't be out this heavy. I suppose I'll have to carry them out to the car.

Loud screaming comes from downstairs. I hurry out of the attic and down to the bottom floor where the single bed on loan from the hospital fills the living room. All his furniture has been pushed against the one wall and a settee stands against the window, blocking out the view to the outside. The place stinks of every bodily fluid and it turns my stomach. You think a person would get used to it but instead, it begins to coat your nostrils and becomes a part of you. Everywhere I go now, I feel as though I smell of death. Even with all the showers and extra deodorant I'm getting through, I hallucinate the smell. He sits up and opens his mouth to speak but he can't, not since losing his tongue. The cancer well and truly took that in an operation that failed to contain it and now it's taking him. My purpose here is over and it saddens me to say goodbye but he doesn't have long and I know he will understand my decision to leave a little early. In a couple of days, I'll call someone to check on him, social services maybe. With cuts and my promise to attend to all his needs, they've literally left me alone, pleased that their workload is reduced. There's still a key safe. They have the number and they keep asking if I need help. Well, now I will finally need them.

It's been handy being at home all the time while I nursed my father through all this, but I've done all I can now. There is only one more person who needs to pay and we have a meeting time. When I've finished with that loose end, my journey to a new life will start. I have my new passport and medical card, so I can start again. The dead part of me can stay here and be nothing more than something I think of fleetingly, what's left is my future. It's a shame that innocents got hurt but if people make bad choices in life, especially when it comes to those they associate with, then a backlash will come. The bigger picture is what's important. Those tiny boys are the bigger picture and I've removed evil from their lives. They deserved more and I have given them that for as long as I can. Only I can protect them and I will. If I can't protect them, we are all better off dead.

I don't fear death, I fear painful life events. Death is nothing. Just like we were nothing before we were born. I don't remember that either.

I will never be scared again. I refuse to be. Coming to terms with the so-called end is empowering.

My father screams in pain so I do the only thing I can. I pour him the largest measure of whisky ever and I hold it to his lips. He pushes it away and grabs his pen and pad. His spidery scrawl begins to form words and I see tears running down his cheeks.

Please let the children go. Please. I love you.

Tears now run down my face as I see his pain. I wish I could have told him what had happened to me. Maybe he could have helped; taken me to the police. He could have been my rock. I think back to that night, the one where I was abandoned by my friend and left alone out the back of that nightclub, to be humiliated and hurt. That was only the start of it. If only that's where the ordeal had ended. That was just the beginning. 'I can't, Dad.' I pause then I hold the glass of whisky to his lips again. This time he drinks with tears in his eyes. We both know what's happening here. He knows that I will soon join him. He can't stand the pain so he has no choice. His old body is riddled and it kills me to think what he's going through.

'Come on, Dad. This will help you.' It will help him. I pour it down and he chokes and guzzles. It's a struggle but he keeps drinking. For a moment, I think he's drowning in the liquid as he coughs it out but he continues to take more liquid. His stare meets mine and he places a knowing and frail hand on my arm. We talked about this so we both know what's happening. I climb onto his dirty bed and lie next to him, holding him as he allows the liquid to take effect. 'You're going to go to sleep now, Dad. I love you. I love you so much.' I hold him as the weight of his bald head falls onto my chest. His breaths are rapid and shallow. I place the glass on the side table and all I see is a bit of residue from the crushed pills stuck to the one side. 'Not long now, Daddy.' Daddy, I called him that until I was about ten. Tears stream down my cheeks. A person shouldn't have to live with this much pain. It is now I wonder if I can live with mine. I hold him and my heart aches as I recall happy memories. Those of him putting me on his shoulders when I was little, or swinging me around. The time he was shouting from around the swimming pool as I competed as a teen and the big hug he gave me when I got my first job. I couldn't have asked for a better or more loving father. He did everything for me. All I want is to be as good as he was. If I am, I know I will have fulfilled my life's ambition. He wouldn't let those children suffer with the parents they'd been dealt.

He falls asleep next to me. Kissing him on his head, I remove my body from his and I sit on the edge. For a moment I think I hear him asking me why I didn't tell him about *that night*. Why I kept the pain to myself. He tells me he could have helped me and this wouldn't be happening now. I know he's right and I know he's not really talking to me. This is just another of the many conversations that run through my head.

I turn to look at him and wonder how long it takes a person to die. Is it a minute, five, an hour or maybe several? All I know is I gave him far too many tablets and a glass of whisky. I lift his frail hand and kiss it. 'I couldn't risk you ever looking at me and being disgusted, Dad. There are some things a father should never have to hear. You were a good dad and I will always love you.'

It's now time for me to leave him. Pulling the sheet up to his chin, I now know he won't wake up. He's not gone but he's not coming back. I can tell by how shallow his breathing has become. Has he found peace? Yes, in the form of a deep sleep from which he'll never wake up. His pain is over. My job here is done and now I have important things to do. Time to get the boys out of here. My phone beeps. The meeting is on.

Running back up the stairs, I listen for footsteps or talking but I can't hear anything. I grab the bags containing the few items I need for my new life and I pop them down by the door. As soon as light comes, we are gone.

FIFTY-SIX

Wyre pulled up next to O'Connor's smashed-in car and Jacob pulled up behind them.

Gina unclipped her seat belt and opened the window. 'What is it?'

'She's not there, guv. There is blood on the bed, on one of the pillows.'

'Any sign of the children?' Gina knew that was a stupid question. Had O'Connor found the children, it would have been the first thing he'd have said but he may have seen a sign or a clue while looking for Heather.

'No sign at all that any children have ever been in that house.'

'Thanks.' Wyre went to get out of the car. 'Wait, we need to speak to Kerstin Godwin's parents. There's nothing else we can do here, right now.' Gina quickly filled O'Connor in with what she'd seen on the *Boyz R Takin it Back* forum. 'If anyone sees Stephen, we need to arrest him and bring him in straight away. He's dangerous. Any sign of Heather let me know immediately. How did she slip out without you seeing?'

'I don't know. There were times I went to the toilet or Smith poured another drink. He walked around the back every twenty minutes but saw nothing.'

'She must have left out the back, or maybe Stephen has her in the car.'

'I only saw him in his car. She said hers was at the garage earlier so she didn't have any transport. We can't discount the boot, though, or her leaving out the back.'

Gina stepped out of the car and beckoned Jacob over. He closed his car door and ran over. 'Guv, I'll stay here with O'Connor until more uniformed officers arrive.'

'Great.' She spotted PC Smith standing outside the door. 'If Stephen comes back, arrest him. If Heather comes back, we need her brought in for questioning. Let's take a quick look around the back of the house.' Gina started jogging to the end of the row, sloshing in every puddle. She cut down the path with O'Connor huffing and puffing as he tried to keep up and they arrived at the back of Heather and Stephen's house. She reached up and opened the gate. 'It's not locked which means she most likely left around the back. Have you checked the garden yet?' Gina thought that maybe she'd run from Stephen after he'd hurt her again.

'Since we spoke, we only managed to get in the house thinking that Heather might be hurt. That's all. No one has been in the garden.' Gina pushed the gate open and took her pencil torch from her pocket. That's when they both saw a small candle in a jar sitting on the bird table but it was unlit, like the flame had been extinguished. Gina hurried over. There was nothing written on this one. It looked like whoever had planned this had not got to finish the job.

Wyre ran around the corner to join them.

'Wyre? Heather and Kerstin. One of them has to be pulling the strings here. Both aren't at home right now. Where are they? What do we know about them?'

As the downpour continued, Wyre spoke. 'Kerstin, we don't know much. She doesn't have a criminal record. Married her childhood sweetheart and divorced four years later. Met Cameron a year later and eventually married him. Mother and father are divorced. She's staying with her mother and stepfather at the moment. Father lives in Cleevesford too. That is basically it.'

'How about Heather?'

'As we know, she works in IT. No criminal record. Mother lives in Birmingham and Dad lives in Cleevesford.'

'Both local. No records. I'll need the addresses of Kerstin's father and Heather's mother and father. We need to widen the search. These women have to be somewhere and so do those children and I want to get to them before anyone else is hurt. We still know there's another victim to go. That candle was there for Stephen; of that I'm sure.'

'There's something else I found, just before we left but I don't know how relevant it is.'

'It could be everything at this moment in time.' Tiredness had been replaced by caffeine-fuelled adrenalin and Gina felt more wide-eyed than ever.

'After speaking to some of Cameron's colleagues, one of them told us that he had a fling about a year ago with someone he met at a sales exhibition. Kerstin was livid and came to his place of work and tipped all his chopped up shirts on his desk after finding a message on his phone. This colleague also said that they soon made up and put it all behind them, after he claimed that it was a drunken mistake.'

'That would give Kerstin motive for wanting her husband, Cameron, dead. It's a start.' Gina grabbed her hair and exhaled. 'Let's get over there now.'

FIFTY-SEVEN

Sonya writhed in the bedsheets, half awake and half asleep. She slipped back into her dream, the one where she was in prison and Erik got to stay with Justin and Charlene forever. She imagined that Erik would forget who she was eventually, that Justin would never bring him to visit. Then she woke with a start, bolt upright, she shook her head to rid herself of the confusion that lay like a heavy fog. The drug hangover, results of a sleep so deep that nothing would have woken her. Erik was still missing. He had to be because the police officer outside her door hadn't told her anything, but then again, she'd been asleep. 'Hey.' Her voice was barely audible and her throat was so dry, she tried again and croaked.

Water. She reached with shaky hands for the jug and poured it all over the bedside cabinet instead of in the glass. Blinking a few times, she cleared her vision. It was still dark outside and she was still in a hospital gown and cuffed to one bar. She shouldn't have gone quite so mad when she was brought in. She remembered hitting a nurse in the face and pushing down a security guard. Maybe they wouldn't have cuffed her had she not but it was like being possessed? Her son had been taken and all those people, they were in the way and she had to get out. She needed to get out, to find him. The abductor had told her that they'd killed him. What was she meant to do?

Her mind kept whirring through everything but she could barely keep her thoughts together. One minute she was thinking about taking Erik to school, the next, she'd flitted to an argument with Justin. She remembered the detective who asked her about any big life events such as deaths; something that might be important.

Think, think.

There was something but she said she'd never betray Kerstin's trust and tell, besides, what did it have to do with her and Erik? Nothing whatsoever. She shook her head as she lay there, listening to her heartbeat thrumming through her ears. What Kerstin told her had nothing to do with Erik's abduction – nothing.

She shouted again. What if she was wrong? 'Hey.' This time it was clearer. She rattled the cuffs on the bed bar as loudly as she could and eventually she got the officer's attention.

'Do you need a nurse?' The young uniformed woman stared sympathetically as Sonya sat up a little more.

'No, I need to speak to the detective, the one who was here before. I have something I want to tell her.'

FIFTY-EIGHT

Gina ran along the row of terraced houses looking for number ninety-two. 'Why haven't any of the houses got numbers on them?'

'It's always the way, guv.' Wyre ran and spoke effortlessly while Gina could feel a stitch coming on. Drains gurgled and thunder rumbled gently in the background.

Rain landed in large cold blobs, covering Gina's face and slipping under her coat and down her neck. Even her bra was now damp. 'Here. It has to be this one.' The front room light was on. Even though morning was breaking, it was still dark and would be for hours. Gina pushed through the stiff waist height gate and it creaked as if it might break if she applied any more force.

Wyre let out a small shriek as she skidded along the mossy slabs then a security light lit them up.

Gina knocked and listened out. A door banged, then a shadow blocked the light in the hall through the window. The figure slid the chain across and opened up. 'DI Harte and DC Wyre.' They held up their identification.

'I don't know where my daughter is, please help me find her.' The woman's tangled light red hair was piled high in a clip on her head. The lines on her face appeared harsh on her puce-like skin. Gina could see the resemblance to her daughter but the woman was a lot shorter and rounder. Like a small apple in a dressing gown.

'May we come in?'

The woman opened the door and led them through the house into a dining room. An old scratched Welsh dresser filled the one wall. Gina edged into the corner, feeling a little trapped. The room wasn't quite big enough for the chairs and the chunky furniture. With every move, Gina elbowed a wall. 'Sorry, we've spoken to your daughter before but we don't know your name.'

'It's Trish.'

'Trish, do you have any idea where Kerstin might go?'

'No. She has nowhere to go. Her house is burnt down, she's lost her husband and I know she doesn't have a lot of money at the moment. I know that because she borrowed money from me and my husband a while back, saying that Cam wasn't doing so well at work. We've all had so many fallouts. I mean, I kept on at her for still being a member of that expensive gym and keeping her nail appointments. I was so angry at the time.'

'Did you argue this evening?'

'A little.'

'Can you tell me what it was about?'

Wyre began making notes.

'It was stupid. She wanted to go out and wouldn't tell me where to. Not that I monitor where she goes, she's left me with the children, that's all. Leo wouldn't settle and I didn't want to be alone with him and be up half the night. I know she's lost Cam and a lot has happened but her children need her more than ever. They're so little. I told her she needed to stay here and be there for them. She'd also had a couple of glasses of wine with us. Instead of her being more relaxed, she seemed hyped about something and kept texting someone on her phone.'

'Could she have been going to meet someone?'

Trish rubbed what looked to be a slightly red eye. Gina imagined that she'd been up most of the night looking after the unsettled children, wondering where her daughter was. 'Maybe.'

'Do you know who she might be going to meet?'

'No, but...' The woman pressed her lips together.

'What is it?'

'Maybe it's a man. She's seemed distracted for a few weeks now. Disappearing off here and there, not telling me where she's been but expecting me to look after the children. I know she's never forgiven Cam for some one-night stand he had even though they'd been playing happy families. I'm worried for her too. With all that's been happening, maybe she's a target for this killer. If she was meant to be in her house with Cam on the night he was killed... maybe they've come for her, lured her into some trap. I don't know... I have so many things going through my head right now.'

Gina couldn't sit around the table any longer, not with two abducted children. It was possible that Kerstin was either the puller of strings or the person that was about to commit the next murder; or both. One more person to go... and that had to be Stephen. If Kerstin had the missing children, where could she have taken them to? 'Are there any other premises that Kerstin has access to? Another house, place of work? That sort of thing.'

'I can't think. She's your classic homemaker, she doesn't go out to work. Wait, they have a holiday home in Devon but it's nearly always rented out.'

Fiddling with her fingers, Gina leaned forward. 'We'll need that address so that we can check it out.'

Trish pulled her phone from the pocket of her dressing gown and scrolled. 'Here it is.' She handed the phone over to Gina with the contact page showing. Gina passed it to Wyre who noted it down.

'I'll get that checked out, guv.' Wyre squeezed her tiny frame out of the almost blocked in chair and left the room to make the call. Local police would need to do an urgent check on the property for any sign of Kerstin or the children.

It was now just Trish and Gina. 'Is there anything else you can tell me that might help us to find Kerstin?'

The woman stared blankly and shook her head.

'How has she seemed?'

'Up until this evening, like a woman who has just lost her home and her husband. She and the children have been devastated.'

'What do you think changed tonight?'

'She changed. She had to be going to meet someone. I can't think of any other reason why she'd run out the way she did.'

In Gina's mind, Kerstin would have had time to leave that candle and jar in Heather and Stephen's garden. 'And where are the children now?'

'They're both in her bed, in the spare room.'

'Have you checked on them?' Gina felt her pulse picking up.

'Not since one in the morning. It took me ages to get them down, the last thing I wanted to do was to wake them up. They're really bad sleepers. I don't know how Kerstin copes with them. I heard about the missing boy on the news, saw the father talking. Kerstin said he and his ex-partner were her friends... the children.' The woman got up and shuffled out of the room before running up the stairs.

Gina followed and almost bumped into a tall man with a neat grey beard who was squinting as the light went on. 'What's going on?' he asked.

'Nothing, dear, just checking on the children. The police are here.'

'Is Kerstin back yet?'

'No.' Trish gently pushed the door open and Gina peered over her shoulder to see the two sleeping children, tucked up in the double bed.

Gina's phone went. 'Kapoor, what have you got?'

'Hi, guv. I'm still looking after Sonya, at the hospital. She's insistent that she speaks to you, now. I asked her to tell me what it was about but she refused, saying she wants to speak to the detective on the case; the same one she spoke to before.'

FIFTY-NINE

Erik stirred and saw that Harvey was still asleep. He was glad not to be alone anymore and he was happier that his best friend was going to go away on an adventure with him. Although he'd miss Mummy, he'd thought about things a lot. Ziggy wasn't just a made-up story that his friend had told him. It was more than that and Erik was a clever boy; that's what all his teachers told him. He knew that the story was real and the bad dinosaurs were too. He didn't want to ever come across the bad dinosaurs, not after what they did.

Soon, he would call Mummy and tell her that he was okay; their friend said he could. Harvey would be okay too. Erik would make sure they'd be fine. He understood who the bad dinosaurs were and what they'd done and now he knew the whole story, everything had changed. He gave Harvey a nudge but he was still asleep.

The door opened with a squeak and his friend crept in, smiling. 'You've done such a good job looking after Harvey. This is for you.' She passed him a plastic dinosaur, this time it was blue, like the colour of the sea. He smiled and took it from her.

'Thank you.' He hugged it closely then he swallowed. He missed the big dinosaur he had at home, the one he'd had for his birthday, and named Big Roar because that's the sound it made when he was playing with it. They were going away and it was going to be a big adventure. He was meant to be happy, like the night before Christmas. 'Can I call Mummy?'

'Of course, I said you could when we got there.'

'But she'll be really worried about me, and Harvey's mummy will be worried too.' He could see that she'd been crying and her hair was a different colour too. Something wasn't right.

'But you know me, they know me. I'll call them and tell them for you. How about that? Then she'll know you're safe.'

He fidgeted in the bed covers. He trusted her to call his mummy but he really wanted to do it himself and not when they'd got to wherever they were going for their adventure. 'But I want to call her now.'

'No and if you keep going on, you're not having that dinosaur.' She snatched the toy from his hands. That had never happened before. He shuffled back on the mattress and bit his knuckle.

'Look, I'm sorry. It's just you can't call her until we arrive. It will be a surprise, okay?' She passed the dinosaur back to him and smiled.

Erik didn't believe her now. Something had changed. His mouth contorted and he began to sob, tears flooding his face. 'I want to call my mummy.'

'Stop crying,' she whispered but he didn't stop. He cried louder, this time hoping that the man monster downstairs would come. Maybe he would let him call his mummy. 'Stop crying,' she yelled as she grabbed his arms and shook him. She thrust a small bottle of pop towards him. 'Drink this.'

He pushed it away. 'Don't want it.'

'I said drink it.'

'No, it makes me sleepy. Don't want to sleep.'

Without warning, she pulled his head back and began to pour the liquid down his throat. After a few minutes of writhing and turning, he knew he couldn't win. She was much stronger than he was. She poured again. He half choked, coughed and swallowed but it was going down. 'You're not my friend, are you?' he asked between coughs.

'Of course I am. I just need a moment to think. Please be quiet while I sort everything out.' Moments later, he felt his eyelids drooping. As he began to drift, all he could hear was her throwing the toys at the wall and yelling. He should have waited until they got to their surprise place and then he could have called his mummy just like they'd planned to. She wouldn't have been so angry. Maybe he should have kept quiet but it was too late now. As things crashed all around him, he couldn't fight the dreams that were taking over any longer. This time, they were nightmares, the evil dinosaur was coming to eat him and there was nothing he could do about it. He couldn't run, he couldn't turn away and he couldn't fight it and his mummy couldn't save him either.

SIXTY

Gina and Wyre passed a man in a wheelchair who was puffing away on a vape by the entrance of Cleevesford General as a woman handed him a box of takeaway noodles. They hurried past the closed café and straight down the corridor until they reached the ward. Gina pressed the buzzer and waited for the nurse behind the desk to buzz them in.

'Too early for visitors, I'm afraid.'

Gina and Wyre held up their identification. 'We're here to see Sonya Baker.'

'Oh yes, sorry. Head straight down to the end of the corridor, last room on your right. You'll see your colleague.'

'Thank you.' Gina left the desk before the nurse finished her sentence. As she reached the end of the corridor, PC Kapoor stood.

'I've just given her a cup of tea, guv. Tried again to talk to her but she said she only wanted to talk to you.'

'Thank you.'

'You both look like you could use a drink too. While you're in with her, shall I grab some coffees from the machine?'

Gina nodded. 'Yes, please.' With her energy dwindling, Gina knew that a bit of caffeine would keep her going. 'How are you coping? I'm surprised you haven't been relieved yet.'

'There's no one to take over, guv. Everyone is out on the case.'

Gina knew the team were all running on empty but all of them wanted to do their best to bring the boys home safely. She entered the small corner room where Sonya sat up in bed under a dim light. Gina sat on the chair close to Sonya and Wyre sat the other side, almost blocking the door. 'Sonya, how are you feeling?'

'I'm really sorry about what I did to the nurse and pushing the security guard over. I thought my son was dead and I wanted to get out and I knew you wouldn't let me. I thought if I got out I could hurry up and save him just in time because as a parent, you think you can always protect your child. But, I couldn't protect him. I did the unthinkable to keep Erik alive and I failed. I'm sorry, please tell the nurse I'm sorry too.'

'We will. What is it you'd like to tell us?'

She shook her head and then stared up at the light, trying to fight back a tear. 'I don't know if it has anything to do with what's going on but I remember you asking if any life events had occurred and I kept thinking of death. I mulled it over in my head. Who'd died? Had someone been hurt? Did anyone mention an accident? I couldn't think of anything, but then I remembered something. It was something Kerstin had said, when she was drunk one night. We were at a wine bar in Birmingham with everyone else. I caught her staring at Cameron as if she didn't know him. We got talking... I can't believe I'm saying this. She's going to hate me and I can't see how it has anything to do with what's happened to my son.'

Gina tilted her head, knowing that breaking loyalties when it came to friends was hard. 'It might not, Sonya, but without knowing, we can't eliminate that it has anything to do with Erik's abduction either. Like you, all we want is your little boy found and brought home.' Gina could see Sonya's thoughts rushing through her head, she'd grimace, then go to speak, then begin to pick her nails.

'I want that too.' Sonya's bottom lip began to quiver slightly, she closed her eyes for a second, swallowed with a click and then opened them again. 'She told me that Cam had confessed to sleeping with a woman once who then claimed that he had raped her. But it was all a mistake, she said. Cam couldn't rape anyone. Kerstin said that the woman was drunk, that Cam was drunk and they both got carried away. Anyway, that was it. I don't know who this woman was or when it happened, although it was way before Kerstin met Cam, years ago. He might have been a student, I'm not sure.' Sonya paused. 'So when you asked me that question, that's all I could think about.' She exhaled and brought her hands down on her lap. 'Kerstin will never speak to me again, now.'

'I'm sure she'll understand. You're doing everything you can for your son. He has to come first. When was this?'

'I can't remember exactly when but it was around July. Stephen had brought his new girlfriend, Heather. There was Faith and Glen. Me, alone, because Justin was obviously seeing Charlene then. And Kerstin and Cameron were there.'

'And how did Cameron seem that night?'

'Tense. I caught him and Kerstin bickering, not that I could hear. I saw the angry expressions on their faces.'

'There's something else, isn't there?' Gina could sense that Sonya was holding back. Silence filled the room and it was soon broken by Wyre turning the page in her notebook, ready to start making more notes.

'I don't know.' She grimaced and continued to bite her already worn down nail.

'Like I said, it doesn't matter how insignificant what you saw may seem. If you saw or heard something on that night, please tell me so that we can look into it. Someone took Erik and it's someone you all know.'

'But Kerstin wouldn't do that to me.'

Someone close to them had taken the children so Gina couldn't deny Sonya's statement. 'What else happened that night?'

'Nothing. It was just a look but it gave me the creeps. I asked Kerstin about it a few days after and she said I was being silly and that what she said about Cam and the rape allegation was nothing, that she'd made a mistake. That night, I also saw Cameron staring at Heather like he was deep in thought or confused. Then I saw Kerstin spot him looking at Heather. I guessed she was jealous because of his one-night stand. She struggled to trust him after that and if Cam even looked in the wrong direction, she'd nudge him and give him an angry stare. When Kerstin saw him looking at Heather, she nudged him so hard, he dropped his drink all over the floor and the bartender had to come over to clean up. There was glass everywhere. Again, I saw them arguing. The music was too loud to hear anything. She came over and announced that they were going and that was it. The rest of us carried on and had a good night.' Sonya took a deep breath. 'I can't see how that has anything to do with Erik but there you have it.'

Sonya grabbed Gina's arm with a pinch that almost pierced her skin.

'I just want to know he's alive, unhurt and safe. Please find him. Promise me you will. I don't care what happens to me, I only care about him.' Tears began to fall over her cheeks.

Gina would love nothing more than to be able to promise Sonya that Erik was all of those things. Alive, safe and unhurt, but she couldn't. 'I'm not going to rest or stop until we find him, I can promise you that.'

Sonya sobbed and used the bedsheet as a tissue, wiping her eyes and nose. 'It has to be Kerstin, it has to be. Things were never the same after that night. I can't put my finger on it, but they weren't.'

Wyre's phone rang. 'O'Connor.'

Gina said her goodbyes to Sonya and they stepped outside the room, promising to keep her updated. Kapoor passed them both a welcome hot drink and she sipped as she listened to Wyre finishing her conversation.

'The cottage in Devon, Kerstin isn't there. It's empty,' Wyre said.

Gina's shoulders slumped and she leaned against the wall. 'Those children have to be somewhere. We need to widen the search. Kerstin and Heather's fathers. They both live in Cleevesford. As far as I'm concerned that's access to other properties.' She turned her attention to Wyre. 'Do we have addresses?'

'Yes, guv. On the system. I'll just get them now.' Wyre began tapping and scrolling on her phone.

'Is Justin Baker conscious yet?'

Wyre shook her head, her black ponytail swishing. 'No, guv. Still out of it. His burns are deep and he's looking at surgery later today.'

'Okay, we'll take one address and call Jacob to take the other. That's two houses to check out and I feel we're getting nearer.' Gina glanced out of the window. With it being almost eight in the morning, rush hour traffic would pick up. They had no time to waste.

As they left the hospital, Gina stopped. 'This all has something to do with that rape allegation and what was said that night. Cameron was staring at Heather. Kerstin makes them leave in a jealous fit. I think there's more to this. They are central to this. We need Heather and Kerstin found now. They are the key to finding the children.'

SIXTY-ONE

I fumble with the central locking as I carry several bags and cases. I'm loaded up like a carthorse, straps across me, bags flapping against my hips with every step I take. With the keys in my mouth, I open the boot and throw in all the bags. I have some things of my father's so that I can remember him. His favourite aftershave will always keep me close to him forever. I think of my new life; new family, new house that I've already paid the rent on and new start-up in Scotland; far, far away. I like my new name too. Sophie suits me. I look like a Sophie and I want to be a Sophie. I don't want to be me anymore.

Through the morning fog, I see my dad's neighbour leaving his house so I keep still. The last thing I need is for anyone to see me. Grey clouds above keep the morning in darkness and the spitting rain makes him hurry.

He turns to walk along the path so I half cover my face with my hood.

'Morning. How's your dad doing?'

Damn, he wants to stop and talk. He also knows it's me but why wouldn't he? I've been attending to my dad's care for months now. Everyone around here has seen me but I didn't want anyone to see me with my new hair colour and the glasses; all carefully chosen to turn me into Sophie. I slip the glasses off and pull the drawstrings around my hood so that it tightens over my face. I can't reveal my hair. I stand on the pavement, trying to distract him from the car I'm about to drive off in. This is a car in Sophie's name. Sophie died when she was little and she would be my age now. It was so easy in the end. 'He's really poorly but we're managing okay.'

'Poor geezer, I know. We're all so sorry to hear how bad he's been. I know some of the neighbours have knocked but I guess he's been too poorly to answer.'

I nod and try not to think of my poor dad and I can't even tell this neighbour that he's now at peace and out of pain. 'He can't manage the door anymore but I'll tell him that you asked about him. He'll be happy to hear about that.' I turn towards the car, hoping that this conversation is over. This man has to get to work soon, surely.

From the corner of my eye, I see the net curtain upstairs flicker and a little yell screeches out of my dad's open front door. 'Sorry, I have to go, my dad is calling.'

The man scrunches his brow and I know why. That didn't sound much like a man in his late sixties. One of the kids has woken up and is walking around upstairs. 'Well, send him my regards.'

'Will do.' I wave. The man stops and looks up towards the bedroom, then he turns to go back into his house. 'Whoops, forgot my phone,' he says overly loud. 'Forget my own head if it wasn't screwed on.'

I run up the stairs and grab Harvey's hand. The confused little boy doesn't resist. I drag him back up to the attic with me and I see that Erik is out cold. I lift him up, struggling to carry the dead weight.

'Am I going home, now?' Harvey asks as he tugs on my coat.

Sweat pools at my hairline and it itches too. I don't think I washed the dye out very well.

'Your hair is different.'

I wish Harvey would shut up because I really need to think.

'Is Erik still asleep?'

'Yes, Erik is asleep and yes, you're going home.' I don't tell him that home is with me in Scotland; either that or we all end this together and be with my dad. This is either the end or a new beginning. I hope it's the latter but I'm prepared for the former. On telling Harvey that he's going home, he follows me obediently and shuts up.

I check my bag. I've forgotten something and I can't leave it. It forms the last part of my plan. I've sent the text and this time I'm going to do the deed myself. One more person must pay for their crime and it is going to happen in the exact way I plan for it to. I hurry upstairs. There it is, a candle in a jar, all ready for my next victim. I leave Harvey alone on the landing. His large hazel eyes make my heart melt. He trusts me like only a child can. I only hope that I can trust him to do what I say. 'Just wait there a minute. Whatever you do, don't move.'

SIXTY-TWO

As Gina pulled up outside the house, a police car pulled up behind her and two uniformed officers waited for her to signal what they would all do next. She glanced in her rear-view mirror and out the front. There was no one around.

Her phone rang and she grabbed it. 'Jacob, what you got?'

'Nothing, guv. We're just at Kerstin's father's house and her father was in but he said he hasn't seen her all night. He spoke to her yesterday and he allowed us to look in the house. There's no one else there.'

Gina glanced up at Heather's father's house and stared at the old net curtain. Several cars were parked up the kerb and on drives.

'Thanks, maybe you should get over here.'

The back door of their target house banged against the frame.

'On my way.'

Another call came straight through.

'Sir.' She waited for DCI Briggs to speak.

'We've had a call from a concerned neighbour about an address that I see is connected to the abduction case. He claims to have seen and heard a child coming in his neighbour, Carl Walton's, house, only Mr Walton doesn't have any young children. The man also claims that Mr Walton's daughter, Heather, was acting strangely on the path just a short while ago.'

'He heard a child.' A child was alive, she only hoped that both of them were. 'We're outside that house now, guv. So the children are in there?'

'The neighbour heard one child. He also said that Mr Walton has late stage cancer and is bed and housebound.'

'So we have a vulnerable adult in there too.'

'Yes.'

'I'm going in.'

'Gina, just play it safe. Remember there are two children involved and we know what this person is capable of. We don't know what she will do.'

Gina swallowed and opened her car door, stepping out into the damp morning. She glanced up and saw the man next door looking out of his living room window. She was going to have to treat Heather delicately. Was Stephen with her and where was Kerstin? So many questions and so few answers. 'We have to save those children,' she said to Wyre. She listened and all she could hear was the hum of traffic and the clopping sound of someone's shoes as they walked their dog on the other side of the road. She couldn't hear any children. The other officers waited on standby. Waves of fear travelled through her body. She couldn't find two dead children, not today... not any day.

SIXTY-THREE

Kicking the jammed front door open with her foot, Gina stepped into the hallway. The door had been left on the latch. The stale stench of excrement and urine hit her first. 'Mr Walton.' No one answered. She held her hand over her mouth and tried to filter the air through her sleeve material as she inhaled again. 'Heather, it's DI Harte. We just want to know that you're okay. Are the boys okay?' She took another step. Wyre followed closely. The other two officers stood at the door. As one went to step in, Gina held out her hand, stopping him. She mouthed the word 'wait'.

Wyre heaved a little and held her hand over her mouth. 'Sorry, guv,' she whispered, as she followed Gina. The closer they got to the living room door, the worse the smell was. Gina pressed the door handle and pushed it open. Her eyes almost stung as the stench coated her nostrils. A full commode sat at one end of the room and several plastic pee bottles were lined up on a shelf. One had spilled all over the carpet. What looked like dried vomit was splattered up the one wall next to the bed.

Wyre stepped out of the room and a PC entered instead.

Gina crept towards the bed and stared at the outline of a body under the covers. She pulled them back and looked at the bald frail man. His skin ashen and his mouth covered in sores. With shaking hands, she reached for his neck to feel for a pulse but she could tell there was no life in him. She shook her head. He was gone. That's when she saw the glass. She leaned over to smell it; whisky, with some crushed up residue on the inside of the glass. 'We need to book that glass into evidence.'

Leaving, she headed back out to the hallway, then she saw blue lights flash against the grey wall. An ambulance had arrived too but it was too late for Mr Walton. She hoped it wasn't too late for Erik and Harvey. Pressure began to build in her head and blood throbbed through her body. With shaking hands, she pushed open the kitchen door. Worktops were covered in plates of old food and rotting bin bags half-filled the room. The PC let out a quiet scream as a mouse scurried across the tiles before making its escape under the skirting board.

Gina backed up and nodded to Wyre who was gulping in fresh air by the porch. 'Heather, I can see how hard it has been for you and your dad. Please come down.'

Not a sound came from upstairs. With every creaky step up to the first floor, Gina's legs became more jellied. She thought back to the photo of Erik that was pinned on their incident room board. The happy little boy with the shaved head and gappy smile. She held a hand to her booming heart and tried to hold back her instinct to scream out. She couldn't afford to alarm Heather. 'Heather, I'm on the landing. Please come out. We can talk.' She had to change tack. Sonya told her Kerstin's secret about what Cameron confessed to. Given the timing and what happened, Gina was going to play a blind hand and hope for the best. 'I know what happened with Cameron, what he did to you. It must have hurt a lot to see him that night at the wine bar.'

Again, no answer. Gina held her hand out to stop everyone from moving. She had to listen for creaks around the house. Nothing, not a sound. Gina pushed the three doors open one after another. Two messy bedrooms and a mouldy apricot coloured bathroom suite and tiles. That's when she spotted the red hair dye box. An empty squirty bottle that contained the dye was lying on the side, the instructions beside it. Then she reached the stairs to the old attic room.

Each step gave her position away as it creaked. The officer and Wyre followed closely. As Gina reached the top door, she pushed it open. 'They're not here.' Sighing with relief, she leaned against the wall to get her breath back. The tension had left her stomach clenching so tightly she could double over and cry. 'But this is where she's been keeping them. We need to put out an ANPR alert for Heather's car. She must have it back.'

'Her red Mini is out there, guv. It's parked on the road just a bit further down. One of the officers spotted it.'

Gina walked around the room, picking up the plastic dinosaurs, seeing sweet wrappers everywhere. There was a small room at the end with a toilet and washbasin in it.

'Damn. Where is she?'

'Guv.' The other officer ran up the stairs. 'The neighbour is out on the path and he'd like to talk to someone. It's the man who called in.' Gina hurried back downstairs. He had to know something. He was their only hope.

SIXTY-FOUR

Gina easily spotted the man in the winter coat, standing by the gate of the house next door. He finished the call he was making saying that he'd be late into work.

'You rang in a short while back.'

'Yes, that was me. Is Carl okay?'

'I'm afraid he's dead.'

'Poor guy. His daughter, Heather said... well, she gave me the impression he was still alive...' The man hesitated then continued speaking. 'He was lovely, Carl. What an absolute shame, the neighbours are going to be gutted. Did you get to the bottom of the kid being there? I only called because I heard about the missing child. I know Heather doesn't have children.'

Gina wondered if asking Justin not to go public about Erik being missing had been the right thing, then she shook that thought away. They had already been on their way over to Heather's father's house despite what Justin had revealed and now their abductor had fled with the children, possibly because she knew they were coming for her. Knowing that she was on the run might cause her to do something stupid in a panic. 'No, there's no child in there. Can you tell me everything you told us when you called in?'

'I saw Heather standing by the road, just by where you're parked now. She must have gone.'

'But her car's parked down the road.'

The man looked in the direction she was pointing in. 'Yes, that's her red Mini. She wasn't getting into that car, though. She got into a silver Daewoo. I wonder why she came in one car and left in a different one. I thought she'd just got a new car.' Gina nodded to Wyre, knowing that she would update the team to be on the lookout for a car of that colour and make. If they come across that car or Stephen's they would be alerted immediately.

'What did she say to you?'

'She said her dad was really poorly. I asked about him. She seemed a little edgy.'

'In what way?'

'Just fidgety. She was messing with her hood strings and I'm sure she was playing with a pair of glasses. I didn't know she wore them.'

Protecting her disguise more like, that's what Heather was doing.

'She also had a bruise on her head, just here.' The man pointed to the side of his temple. 'I think I could see it because her hair was scraped back so tightly in her hood. I think she'd just dyed her hair as there was a line of it along her forehead.'

Gina's mind flashed back to that image she saw on the *Boyz R Takin it Back* forum, the one Stephen had posted of Heather.

'Did you see her leave?'

'No, I went in the kitchen to call you from our landline. I have a mobile but don't get a good signal in the house so, no, I didn't see her leave. I did notice something strange. When I was speaking to her, I saw that there were two child car seats in the back of the Daewoo. When I heard the child calling, that's when I knew something odd was going on.'

'Did you see the child or hear what the child said?'

'No, all I heard was a childlike call and the net twitched in the front bedroom. I knew it couldn't be Carl as he hasn't been up those stairs for nearly a year.' The man paused. 'Is it the missing boy on the news?'

'We don't know at the moment. Is there anything else you can tell us?'

'No, I wish there was. Sorry.'

Jacob pulled up and hurried over. 'Guv, I've just had a call.'

'Excuse me.' Gina left the neighbour with Wyre and followed Jacob. 'What is it?'

'Stephen's car has popped up on ANPR. He came off the Cleevesford Bypass only fifteen minutes ago. Mulberry Lane leads to a country road that is about two miles long. It winds through the farmland. He hasn't come out the other end as there's ANPR on that road too. He is still there.'

'We need to get there now. Any sign of the silver Daewoo?'

'The alert has only just gone out.'

'Call in and make sure that both ends of the road are being monitored. If Heather is with him or meeting him, I want them kept there. Let's go.'

SIXTY-FIVE

Gina raced through the morning traffic and overtook everything on the dual carriageway. The rain had started falling like a sheet from the sky. Flash flooding had been expected. Wyre held onto the dashboard as she took a corner into Mulberry Lane. A police car had just pulled up at the junction. She placed her foot on the brake as the lane got narrower, until it fed into a single-track road with pulling in places. She glanced in her rear-view mirror and saw that Jacob had also turned in and was sticking close by.

The road dipped and weaved then suddenly the passenger side of her car was half plunged into a verge. She pressed and pressed on the accelerator until the tyre found some traction out of the mud. Another huge puddle ahead completely splashed the windscreen. As Gina turned on the windscreen wipers, she saw movement ahead. Maybe it was a bird or a fox. No, it was definitely a human hand. The rain eased off and became nothing more than a sprinkle. This wouldn't last. Turning off her engine, she gently opened her car door and stepped out, edging closer so that she could get a better look. Long willowy finger-like branches reached down, entwining with the brambles below. She pulled them back and peered through the gap to see what was happening. Jacob pulled up behind her.

She held a hand up and placed her index finger over her lips, indicating that he and the other police cars stopped where they were and remained silent. There was no room for error with there being two children involved. A tremor began to travel to Gina's fingers but she remained as still as possible behind those branches.

It looked like Heather was shouting at Stephen but she couldn't hear the words that were coming from her mouth. In her hand she held a petrol can and she began sloshing it around Stephen's legs and feet. Rain began to pelt and red streaks began to run down Heather's face. The urge to run in was overwhelming but Gina held back. She wasn't meant to have anything to do with Stephen during the course of the case.

'We need to do something. If she sets him alight...'

'Just wait a second. We don't know where the children are. Can you see them?'

'Not from here. I can see her. Is she bleeding?' Wyre tried to step in closer, scrunching up her eyes to get a better view.

Gina pulled another branch back and budged over. 'It's hair dye. She obviously ran out of time this morning and didn't get the chance to wash it all out properly. I'm more concerned about that petrol can and the way she's pouring it. Can you see Heather's car?'

'No, it must be further down the lane. Can't see Stephen's either yet.'

Jacob crept closer to them, through the puddles and broken up tarmac.

Heather shouted again but Gina still couldn't make out what was being said. All Stephen did was sneer. He wasn't afraid of her or her petrol can. In an instant, Heather opened the cap and flung another stream of the flammable liquid at his arm. He started swearing and shouting, then he lashed out, punching her in the nose. Blood began to stream and in what looked like a panic, Heather pulled out a lighter and lit it, holding her nose as she chased Stephen onto the field. Both of them ran but Heather was much fitter. It didn't take a lot for her to catch Stephen up, even with a bleeding nose.

'I can't see the children so we need to intervene now.' Running towards them, Gina leaped over a pothole and sprinted towards the entrance to the field. A dip in the ground took her by surprise and her ankle crunched slightly.

'You okay, guv?'

'Yes, just stepped in a hole.' She glanced up but still couldn't see the Daewoo or the children but she could now see Stephen's four-wheel-drive. He must have picked Heather up and brought her here. Gina's heart pounded. Heather must have left the children somewhere in her other car, but where? Maybe this was how it would all end, finally with her and Stephen. The man that had and was still causing her so much angst was about to be set alight. A part of her didn't want to catch up and stop Heather. She thought of Hetty and how bad things could get and she continued running and limping.

Whoosh.

The petrol on Stephen's arm lit up and Heather held the petrol can above his head as he squirmed on the earth, dragging his flaming body through the mud. He rolled over to try to extinguish the flames but it was no good. The accelerant was doing its job well and Stephen didn't seem to have the strength to fight it. His skin singeing, he tried to reach up towards Heather and half mouthed the words sorry. Gina slid towards them trying to maintain her upright position with all she had. 'Heather, stop... please.' Her voice was more of a crackle.

The woman's wide-eyed stare pierced through Gina, making her shiver.

'I know what you've been through. Sonya told me about what Cameron did. You were the woman he was talking about, weren't you? The rape?'

She shook her head and bit her lip, dye starting to sting her eyes. 'You don't know the half of it and as for him, he's scum.'

Gina didn't doubt that for one minute but she had to do what was right. She needed to know where the children were and to find that out, she needed to diffuse this situation. Heather laughed manically and held the petrol can above Stephen's face. Gina launched her aching body towards Heather in the hope of knocking the can out of her hand but the petrol sloshed as it fell and splashed on Stephen. His piercing screams were like nothing she'd ever heard before as the flames licked at the skin on his chin and cheek. Heather quickly regained her balance then roared and slammed her body onto Gina's, pinning her to the floor. Jacob hurried over, pulling her off Gina but Heather refused to let go, raking Gina's hair with her hands, taking a clump with her.

Stephen gripped his chest and began to gasp for breath; the shock, maybe the trauma had sent him into cardiac arrest. His screams were like those of an animal being attacked, loud and piercing. Then the silence was haunting, he could no longer scream as he gasped for breath, flames licking at his clothing. A fire engine sounded in the background. Stephen stopped writhing, giving up on saving himself. A mass of flames filled the air as his clothes continued to burn. Gina crawled over to him, removed her coat and began patting it over the flames on his torso. The one side of his face was starting to melt. Grabbing huge handfuls of damp, cold mud, she began rubbing it into his stubble, using anything at hand to help. With the fire diffused, she removed her coat from Stephen's body where a plume of smoke filled the air. His skin was charred and red, flesh under the skin showing through. Gina turned away and took a deep breath, the smell of cooking flesh turning her stomach. Then she turned back to see a lifeless man who had gone out of his way to cause her so much pain, who would never leave her alone for as long as he lived. She felt for a pulse, it was faint. 'Jacob, go and wait for the fire engine and direct them here, paramedics too. It looks like cardiac arrest and major burns.' He nodded and turned back to the road. 'Wyre, don't let Heather get away. Chase her.'

Heather was already halfway across the field.

'But, Stephen. You shouldn't be here with him, guv.' Wyre glanced at Jacob.

'She's right,' Jacob said.

'But I've also hurt my ankle so I'll never keep up with Heather. I have to stay here. We need a paramedic and we can't let Heather get away. Just please go get Heather. We need to know what's happened to the children and where they are.'

Jacob scrunched his brow and nodded to Wyre.

With both of them gone, she stared at the man who resembled her abusive ex and all she could see was the man who'd beaten, raped and mentally tortured her. It would be so easy to let him slip away, just like she had done with Terry. Those words she whispered in Terry's ear sent a shiver down her spine. It was like she was reliving that moment all over again. She was back at the bottom of the stairs waiting for a drunken abuser to die, she felt the same.

She felt for Stephen's pulse again, it was weak. Thunder cracked and another rain shower fell, soaking them both. The fire engine would be trapped in the lane and the ambulance would be trapped behind that. She held his life in her hands and stared at the dying man. She wondered what Pete Bloxwich would report after this incident. There was also a chance she'd be suspended if anything happened to Stephen. Being with him now would come back to haunt her if she let him die. Wyre had pointed out that she shouldn't be attending to Stephen but she'd sent her away to chase Heather. There was nothing badly wrong with Gina's ankle. Yes, she'd crunched it slightly in the mud but pain; there was none.

It was just her and Stephen. She had seen what he'd done to Heather and she knew what Cameron had done to her too. Monsters are sometimes made and they had created the monster and she came for their lives. Swallowing, thoughts of the children came back into her head. Harvey and Erik. She thought of the lives ruined. What had Sonya ever done to Heather and the same with Faith? Both women had to live with what they'd done forever. Both women still didn't know if their children were alive. And Kerstin was still missing.

Gina snapped out of her thoughts and got on all fours, her knees sinking into the earth as she massaged Stephen's heart until two paramedics found their way through. He wasn't going to die today, not if she could help it. Shivering, she moved out of the way so that they could take over. There was no way she would risk her career being over and a huge internal investigation. She watched as the paramedics worked. He took a small breath and part opened one eye. He went to lash out at Gina but he flinched at the pain and withdrew, screaming for help. 'You're okay, Stephen. You're going to be okay. Good job we were here.' She didn't gush or look pleased and she could tell that he knew that without her, he would have died.

She heard him try to swear but the oxygen mask went on, cutting him off as he gasped, the strap burrowing into his burnt flesh. Gina could only imagine the agony he was in. So much for him appreciating her making sure he stayed alive. She held that power in her hands. Just one look at him told her that he was going to find life hard enough from now on.

Wyre began marching back over the field dragging a hand-cuffed Heather along. Gina struggled to stand, her whole body crying out for a break and a drink but it wasn't over yet. They still had two children to find and the only person who knew where they were was being marched back over a field. Unless... she stared at Stephen's car. Half running and half limping due to her muscles seizing up, she snatched the car door open. Stepping up into the cab of the four-wheel-drive, she snatched his phone out of the holder. On a normal day, Gina would have punched the air at finding a phone that wasn't password protected, but there wasn't time for that. She scrolled through his activity. He'd used satellite navigation to get here and his last few locations were also stored. She opened his texts and could see the chain of messages from Heather telling Stephen she'd left him last night. Him replying saying he'd kill her. She'd then given him the location of the riverside car park, which was only a mile away. Her stomach dropped. 'Wyre, book her in and take her to the station.' Jacob ran over. 'Jacob, the last but one location stored on this phone was the riverside car park.' Gina stared at Heather. 'What have you done to the children?' She imagined Heather making good on her promise to the mothers. Fail and your children die. Were they in the bloated river, carried away with the floodwater? She could barely hear anything over the sound of the torrential rainfall. Another downpour, more flash floods. She visualised their little drowned bodies being swept downstream. The rocks, the currents, the weir. 'Heather?'

'What anyone who cared would have done. They're in a good place. All I wanted them to do was to be quiet... and they wouldn't...'

SIXTY-SIX

As Gina pulled up on the road by the river, she could see that the car park was flooded, and the path that led to it wasn't much better. Wyre stepped out of the car and stared at the scene in front of them. Neither was equipped to deal with a car that was about to be swept into a burst river. Jacob pulled up behind, followed by another ambulance. A look of defeat on everyone's faces. No doubt a fire engine would follow. She swallowed as she saw the car that the neighbour described Heather driving parked right on the edge of the bank, river water racing around the lower end of it, rising second on second. Gina half ran and limped towards it but the gushing torrent swept it towards the edge of the river.

'No.' She reached the edge of the floodwaters just as the car toppled into the river. They were too late. If only she'd left Stephen and focused all her attention on not letting Heather run off into the fields in the first place. Tears of regret filled her eyes and she knew they'd stay with her forever. More baggage to carry around. The bag of regret and secrecy was so full, that alone would sink her. Who needed a burst river and a flooded bank?

The car got smaller and smaller as it bobbed away, ferociously dragged downstream. A strong gust howled and a tree branch snapped, that too fell in and followed the car; swirling and dipping, only to be thrown back up in violent splashes. The sound of the sloshing weir ahead gave away that the car was being bashed around. Gina began to plough through the water, past her knees and it hit her thighs. There had to be something they could do. No longer could she see the ledge and the water was even higher. Rain bucketed down in thick sheets and thunder brewed in the air; growling before crashing. A flash of lightning struck ahead.

'Guv, get back.' Jacob grabbed her by the shoulder just as a large branch fell from the tree above. Her legs were numb from the cold water, taking some of the pain in her ankle away. Her body began to uncontrollably shiver. They'd lost the children. The boys had to be in the car. 'A helicopter has been despatched. We'll follow the car downstream.'

She shook her head. 'It's too late. We're too late...' A tear slid down her face and mingled with the rain. Grit stung the corners of her eyes. No one would know she was weeping for the children, not with how drenched her face was. She didn't want them to see her crying. She wondered if the children were already dead or had they been trapped in the car and swept away? Were they now being tossed around in the River Avon as the car filled with water, gasping for every little bit of oxygen they could get into their little lungs? 'No,' she yelled.

'Guv!'

She left Jacob standing knee high in river water and sloshed her way downstream, along the bank. As she got to higher ground, she managed to pick up the pace her ears tuning in to the sound of the weir. Her clothes, her boots, her hair, all sodden with water and weighing her down. She pushed on, hearing Jacob calling from afar. She couldn't see the car at the weir. It had gone even further downstream. She hobbled until she finally spotted it, face down on the opposite side of the riverbank with only the boot sticking up. If the children were in the car, there was no way they would be alive. She moved to the edge, trudging through the water and stood there, watching and trying to build up the courage to do something. Do what? She could swim. In her mind she could see the children with their mouths pressed to the top of the car, knowing they were sinking and not being able to escape. If she didn't at least try to rescue them, she'd never forgive herself. Help from the technical rescue team would be too long arriving.

Another large gush sent the river swelling again and water began to pool around her knees. She removed her stab vest and dropped it to the ground, then watched it get dragged under the water before bobbing back up further down. In a matter of seconds, it was gone. Cold, so cold; and the water would be icy, especially once it reached waist height. She was strong, she could do this. She closed her eyes, took a deep breath and ran towards the river.

'What the hell!' Jacob yanked her back for the second time that day. 'You go in there, you die. No one will be saved.'

'The children are in that car. They're dying.'

'Help is on its way. You and I aren't equipped to deal with this. I'm not letting you put your life at risk.'

'It's my life, I'll do what I like and I can't live with myself if those children die.'

'Well it's my decision, Gina. I'm SIO and I'm ordering you to step back.'

'That's bullshit, Jacob. You're only SIO because of Stephen. He isn't here and two children are dying as we speak.'

'Gina... please. They're already dead. No one could survive that.' As he spoke the rest of the car sank before bobbing up and down again. It had been swept away and neither of them could see it anymore.

'I could have tried. I failed.' Tears streamed down her face. Nothing mattered. What people thought of her didn't matter. She was now merely a mother who would have to tell two other mothers that their children were dead and not only that, they'd died a horrific death and suffered. She sobbed and spluttered as she looked down.

A look of sadness washed over Jacob. She'd never noticed any sign of ageing in him before but his frown line was now prominent. She knew that the death of two children who could have been saved would age anyone instantly. She glanced at the river again and wondered if she was being too harsh. There's no way she would have survived or saved those children. Jacob placed a caring arm around her shoulder. 'Come on, guv.' They stepped out of the water and back towards the trees.

'I'm sorry,' she mumbled.

'Don't be silly.'

'No, I am. I shouldn't have spoken to you like that. You're a great detective and a great SIO. I made a stupid decision and would have gone through with it if it wasn't for you.'

'Apology accepted. You're right though.'

'About what?'

'I'm only SIO because of Stephen and I haven't really acted like an SIO at all. I've just coasted along with you taking the lead. Why? Because you're better at it.'

'No, I took over and I should have stepped back. Maybe if I had, we wouldn't be in this position now.' She swallowed. 'You made the best SIO decision ever just then. I thought with my heart, no consideration of the consequences. You used your head. If I'd have jumped in, it would have been the most foolish thing ever and I'd have saved no one. We all have to live with losing the children. That loss is a team effort.' She wiped another tear away.

'Heather took the children. We didn't.'

'We were too slow, Jacob. We failed just like Sonya and Faith, and those children paid the price.' Gina paused and glanced around at the bleak landscape that was set to get worse. They had to get away before the river rose even more. Very soon, the woods would be under water, just like they had been in earlier floods. 'Did you hear that?'

'What?'

She could barely hear him over the weather and roaring river but there was a moment, more like a second. She'd definitely heard a sound. 'That.'

'I heard it.'

'It's got to be the children.' A helicopter flew above, the noise taking away the slight squeaky sound she'd been trying to tune in to. 'Damn, I can't hear it anymore.'

'Which direction did it come from?' She could just about read Jacob's lips.

Instead of answering, she pointed right at the wooded area that was about to be taken by the river.

Jacob stared at the danger that unfolded. It would take both of them and they'd both be risking everything. He nodded.

Gina trudged through the water until it reached her waist. The pull was strong. As the helicopter turned in the other direction she called out. 'Harvey... Erik.' Then came a piercing scream. Her eyes fixed on the writhing figure, water reaching the figure's chest, her red hair floating on top. Gina began the descent into the slight dip. What felt like a tsunami of water lifted Gina off her feet and she knew that she'd never see Hannah or Gracie again. It was as if hands were reaching from below, entwining themselves around her legs. As her head ducked under, she held her breath but she was running out of oxygen. She needed to breathe. Her end had come.

SIXTY-SEVEN

With a gasp, Jacob dragged her with one arm to the surface and wrapped a rope around her waist. That's when she saw the chain of people reaching back. She was at the end, then Jacob and three firefighters. Wyre waited back in the distance, hand over her mouth while she frowned. She glanced back to see if she could see Kerstin's red hair.

'You can reach her, guv. We've got you now.' He gripped the rope.

Reaching just that bit further, she grabbed onto the tree that Kerstin was leaning against. That's when she saw how deathly pale her face was. Blue lips chattered back, making no sense. 'Kerstin, grab my hand.'

The woman sobbed and turned her head. 'I... I'm tied to the tree.'

Gina reached down but couldn't feel the rope. She took a deep breath and through the murky water she caught sight of a strand of blue rope. Coming back up, she hugged the tree, latching her legs around it loosely as she reached under. It was double knotted. As she went for the second knot, she caught sight of the mighty swell and she knew what was coming. Just as the smash of water hit them, the knot came undone and Gina managed to grab one of Kerstin's arms, then they were both plunged into darkness.

The rope around her waist was being tugged but it felt too slow. Gina could feel Kerstin's grip loosening then it was only Gina holding on. She couldn't let go of the breath she was holding. A large stick bashed her head as it charged past. *Don't let go, Gina.*

Her fingers were slipping. Just as she was about to let go, Jacob pulled her out. The whole line was moving further back and winching them in. Kerstin gasped as her head broke the surface. Bodies sliding through mud and roots, they both sat shivering. A paramedic ran over with a couple of foil sheets, popping them over Kerstin and Gina's shoulders.

'We have to get out of here, guv. The whole area is on a red warning. A bridge has been taken ahead. It's absolute chaos, everyone is being evacuated from the area.'

'Kerstin...' Gina shook the woman.

Her chattering teeth stopped her from talking and her stare was wide.

'She's suffering hypothermia and is in shock. We need to get her to hospital, now.'

'Wait. Kerstin, where are the children? Have you seen them? Were they in the car?'

'They...' Tears slipped down Kerstin's face and she screamed in pain. Gina saw the blood that was now dripping from her shoulder. 'They went that way... I... I told them they had to run. They...' Her eyes began to droop.

'Kerstin.'

'They tried to save me but it was too dangerous... I told them to leave me.'

Gina stared in the direction that Kerstin pointed in and she hoped they weren't too late. A large tree completely collapsed as the river breached their area. 'Get her out of here, now.' Without hesitation, the firefighters and the paramedics all worked together. She glanced up at Jacob. 'The children went that way.' After coughing out the river water from her lungs, Gina hurried towards the fallen tree and fought through the branches to take the fastest route. Sloshing through the wood, she continued on. That's when she saw a flash of red, like a little raincoat drifting away with the water. 'Erik, Harvey!' Nothing, not a sound.

'Gina, be careful.' Jacob hurried up behind her.

'They came this way. That coat has to belong to one of them.' The rain came down in a much heavier burst once again. The cold had reached her bones and she was running stiffly, the struggle getting harder now with every step.

'We don't have long.'

A voice from back where they'd come from called, 'The helicopter spotted something over that way.'

Gina held a hand up. 'That's the way we're going.' The dip led to more water that came up to Gina's chest. She reached under for the children but couldn't feel anything. What had only hours ago been simple woodland was now a quagmire that was likely to threaten life. Cleevesford wouldn't forget this flood in a hurry. She glanced to the right where what looked like the whole of the woodland was being thrashed by the river, then to the left, that's when she saw the boy clinging to a branch up a tree. 'Erik, are you okay?'

The boy stared and flinched when Gina reached out. Shivering, he clung to the tree, not allowing her to help him as she reached out.

'Erik, I'm Gina, I'm with the police. We've come to help you.' After a few seconds, the boy reached out to her and she lifted him down, trying to keep him out of the water. She passed the frightened little boy to Jacob, knowing that there was another little boy out there somewhere. She couldn't see anyone else. 'Erik, where's Harvey?' The boy pointed towards the road and Gina had never felt so happy in her life to see Harvey sitting higher up, his side firmly against a tree.

'I'll get Erik back.'

Gina nodded as they headed out of the deeper water. A firefighter joined them and a paramedic trudged through and took

Erik. She hurried up the hill and kneeled down beside the boy. 'Harvey, we've come to help you and Erik. Are you hurt?'

He shook his head. 'I'm cold.'

'I'm really sorry that I'm soaking wet and cold too but do you mind if I carry you out of here and get you to safety?' She didn't want to alarm him, he'd been through so much.

He nodded. She reached down and lifted the tiny child up, gripping him tight. When she had seen that car bobbing around past the weir, she thought that had been it, but now here they were holding two shaken up and cold healthy children and she couldn't be happier.

'Guv, run. There's another surge.' Jacob and the rescue team began sprinting away from the river.

'Hold on tight, Harvey. We're going to have to run for it.'

'Don't let me go... I'm scared.'

'I won't let you go. I promise. Are you ready?'

As he nodded, Gina battled through her stiffness and shivers. Just as the waters were about to reach her she threw Harvey ahead onto what was an old elevated pavement, she grabbed onto a low hanging branch just as the water hit. Fighting against it, she dragged her body up next to Harvey's and he ran over to her.

'I want my mummy,' he cried and yelled, but he was finally safe.

'This very nice lady is going to help you, Harvey. You're going to be okay.' She couldn't promise the poor lad anything about seeing his mother and he had just lost his father. As Wyre helped Harvey, Gina lay on her back, chilled through as the rain pounded down.

'Come on, guv. I hope you have a change of clothes at the station as Heather is ready to be interviewed.'

'I do and bring it on.' She really wanted to know what Heather had to say for herself but that would be after a sit in front of a heater with a hot cup of coffee.

SIXTY-EIGHT

Darkness had fallen and seven people had been declared dead because of the flood. Another twelve were in hospital. A bridge had been swept down the river, several roads were unusable and five people were still missing. This was the worst flooding Cleevesford had ever seen. The woman she stared at had left two children in a car by the riverside knowing that the area was prone to floods. She also tied another woman to a tree knowing the same thing. She'd abducted two children and coerced their mothers into murdering two men under the threat that they would never see their children alive again. Her list of crimes was unforgivable. Gina swallowed knowing that Heather was all that and she was also a victim of Stephen's abuse and she would make sure he paid for what he'd done when he was deemed well enough to be charged. Jacob would have the pleasure of arresting him as soon as he'd been treated. Even though she saved Stephen's life, she wasn't allowed anywhere near him and she understood that. There's no way on Earth she would ruin everything by contacting him now in any way or form. Regardless of what Heather had done, he would pay too.

The tech team had gone through Heather's many tablets, laptops and burner phones and found a whole load of files containing photos of what Stephen had done to her along with all the messages she'd sent to Sonya and Faith. She'd also kept an abuse diary and had even managed to record some of the incidents with a hidden camera. All that would help with her case against Stephen. There were also lists of notes documenting the habits of Glen, Cameron, Justin and Stephen. She'd been watching them carefully while she planned what would happen to them.

Gina's phone pinged. She grabbed it and looked at the email.

Tick-tock, Gina. Time is running out. I have an article to publish!

No... his time was running out and he didn't even know it. She was badly looking forward to confronting him. She was going to throw that thought right back at Pete Bloxwich. One word from her and everyone would know what he'd been saying online. He'd never work again. They both had the power to bring each other down, she only hoped that would be enough to shut him up once and for all.

'Right, Heather. Start at the beginning.'

Hair dye still streaked her head and cheeks. She touched the sore on her head. 'As soon as I met Stephen, I knew I had to have him in my life... not like that though. It wasn't some soppy love at first sight. I recognised him from my past. Eight years ago to be precise and around this time of the year.' Heather slapped her lips together before sipping a bit of water.

'And.' Gina didn't want her to stop. She knew what Heather was going to say. It wasn't just Cameron and the attacks had been specific.

A lone tear drizzled down Heather's face. 'I was at a nightclub in Birmingham, with Sonya of all people. We were friends back then after going to the same college. I noticed she'd disappeared and I went looking for her. I wondered if she was okay so I checked outside but she wasn't there. I walked around the building and stopped by the bins because I felt a bit sick. That's when Cameron appeared. He began touching me, asking if I was okay. He was drunk but not too drunk...' Heather gasped in a lungful of air. 'Anyway, he began to touch my face. That's when I spotted the other two who I now know to be Glen and Justin. They closed in on me like a pack of wolves, laughing at me, tugging at my bra strap and pushing me about. It all happened so fast.'

A lump formed in Gina's throat. She remembered how Terry used to corner and mock her. 'What happened after that?'

'Isn't it obvious?' She paused for a moment. 'Cameron threw me down onto the rubbish. While the other two held me down, he raped me. That's when I noticed Stephen come around the corner. I'll never forget the words that came from Glen's mouth. "Stevo, keep a lookout. We're all just having a good time, aren't we, bitch?" and Stephen did exactly that. He laughed at me, lying there pinned down. Glen was next. I'll never forget the punch to my stomach and the way he splayed his hand over my face. Justin seemed a bit unsure but the others mocked him into raping me, including Stephen... not one of them cared who I was, looked at my face or said anything after. Stephen just grabbed my phone that had fallen on the floor and found my number. He then sent me a text saying what a good time we'd all had and thanking me for inviting them all to have a bit of fun, that he loved my fantasy idea and that we should do it again sometime. It was like he was some sort of expert at covering his crimes up.' She swallowed and paused, her bottom lip quivering. 'He threw it at me like I was some discarded piece of rubbish. That's when he lit a cigarette and dropped the match on me. It caught my top. They all laughed at me as I slapped my chest to put it out then they all went back into the club as if nothing had happened. I never reported it; that was my big mistake. That message Stephen had sent to my phone, I thought I'd never be believed. I lay there amongst the rubbish in the dark alleyway for over fifteen minutes before I could even move.' Heather grabbed a tissue from the box and wiped her face.

A sickening swirl began to wash through Gina's stomach. What she was hearing was more revolting than she'd ever imagined it could be and she hated those four men more than ever.

'When I got myself together enough to stand, all I wanted was my friend, Sonya. I called and called her over again but she didn't answer. I later found out that she went home with some guy and didn't tell me. I know we weren't really close friends but leaving me was unforgivable. We went out together. We were meant to be looking out for each other. I had no one. Eventually I got a taxi home, took a shower and nursed my wounds while I kept thinking about what had happened. It was so... surreal. I didn't hear from Sonya for over a week. She'd spent all that time with her new guy, not once returning my calls so I ignored her after that. Our friendship was over.'

'Is this why you did what you did?'

'I wish that was all that had happened. No, there was more, lots more. I did what a sensible person would do. The day after, I took the morning after pill, then I tried to forget it... it doesn't work like that, though.'

'Like what?'

'You can't forget an attack like that. From then on, I'd constantly look over my shoulder. I knew that the man called Stephen had my number. I got rid of my phone after a couple of weeks and didn't even tell Sonya my new number. When I saw her around and about, I ignored her, told her I was busy. I can't explain how frightened I was. No longer would I go out dancing and having fun. It was like my life was over... a while later, I began having the most awful stomach cramps, heavy periods and nausea. They'd given me chlamydia, which had led to pelvic inflammatory disease. After several recurring bouts that antibiotics seemed to fail to fully shift, I was referred to a specialist. Then more tests came. I was left infertile. Told at twenty-two that I would never have children because of what those men did to me. I sat there and listened to some health worker telling me the consequences of unprotected sex and it hurt so much. I'd always used condoms. Those men raped me and they took my future with them. I hated them more than anything and I vowed that if ever I saw them again, I would make them pay with everything I had.'

'Which is what you did?' What a mess of a case. A part of Gina wanted to reach out, hug Heather and tell her that everything would be okay, but it wouldn't. She wished more than anything that Heather had reported her rape on the night it had happened. Gina knew first-hand how those feelings of hate and anger can manifest themselves and she could see the rage in Heather. She thought of Erik and Harvey being left in a car next to a flooding river and knew that Heather had taken her revenge too far to gain enough sympathy in court. In some cases there were no winners and this would be one of them. Sonya had been guilty of nothing more than being a bit of a bad friend on one night but she had paid a huge price. Faith had done nothing but marry Glen. Heather had left Kerstin tied to a tree next to a bursting river.

'Yes. I saw Stephen in a pub a few months ago. I recognised him straight away but he had no recollection of who I was. It's not surprising, it was dark that night and none of them were looking at my face. I remember shaking like mad then running to the toilet and vomiting so hard. All those memories came back with a punch but I couldn't let what I saw as an opportunity go. I flirted with him, got his number and started seeing him. He was a complete pig from the start but I knew I had to find out who the other men were. He said he'd been living with a woman in Scotland for a short while and had just split up, I told him I was single and that I worked at home in IT, while also caring for my dying father. He'd moved in with me within a month, citing that he was about to be thrown out of his room but the plan was working. He introduced me to his friends one night at a wine bar in Birmingham. They all had pretty wives and nice families. Those men hadn't suffered one bit for what they did to me. That's when I recognised Sonya, and she was now married to Justin. One of my rapists. The men didn't recognise me, which makes me wonder if I was the only one. I always did wonder if they hunted their victims in packs.'

'So, that's when you met the wives of the men who raped you?'

'Yes. They were so nice to me, so warm and inviting. Faith was insistent that I try their gym when I told her my circumstances and that I never went out much. She had a free pass for a month and they all said I should join. I knew that would keep me close to the men too. I also knew that I had to come up with a plan. Sonya was going to be first to be punished. Had she not abandoned me that night, I wouldn't have gone outside to look for her. I spent months getting to know them all, getting to know their routines and habits. I kept away from too many meet ups, knowing one day that one of the men might recognise me. I mean, my hair was different. I tried to wear my reading glasses in their company. I didn't dress the same. Gone were the dresses. I was a jeans and sweater person now. Back then, I was fuller figured. We met a few more times at the wine bar and in Faith's garden for various get-togethers in the late summer, but I'd mostly visit the wives when the husbands were out or at work. I got to know them, their houses and the layouts, their habits. I knew that Glen slept on the settee a lot when he'd had a drink. I knew that any time Kerstin was having problems, she'd stay with her mum and stepdad. I knew that Cameron didn't really get on with his mother-in-law. Things all seemed to fall right for me. This was before I had a real plan. This was just the prep.'

Heather's now red hair had half dried like twigs around her face. Her skin mottled and pale gave her a ghostly look. 'Tell me about that,' Gina said.

'I knew I was going to make them all pay. The wives must know what their husbands were like. Glen was horrible all the time, to Faith and everyone around him. She had the opportunity to leave him for Aiden but she stuck around like an idiot, which made me angry.'

A flutter in the stomach made Gina shift positions. It seemed harsh, Heather calling Faith an idiot. Gina knew how hard it was to leave an abusive relationship, especially when there are children involved.

'The plan had to be set in motion sooner than I'd have hoped.'

'Why?'

'Cameron started looking at me more when we all went out

one night. It was at the regular wine bar nights. I saw a flicker of recognition in his face. I remember feeling like I had to get away so I hurried to the toilets. When I came out, he was waiting and he kept asking if we knew each other. Of course I said no. I could tell that he was unsure at this point as a smile returned to his face, that's when Kerstin came around the corner. She looked confused for all of a few seconds but Cameron made it sound like I'd come over ill and he was just checking on me. I played along and made my escape from his questions. That's when I realised how stupid Kerstin was. Her husband was a rapist and he looked as suspicious as hell when she saw us, yet she was so easily appeased by his explanation. I realised that all of them should pay in one way or another. That's when my plan took shape. For a moment, I saw another way out. With my father dying and my property only being rented, I wondered if I could still have it all. If I got the wives to kill the men, that would keep me out of it. The only way to get them to do what I wanted was to take the children. I'd already met the children. I'd even babysat for them sometimes when Faith wanted to meet up with Aiden or when Sonya had to work over. Oh, here's a good one. Kerstin had recently asked me to babysit for her two. No one knew she'd been seeing the woman at the gym, Alannah. I got it out of her eventually. Her marriage sucked anyway as Cameron was a rapist, cheating scumbag. Anyway, that wasn't any of my business. I became the good, dependable friend, got to know all the children and wormed my way into their lives. As for Erik and Harvey, I just told them we were going on an adventure. They were really happy about that and they came with me.'

'What were you going to do with the children?' Gina furrowed her brow.

'I had this place in Scotland all paid up for six months. A little lodge by one of the lochs. All done online. I took the identity of a dead woman called Sophie Dyson.'

Gina glanced at the notes. The car that had been swept downstream had been registered to someone of that name.

'I was going to live up there, with them, being happy. We were going to eat sweets all day, play dinosaurs and have lots of fun. I wanted them to remember me but I also wanted them to know what their dads did. I made up this story about Ziggy the dinosaur. Ziggy was me by the way. I told them everything in a way they'd understand. Those children know exactly what their daddies did. They deserved to know the truth.'

'You told Sonya and Faith to leave candles at the scene?'

'Candles of remembrance. I wanted a candle lit for the old me, the one who had died that night because that's what happens. When someone does to you what those men did to me, they kill a part of you and that person is gone forever. When I saw Stephen again after all that time, I felt like the phoenix who was about to rise from the ashes. I wanted to make them pay in the worst and most painful way possible. Being burnt alive has to be up there with the worst. That's how deep the anger and hatred runs. But just remember, I loved those children. I loved them so much, I felt they deserved more than what they had. I would never have hurt them.'

'You left them in a car by a swollen river during the floods. You risked the lives of all the emergency services that day. If the children had done as you'd said and stayed in the car, they'd be dead too and so would Kerstin.'

Heather slammed her hand on the table. 'I didn't know the river was going to burst. I was going to finish up with Stephen, go back for them and leave.'

'How did you get Kerstin to meet you?'

'That was easy. I told her that Stephen had beaten me up and not to tell anyone and to meet me. When I met her in the woods, I then began to set her totally straight about what Cameron did and she kept denying it, that he'd told her he'd slept with some woman and then she'd said he'd assaulted her after they'd had sex. She believed that disgusting animal over me. I tried to tell her what the others did but she kept saying I was mad and lying and who'd believe me as I'd taken the children? I had enough of trying to explain in the end. All I wanted was to find one person who would believe me. I stared at her for ages, wondering what to do. I had the petrol can and the lighter. It was then I realised the enormity of what I'd made Sonya and Faith do. I couldn't set her alight so I decided to leave her there for the time being.'

Gina bit her bottom lip. Heather was speaking far too freely given the trouble she was in. 'Why didn't you want a solicitor?'

'There's no point. I know what I've done. You know what I've done, in fact I want my story to come out. I want everyone to know why I did what I did. I want every bastard person who's raped in the past to look over their shoulders for the rest of their lives. I want victims' who've been hurt to feel like they can take these matters into their own hands. You work for the police. You know about the lack of convictions for rape?'

Gina had to agree. The conviction rate was dire.

'Rape is a crime that most perpetrators get away with. I made them all pay. I never meant to leave the children by the river and I sincerely didn't know the river would burst. You can see how honest I've been about everything. I swear I never wanted to hurt Harvey and Erik. I just wanted to love them.'

'They say you kept giving them drinks that made them sleepy.'

'It was only until we got to Scotland. I didn't want my dad to be disturbed by them as he was so ill... they were just sleeping tablets... I guess you found my dad?'

'Yes.'

'The law, your law, allowed him to suffer in the way he has for months and he'd beg me to help him escape the hell he was living in. Your law allows rapists to get off charge free. Your law stinks. My law saved my dad from any more pain. He wanted to go. I lay there with him in my arms as he slipped away from this misery society forced him to live in. My law has taken two evil men off the streets and has definitely made another two think twice about what they did. Your law is going to make sure I now suffer.'

'Suffer?'

'I'm dying. I was told a few weeks ago that I have terminal

ovarian cancer. I had nothing to lose and less than a year to live if all goes well. All I wanted was to spend some time with the children, to play the part of a mother. Being a mother one day was all I ever wanted until those evil men took that from me. Being a mother was my only wish but I guess me taking the children to Scotland is off the cards now. I'm probably not going to be around for the trial so do your worst. It's a complex case, I know that much, so I can imagine how long all this will take to get to court. I know I'm in for a painful ride but that's the risk I took when I started this. Some things pay off, some things don't.' Heather placed her head in her hands and stared at the desk. 'Did you find the files? The ones on my computer.'

'The ones documenting your abuse?'

'Yes. I want to give a full statement and I want Stephen prosecuted. I was also monitoring his internet use and everything he did online. He's in approximately ten women hating groups and shares photos of what he's done to me with pride. All the evidence and links are there. He also confesses to *bashing his gobby exes* – his words – you might want to ask a few of them for statements. That should tighten your case. If you make people like him pay, you don't create people like me. Do your jobs.'

'Heather, you didn't give us the chance to do our jobs when it came to your attack, but we will certainly be arresting Stephen for what he's done.'

Tears drizzled down her face. 'You know, it's only in this past minute I've accepted I'm actually dying. There's something about saying it out loud. I don't have anything else to say. Can I go back to my cell, please? I like the cell and I'll get used to it. It's the safest I've felt for years. All's well that ends well, as they say.'

She stood and Jacob leaned over and stopped the tape. The camera in the corner of the room continued recording. She stood facing the door in standard issue grey track bottoms and a grey sweater.

'Of course.' Jacob left the room to take her back and Briggs came from the room with the one-way mirror.

'You okay?'

'Yes... I mean no. All this stemmed from what they did to her. I can't get my head around it. I can't get my head around the fact that Stephen was a part of it and I feel like because of him, it all comes back to me.' She glanced up at the camera and took Briggs into the corridor and carried on speaking in a hushed tone. 'I'm sitting there telling her that she didn't give us the chance to help her convict her rapists back then when I didn't report Terry. I did the same as she did. I'm as bad.'

'You're not bad. She's not bad. No one is entirely bad or good and sometimes good people make bad decisions.'

'You're right. I'm not good though. I care and I try but this world pushes me to my limits.' She clenched her fists as she thought of Pete Bloxwich and the fact that amongst all this, she had to deal with him too. 'Right, I suppose I best call the CPS. This is going to be one of the hardest cases to unravel that I've ever had to deal with.'

'You and me both. Let's do that together. It's going to be a long night. I have some crisps in my office and I know there's a fresh pot of coffee on the go.'

'That's music to my ears.' She paused. 'I hope they don't come down too hard on Sonya and Faith. Doing what they did while they thought their children would be killed.'

'We can only put over the facts and evidence.'

'Life truly stinks. How's Kerstin?'

'Being treated in hospital, along with the others. We have more uniform guarding rooms right now than we do on the streets. PCs Kapoor and Smith are handling that side. I do have a bit of good news, well as good as it can get considering what's happened.'

'Go on. I really need something to cheer me up right now.'

'Harvey and Erik have both been reunited with grandparents and are safe and well. A professional team will be speaking to them when they've had a chance to warm up and rest but they are both finally with family and safe.'

'Did they say anything about what happened?'

'They kept going on about Ziggy the dinosaur, something to do with a story. As I said, the professionals will be working with the children. It's going to be a long hard road to recovery for them too.'

'One night, four men and a brutal attack. This is where it led. We have to campaign to do more for rape victims, to encourage them to come forward and not let cases get dropped so easily.'

'Let's get this case wrapped up and you're right. We must.' Briggs paused. 'I know this case is complex. The CPS are coming back to me soon but do you want to head over and break the news about Erik to Sonya? I think one of us should tell her in person.'

Gina nodded. She did want to do that.

'We'll talk about your interference in the case when it comes to Stephen, later.'

A serious expression spread across her face.

'It's not going to be that bad. Don't fret. I do however have a few boxes to tick.'

She exhaled. The worst of the day was over but there was still so much to do.

SIXTY-NINE

Erik snuggled up in the big bed, the spare one at his nanny's house. Tomorrow, someone was going to come and talk to him. They wanted to know what it was like staying in the attic. They would talk to Harvey too. Erik wondered if he would see his mummy soon but his nanny said it might be a while. They said his mummy and daddy were a little poorly and he'd be staying at Nanny's. He didn't mind. Nanny would take him to school and he was happy here.

He lay his head on the soft pillow, his eyelids closing as he felt sleep taking over. Not in the same way as the drinks he'd been having but in a tired way. It had been a long day running from the river. It had also been scary. When they found his mummy's friend tied to a tree, she told them it was a game and that they should run as far away from the river as they could, so they did. Erik couldn't keep up and the water followed him. He had to climb a tree while Harvey kept back and waited for him. They hoped the water would go so that he could climb down. That's when all the people came and rescued them.

He clutched one of his old teddies, missing his dinosaurs. Then he thought of Ziggy and what those horrible dinosaurs did to her. He wasn't silly, he was a big boy. His teacher told him how clever he was. He knew that Heather was Ziggy and that his daddy was one of the bad dinosaurs. Harvey knew the same too. Both of their daddies had hurt Heather. His daddy wasn't a nice person. His mummy had left Heather alone that night which is why she got hurt. His mummy hadn't been very nice to Heather but Heather had told him that he should forgive Mummy. He loved Ziggy the dinosaur even though she did make him sleep a lot. He loved the sweets and the adventure and the dinosaurs that she gave to them and he really wanted to go on the big adventure to Scotland. Maybe one day.

For now he was safe with his nanny and he hoped he could stay with Nanny forever. At least Nanny is a good person. He let out a little snore and woke himself up a little. Actually, he didn't want to ever go home. Although it was scary at the end, he'd miss Heather or Ziggy as he would always call her in his mind.

SEVENTY

Sonya lay there in the semi-darkness of the room. The night light was gentle and directed to the corner of the room. Nurses bustled in the corridor, dragging equipment around with them on bumpy wheeled trollies and another police officer had taken over guarding outside the room. Her heart filled with pain for her son. She could take whatever happened to her but Erik, he didn't deserve anything. He was just a little boy. Her little man. Someone knocked on the door and entered gently. 'DI Harte?'

'Sorry to wake you.'

'I'm not asleep. I feel as though I'll never sleep again. Have you found him?' She swallowed, not wanting to hear the words that came next. In her mind Erik had died. The promise of him being set alight had run through her mind like a broken record.

'I wanted to come here and tell you myself. Erik is safe.' The DI smiled and sat beside her on the chair.

'Who did this to me?'

'We have charged someone. Heather Walton.'

'Heather? But she's my friend. How could she? Was he hurt?'

'No. Erik is doing well.'

'What happened?' Sonya swallowed and took in the worry lines around the detective's eyes. She knew it was going to be a long story and it was. After DI Harte had finished filling her in, she felt a trickle of a tear running down her cheek. She barely knew Heather in the past. Their friendship had been brief and had only consisted of a few nights out, sometimes with other friends. When Heather hadn't returned her calls back then, she'd thought nothing more of it and moved on with her life. If only she'd not gone back with that man at the club, the one she'd met. None of this would have happened. 'What will happen to me?'

'We're talking to the CPS at the moment. This is the most complicated case I've ever had to deal with but you will be charged with murder. I'm so sorry. It's looking like you'll get bail due to your cooperation and previous character so you'll be able to discuss everything further with your solicitor. I know you and Erik have been through so much.'

Sonya paused for a moment as she digested everything and she swallowed. 'What will happen to Justin?'

'We will be questioning him for the historic rape.'

Sonya laid her head back. It was all such a mess. She closed her eyes and smiled. Nothing mattered anymore. Erik was alive. Her son was okay.

'Can I see my son?'

'Leave it with me. I'm sure I can arrange that. He's safe with your mother at the moment. I suggest you work on getting yourself better in the meantime.' The DI stood and did her coat up.

Sonya could see how tired she looked. She had a sore on her nose and fine scratches on her face. 'Will you stay with me for five minutes? I don't want to be alone.'

She smiled and sat back down. 'Of course.'

Sonya lay there and closed her eyes. Her son was safe. That's all she wanted to know. Finally she succumbed to her body's exhaustion and closed her eyes. Sleep was beckoning.

While driving, Gina's mind kept replaying the events of the past few days and what would happen to Sonya, Faith and Heather. Sonya had been charged with murder and was granted bail with conditions until her case was heard. Her mother had been given permission to bring Erik to the hospital and from what Gina had heard, the reunion had been a tearful one. Gina understood the power of a mother's love more than anything. She loved her own daughter and granddaughter immensely, even if she didn't show it often.

Faith had been charged with arson with intent to endanger life. Again, she had been bailed on condition that she checked in daily and stayed with her parents. Both women had committed these huge crimes, but they'd also helped the investigation and had previous good character. Heather had accepted her charge of child abduction. She had refused a solicitor and had barely spoken a word since to anyone.

Gina took a deep breath as she neared her destination. Knowing that Stephen was finally going to pay for his crimes gave her a sense of peace. There was one more person she had left to deal with today and with that thought, her stomach turned.

Gina pulled up in the car park, the exact one that Pete had asked her to meet him at. The early morning workers were all driving through the rain to get to work, all in a hurry. Water splashed from the verges onto the pavements and an angry pedestrian in a mac got drenched.

Pete pulled up next to her. She watched the man get out of his car and get into hers. 'So you finally decided to tell your story.'

'Stephen has been charged with assault. Your source is looking less credible by the minute. Domestic abuse, by the way, but you already knew what he did, didn't you?'

'Gina, Gina, how would I know that? And it doesn't matter what you've charged him with. This is about you. It's about what happened to his brother, Terry. It's about truth and justice. It's about a mother being able to sleep at night.' He smiled and nodded righteously.

'You know what, BeeMan, you're right. Everyone deserves to know everything about everyone, wouldn't you say. I bet your editor would like to see what I have.'

Pete's grin turned into a stark stare. She saw his Adam's apple bob as he swallowed.

'I know all about BeeMan. I know who he is and what he's said. Some pretty disgusting stuff. I think it would be in the public's interest to know who was delivering their news. You really are a piece of work.'

'You know nothing.'

'We have all Stephen's devices in custody. The wording you chose in your awful and nasty emails to me, that's what gave you away. Honeybee, beady little eyeballs – I couldn't fail to recognise your wording anywhere. You can say what you like about me even though we both know it isn't true. We will both have muddy water over us and we know mud sticks; that is a problem for me, even though you lie. I looked into your life. You have two lovely daughters, a sister, a little niece and your mother. What a sweet looking old lady. I bet they'd enjoy hearing what you think of them, being women. Your readership is half female, I bet they'd love to know the real Pete too. You know what, I could do this. I could get through it and be fine. Firstly, there is no evidence of what you, Hetty and Stephen accuse me of. What we do have is a bitter old woman, a disgusting women-hating journalist and an abuser of women's words against mine. I will be fine in the end because I'm innocent. I'll be suspended while they investigate then I'll be back, stronger. That would upset me as I love my job. You, Pete, you seriously need to consider who you mix with. You lack credibility. For the tape in your pocket, Pete Bloxwich, I have never done anything wrong. I am a victim of your hate campaign against me as a police detective and a woman. Also, you are more than a contributor on the women hating online forum, the *Boyz R Takin it Back*, you own the website domain. I delved a little further and it came back to you.' Gina swallowed. It wasn't easy running on no sleep and too much coffee. She felt her fingers trembling and she knew that Pete could see.

He clenched his teeth. 'I don't know what you're talking about. There is no hate campaign and I will do all I can to stop any from starting. I totally respect what you do and that you're a woman. I guess that's all.' He pulled his phone from his pocket and put it in aeroplane mode in front of Gina.

'Turn out your other pockets.'

He did as instructed and there was nothing there. 'You did it though, didn't you? You let him die. You wanted him dead?'

'Who are we talking about?'

'Terry, your ex-husband.'

'I loved my husband. He fell down the stairs when he was drunk. I don't know where you got the idea that I wanted him dead from, but this is hugely distressing for me so please leave.'

'He beat you though, didn't he?'

'That is no business of yours, Mr Bloxwich. Get out of my car or I will arrest you for harassing me.' Gina pulled out her own phone, which had been recording everything. He went to grab it but she blocked him, smashing his hand away. 'No, you don't.' He went to grab it again and caught Gina's arm with his hand. 'Right, out now or it'll be an assault charge. Imagine that, assaulting a police officer. For the tape, Pete Bloxwich has just hit me while trying to grab my phone.'

He pushed the door open. 'Bitch,' then he slammed it before hurrying off into the dark morning rain. She watched as he jabbed a button on his phone, opened the passenger door and threw it in with force. He kicked the door as he closed it, went to the driver's side and wheel-spun out of the car park. A trickle of tears slipped from Gina's eyes and she shook so hard, she dropped the phone. Each time she tried to pick it up from the footwell, she missed or dropped it again. Briggs opened the door to the passenger side.

'Thanks for having my back, again.' She leaned into his warm chest and allowed him to envelop her in his embrace where she sobbed until there were no more tears left to cry. It was over. Pete was gone. Stephen was going to be doing time and Hetty was nothing without them. It was finally over.

'I'll always have your back.' He kissed her head.

She wondered if that was true. If he knew what she'd said to Terry as he breathed his last, he'd wonder who he'd ever got involved with.

* * *

Thunder clashed and rain poured. Hannah cried like it was the end of the world from her cot. Her husband lay there dying at the bottom of the stairs. Make the call or not? No, she'd wait until the point of no return. That was a large crack of his head when he landed and Gina could see the blood beginning to seep out. His stare had been wide for a few seconds and he couldn't speak. 'Terry, I can't let you live,' she whispered in his ear. They say that hearing is one of the last things to go before a person dies but Gina wasn't sure. Maybe that was just something silly she'd heard. 'I knew this moment would come one day. Hannah and I will be just fine without you. It was either going to be you or me one of these days. I chose me and I won't let you hurt my child again.' For the first time ever, he'd walloped their baby daughter, just before he left for the pub. For so long, she'd cowered as he'd hit her. She'd stood in front of her crying baby's cot to hold him back and he'd attacked her instead. She finally did what she had to do, for her child. Terry had to die!

A LETTER FROM CARLA

Dear Reader,

I'm hugely appreciative that you chose to read *Her Dying Wish*. As a story, I loved the planning and the characters that developed during the early drafts. I really wanted to explore what people would do if they were pushed to their limits and Sonya's story enabled me to do that. At times it made me shiver at what I put her through.

If you enjoyed *Her Dying Wish* and would like to keep up to date with all my latest releases, just sign up at the following link. Your email address will never be shared and you can unsubscribe at any time.

www.bookouture.com/carla-kovach

Whether you are a reader, a tweeter, a blogger, Facebooker or a reviewer, I really am appreciative of everything you do and as a writer, this is where I hope you'll leave me a review.

Again, thank you so much. I'm active on social media so please feel free to contact me on Twitter, Instagram or through my Facebook page.

Thank you, Carla Kovach

facebook.com/CarlaKovachAuthor

twitter.com/CKovachAuthor

instagram.com/carla_kovach

ACKNOWLEDGEMENTS

So many people are involved in bringing a first draft to a finished book, which is why I'd like to say a few words of gratitude.

Thank you massively to my editor, Helen Jenner. As always, her input into this book has been invaluable and brilliant, and I look forward to working on the next book with her. I'd also like to express my gratitude to Peta Nightingale too, who keeps me updated with my contract information and much more.

I adore the cover so thank you to Lisa Brewster for her work in giving my latest book a brilliant face for all to see. It's perfect!

Noelle Holten, Kim Nash and Sarah Hardy make up the fabulous publicity department. I totally appreciate the constant energy and enthusiasm that they exude. Publication day is made super special because of them.

Bloggers and readers deserve a big thank you too. I'm always thrilled that they've chosen my book to read and all because they love reading. Much appreciated.

The Fiction Café Book Club are a lovely group on Facebook and I'm happy to be a member of this supportive and positive reader community. Their enthusiasm for books is contagious and I love contributing to this page and reading their posts.

I'm also mega grateful to the huge happy family that is the other Bookouture authors.

Beta readers, Derek Coleman, Su Biela, Brooke Venables, Anna Wallace and Vanessa Morgan, are brilliant too. I know they're all busy with their own writing or work but they always give me time and early feedback, which is really helpful.

I also need to say thanks to my two writing buddies and fellow authors. This is a second expression of gratitude to Brooke Venables and a huge thanks to Phil Price. We've formed a fun little support group and I love being a part of it. The check-ins and support are second to none. And the coffee meetups where we share our progress are fun too.

And then there's the experts. I'd like to say a big thank you to fire scene expert, Nigel Adams, who is also a huge bookworm and blogger too. I'm also grateful to former DCI Stuart Gibbon of Gib Consultancy for answering my policing questions.

My husband, Nigel Buckley, has been so supportive so I'd like to say the biggest thank you ever to him. He helps to keep me on target with all those encouraging words and cups of coffee when he knows I'm racing for a deadline.

Made in the USA
Columbia, SC
25 April 2022

59462428R00193